secrets

the ivy
secrets

BY LAUREN KUNZE

IN COLLABORATION WITH
RINA ONUR

GREENWILLOW BOOKS
An Imprint of HarperCollinsPublishers

Thank you to everyone whose continuing efforts have made this series possible:
to Greenwillow Books; to the Stimola Literary Studio; to family; and to friends.
Special thanks in particular to Susan Adler, for her unwavering tolerance and
support; to Anna Riker and Corey Reich, two exceptionally enthusiastic early
readers; to the former Harvard undergraduate who answered many pressing
campus-related questions; and to Christina Hoffman, who has allowed the author
to live with her on more than one occasion and still loves her anyway.

The Ivy: Secrets
Copyright © 2011 by Lauren Kunze

The text of this book is set in Adobe Caslon
Book design by Christy Hale

Library of Congress Cataloging-in-Publication Data
Kunze, Lauren.
Secrets / by Lauren Kunze with Rina Onur.
p. cm. — (The Ivy)
Summary: Returning to Harvard University after Thanksgiving break, freshman
Callie is determined not to make the same mistakes that have alienated her
friends and roommates, but secrets soon lead to social drama and heartbreak.
ISBN 978-0-06-196047-5 (trade bdg.)
[1. Universities and colleges—Fiction. 2. Roommates—Fiction.
3. Interpersonal relations—Fiction. 4. Dating (Social customs)—Fiction.
5. Secrets—Fiction.] I. Onur, Rina. II. Title.
PZ7.K94966Se 2011   [Fic]—dc22   2010042023

11 12 13 14 LP/RRDB 10 9 8 7 6 5 4 3 2 1
First Edition
Greenwillow Books

FOR MICHAEL J. KUNZE

ONE

Notes on Triangles

Dear Students:

A very warm (or rather, frigid, as the weather would have it) Welcome Back from Thanksgiving break! Particularly to returning freshmen, if you are returning, that is. (A surprising number of individuals can't even manage to hang on until the end of the semester, when some of you will be asked to leave due to grades. Two below a C and you'rrrrrrrrre out!)

As for the rest of you, how was home? Get any diet-inspiring questions about when the baby's due? Did the phrase *best friends forever* ring hollow when you struggled to remember—or forced yourself to laugh at—the inside jokes you once shared with your high school besties? After you hugged that boyfriend or girlfriend whom you hadn't seen since summer ended, was there an awkward lull in which you realized that you no longer have *anything* in common?

That's what I thought. Fear not, though: it's all totally normal, and I say, "Out with the old and on to the next." With that in mind, here's what you *should* be worried about instead: EXAMS. We're nearing the end of the semester, and ladies and gentlemen, it's almost time for the moment we've all been dreading. . . . There's only one more short week of classes before reading period begins, followed by your first-ever finals Harvard Style. Don't freak out just yet. There's still time to get back on track, starting with my five tips for a fresh start.

1. Don't sweat the small stuff.

Your grades. Surprise! They're no longer perfect like they were in high school. It's called a curve, people, as in the predetermined distribution of grades and not the new weight on your hips. So either make peace with that B- or start amping up your game: turn in extra credit, go to office hours (wearing something seductive) to "go over the class material" (i.e., flirt) with your professor, or pitch a tent in the library and hit the books. . . .

For those of you who are still vying for a spot on a magazine, newspaper, team, so-called Sorrento Square humor organization, or whatever other extracurricular activity you're hoping to use to buff up that résumé, you are also now entering the final rounds of COMP: GAME FACES ON, FROSHLETTES.

2. Break up with your boyfriend or girlfriend.

If you missed the annual Turkey Drop (when a college freshman breaks up with his/her longtime high-school lover on the first day of Thanksgiving vacation, shortly after that awkward hug), you need to TCB (that's Take Care of Business). Immediately. Those who are still with significant others from high school—ew—I have no words for you except *Congratulations*: you are now stuck until winter break and may even end up living the lie through Christmas, New Year's, Valentine's, and well into the spring. (FYI, breaking up through e-mails, texts, and even phone calls are tacky.)

For the wiser contingent of the student body who came to college sans anchor: if you paired up with somebody in the fall, unless they're THE ONE (e.g., have world-saving super powers and can pull off a leather bodysuit better than Keanu Reeves in *The Matrix*), I strongly suggest you end it now. If you don't, you run the severe risk of getting saddled with the same scrappy boy/girl from across the hall—aka the first person who could stand your presence for more than five minutes—for the next four years of your life and beyond. Once college ends, you'll wake up one day to find yourself married and thirty, wondering why your ass is fat and you've never actually been on a real date.

3. Reinvent your schedule.

Sleeping during the day and working all night is cool if you're a vampire, but personally I think that trend was *so* last fall. Why not give living like a normal human being a try? Grandma Thorndike always said that nothing good happens after 2 A.M. . . .

4. Don't let your appearance or physical or mental health "go" just because it's below zero degrees outside.

Sweatpants are never okay, with the possible exception of the gym. They should be illegal. In fact, sometimes I fantasize about following in my favorite uncle's footsteps and going into politics just so I can turn this particular dream into a reality.

5. Wash your sheets and towels.

For crying out loud! I know how many of you haven't gotten around to it yet. . . . If you left your windows open so the sheets have had a chance to air, don't put off washing them any longer. Do it now! However, if there are any mysterious-looking growths, regardless of color, texture, or size, do *not* take them into your science lab for analysis but rather: BURN IMMEDIATELY.

So nice to have (most of) you back!
Alexis Thorndike, Advice Columnist
Fifteen Minutes Magazine
Harvard University's Authority on Campus Life since 1873

The Reasons Why You
Need to Move Out Immediately:
A Manifesto
by V. V. V.

1. You hooked up with Gregory at Harvard-Yale when you _knew_ how I felt about him.

2. You screwed up our entire room dynamic.

3. You blew it with Clint.

4. You're an all-out terrible person.

5. There is no hope that I will _ever_ forgive you. We will never be best friends _ever_ again.

Callie Andrews stared at the "Manifesto" that Vanessa Von Vorhees, roommate and former "best friend," had taped to the window above her desk. She chewed on her pen while she considered how to respond. And, not for the first time that day, she wondered if coming back to Harvard had been a huge mistake. . . .

She had arrived in Cambridge late last night. In truth, she hadn't seriously entertained the idea of not returning for more than a few hours. After all, what could she possibly say to her parents?

Hey, Mom, remember Evan? You know: my jackass boyfriend from high school? Well, turns out he made a secret sex tape of us because some of his old soccer teammates dared him. No, I didn't know about it at the time, but get this: now my arch nemesis has a copy and there's no telling what she'll do. Yeah, her name's Alexis Thorndike. She's real swell; you should meet her. . . .

Yes, Daddy, Economics is going great!—as she slides the letter from Harvard, the one warning her of an imminent *C,* the first in her life, behind her back—*but did I tell you about all of my new friends? Well, there's Vanessa, that's my best friend. We're really close, even though I walked all over her to get into a social club that I didn't really care about belonging to in the first place and slept with the guy she*

liked—oh, and did I mention that I had a sort of boyfriend at the time?
It's okay, though, because we were on a sort of break. . . .

Imagining how it would all play out was almost funny. Almost.
Though, ironically, if she told her parents the truth, they'd
probably laugh and assume she was kidding. This was known
as the Jessica Stanley Style of Parenting (that's *parenting* as in
how to control one's parents). Jessica, Callie's best friend from
high school—a relationship she had thankfully managed *not* to
ruin from three thousand miles away—was in the habit of telling
the truth in a sarcastic tone. *Hey, Mom, just going out to do some*
underage drinking, you know, might have sex with my boyfriend,
but I'll be home by curfew! To which Mrs. Stanley inevitably
responded, *Oh, ha-ha, honey, very funny, how you do love to torture*
your poor old mom.

Jessica had been an absolute angel over the break, but now she
was safe at Stanford while Callie was back here in hell. Shrouded by
the cloak of night, Callie had crept onto campus in the wee hours
of the morning, slipped through C Entryway to Wigglesworth
Dormitory, and mounted the stairs that led to that familiar, big
brown door.

Only this time something was different. On the board that used
to read DANA, CALLIE, MARINE, & VANESSA, somebody—most
likely Vanessa—had done her best to rip down Callie's name, so
that now it looked more like: DANA, A E, MARINE, & VANESSA.

As far as omens go, this one wasn't promising.

The common room of suite C 24 was dark when she stepped
inside. The doors to the bedrooms were all shut; everyone was

obviously asleep, and since the Marilyn Monroe poster was still hanging intact on the door closest to the bathroom, she assumed that Vanessa's attempt to transfer out of the room—as she had furiously vowed to do before they'd left—had proven unsuccessful.

Well, that was too bad. Callie had had a lot of time to think over the break, and as a result . . . she was more confused than ever. She had betrayed not only Vanessa but also Clint, who was perfect: smart, handsome, older, attentive, chivalrous, and just . . . well, . . . *perfect*. He had broken up with her (or had he; she still wasn't sure what *I need a break* had really meant) when they were on the verge of becoming intimate. She had completely freaked out, offering no explanation. (Since, really, how could you possibly hope to explain a panic attack induced by thoughts of your evil ex-boyfriend and his awful hidden video camera? Running away as fast as you could was surely a preferable alternative.) Naturally, in a typical perfect-guy move, Clint didn't care that she wasn't ready to go all the way—instead he was upset about her refusal to open up.

Then, as if she hadn't screwed up enough already, she slept with Gregory: Gregory whom she *hated* with every fiber of her being. Except that lately the "fine line between love and hate" was starting to look very, very blurry. . . .

Even if Gregory *were* right for her—which he wasn't, as she frequently reminded herself—it was *still* wrong: very wrong to have slept with your best friend's crush, wrong even if he clearly didn't like her, wrong even if you thought you might be in some serious like with him, and especially wrong if you already had a perfectly wonderful sort of boyfriend even if you were on a sort of "break" at the time.

Some of that wrong, however, ought to be canceled out by Vanessa's equal if not greater betrayal: she had revealed Callie's biggest secret to Callie's worst enemy, and as a result Callie hadn't slept well or eaten right in a week, waiting for Lexi to make her next move. Over the break Lexi had stayed completely silent, which turned out to be far more torturous than if she vocalized whatever horrible things—taunts, blackmail, coercion—she might have planned. Now, with the second round of *Fifteen Minutes* magazine COMP results right around the corner, there was no telling what Lexi would do to prevent Callie from joining *her* publication even though Callie had given up everything—sleep, HBO, sanity—in her efforts to join the magazine.

Normally when you have a recurring nightmare about finding yourself naked in front of the entire school, you awaken and realize it was only a dream. But in Callie's case, the nightmare would be true: monsters (Lexi), demons (Vanessa), and nudity.

Sighing, Callie stepped inside her tiny bedroom without bothering to turn on the light. She had been so eager to return to California after what happened at Harvard-Yale that she had left her room—with its twin bed, desk, dresser, bookshelf packed to capacity and old soccer photos lining the walls—in a state of disarray: clothing strewn across the floor, books out of order, stacks of old assignments and COMP papers piled on her desk next to a stale cup of coffee (late nights + insane workload = hopelessly addicted), and sheets tangled at the base of her bed. Abandoning her suitcase in the middle of the fray, she sank onto her mattress and, fully clothed, pulled the covers up to her chin.

She was too exhausted to clean tonight. The mess could wait, and they, the long list of people who were avoiding her or whom she was trying to avoid—Vanessa, Lexi, Gregory, and Clint—could, too.

And so Monday dawned like a fresh rose in springtime. Sunlight slanted through her window, beckoning her to gaze out across the magnificent Harvard Yard. A fresh blanket of snow glittered in the morning light. Today would surely be a new beginning. She was older, wiser, and completely—

"Completely FUCKED!" She heard a voice—Vanessa's—yelling from the common room.

"Calm down," another voice said, maybe Mimi's, maybe Dana's. "You knew your chances of transferring were slim to begin with—"

"Yeah, well . . . the BITCH," Vanessa said loudly, presumably aiming her words at Callie's door, "is BACK. She had better..." Callie heard footsteps and gathered that Vanessa was now standing right outside. "She'd BETTER STAY THE HELL AWAY FROM ME IF SHE KNOWS WHAT'S GOOD FOR HER."

Callie rolled over onto her stomach and pulled a pillow over her head. Before long, she was back asleep.

Several hours later she awoke. More voices were coming from the common room. Wary of a run-in with Vanessa, Callie strained to hear, trying to pick out the simpering Judas-Brutus tones of her ex "best" friend.

Instead she thought she heard a British accent. Its owner spoke in a pleading pitch, "Please . . . you've got to help me. I can't do it alone anymore! Please, just say yes. I *need* you. Without you, I don't think I can survive."

Hmm . . . was OK finally confessing his love for Mimi? A little desperate, wasn't he?

"I know I'm behind . . ." Then there was muffled murmuring, a girl's voice but Callie couldn't tell whose, followed by OK again: "No, I wouldn't say so far behind that I can't possibly catch up."

Callie almost giggled. From the sound of it Mimi was telling OK that she was too mature for him; well, that was certainly true.

"Look, I'll pay. Just name your price."

Wait a second—that couldn't be right.

She poked her head out from under her covers and, like a warrior surfacing from a bunker after the dubious declaration of cease-fire, she opened her door a crack.

Left: no Vanessa.

Right: no Vanessa.

Common room: OK and Mimi . . . and Dana, her face set in a characteristic frown, were sitting on the futon couch. No Vanessa. All clear!

"Callie, darling! *Bienvenue en enfer!*" Mimi cried, running over to embrace her. "That is French for," she continued, gesturing at Dana and OK, who, had a calculus textbook open between them, "welcome to hell."

Dana stiffened. "Mimi, if I've told you once, I've told you a hundred times. It doesn't matter what language you speak in. *He* hears *everything*. Hi, Callie."

Mimi rolled her eyes.

"Blondie!" OK cried, leaping to his feet and locking Callie in a tight embrace. "Blondie, thank god!" Dana blew a frustrated gust of air through her lips. "Do *you* know how to take the integral of a trigonometric function?" OK continued.

"Um, yes, but why—"

"Okechuwuku Zeyna," Dana cut in, and from her tone Callie was surprised that she wasn't actually wagging her finger. "How on *earth* do you expect to take the integral of a trigonometric function when you still haven't learned to do derivatives?"

Mimi cupped her hands to her face and whispered, "Somebody got a letter over Thanksgiving break warning that he is failing his math class—"

"Hey!" OK cried, frowning. "A D is not a—"

"Is not a passing grade," Dana interrupted. "Now I will help you, but you do understand that you're going to have to actually work?"

"What, you can't just telepathically transmit the integrals into my head?"

Dana's expression remained unchanged.

"All right, all right." OK sighed, sinking back onto the couch. He flipped his book to somewhere in the middle.

"Best to start from the beginning, darling," Mimi urged, plopping down on the other side of him and pretending to examine her fingernails.

"Listen, you," said OK, seizing her forearms with both hands, "I may be behind, but I'm not a *total* idiot."

"Oh yeah?" said Mimi, cocking one eyebrow. "What is a trigonometric function, exactly?"

"It's a . . . well . . . it's a . . . Well, you know, it's one of those things that's difficult to say *exactly* what it means. Like the word *surreptitious*: you *know* what it means and could use it in a sentence, but nobody could really say the exact definition."

"Surreptitious, an adjective: obtained, done, or made by clandestine or stealthy means. Middle English with Latin origins in *surrepticius*, from *surreptus*, the past participle of *surripere*, to take away secretly," Dana recited instantly.

OK's mouth fell open in a manner that made him look the way a caveman might if he had just been handed a cigarette lighter.

"I think I'm going to need to raise my price," Dana said, flipping to the beginning of the book. "Now let's see, where shall we start? Do you at least know your limits?"

"He definitely does not know his limits!" Mimi shrieked, swatting at OK's hand, which he had *surreptitiously*—or so he had thought—placed on her knee.

"Sure I do," said OK, smiling wickedly. "The limit, much like your beautiful self, is what I, the function, or f of x, approaches—moving closer and closer to," he said, enacting his words and scooting closer and closer to Mimi. "But he can never," he continued, inching closer as Mimi leaned away, "quite"—he spread his arms—"get there!" he concluded, throwing his arms around her and burying her beneath him.

Dana shook her head in disbelief and looked at Callie. "You'd think studying calculus is the one time we'd be safe from all this … flirting." She wrinkled her nose.

Callie laughed. "Looks like you've got your work cut out for you."

"*Ahem!*" Dana coughed, clearing her throat and tapping OK's shoulder. When he failed to react, she grabbed him with a strength that seemed to surprise even her and threw him back against the couch. "*You* will stay right here. And *you*," she said, pointing at Mimi. "If you insist on staying, kindly sit in the armchair *over there*."

"Yes, ma'am." Mimi laughed. She made her way to the overstuffed armchair where Callie was sitting and perched herself atop her roommate's lap.

Callie smiled.

"Missed you, *ma chèrie*," Mimi whispered, wrapping an arm around Callie's shoulders.

"I somehow get the feeling that you're the only one." Callie sighed, watching while OK squinted at the notepad on which Dana was patiently drawing.

"*Tut, tut.*" Mimi clicked her tongue reproachfully. "You two …"

"I heard her this morning," said Callie. "She sounded angry."

"This is a triangle. Do you know what a triangle is?" Dana asked OK.

"A triangle—bless my boots. You mean that three-sided thing isn't a square?"

Callie and Mimi burst out laughing. Dana silenced them with

a glare. Mimi looked thoughtful. Turning to Callie, she said: "Yes, Vanessa is angry. Almost as angry as Mama the time she caught me finger-painting on her Chanel suits . . . *Pourquoi pas*: I was six and I had run out of paper!"

Was she kidding? As always, it was nearly impossible to tell.

"But seriously," Mimi continued, "you two are so close. You will work it out."

"I don't know . . ." Callie murmured. She stared at the floor, wondering if Mimi knew about the tape. She certainly knew about Gregory at Harvard-Yale: he and Callie had hooked up in her shared hotel room, and even though Gregory had been gone, in mysterious Gregory fashion, by the time Callie had woken up that morning, Mimi had been the one to locate her underwear on the other side of the room. *Oops.* Mimi had spent that night across the hall in OK's hotel room. In fact . . .

"What's going on with you and Mr. Cotangent-ly Challenged?" Callie whispered.

"I do not know what you are speaking about." Mimi grinned. "Though one might ask *you* the same question about—" She paused when Callie winced, almost as if she were in physical pain.

"Sorry," Mimi muttered.

"No, it's okay—" Callie started.

"What?" asked OK.

"Ugggg. Sorry, no, not you." Callie moaned.

"Hey! Back to work!" snapped Dana.

"Fine, fine, sorry, back to cosine . . . fascinating . . ."

Callie laughed. "It's *all right*," she said to Mimi. "I haven't heard from him since Harvard-Yale."

"Wait," said Mimi. "Which one?"

Callie half laughed, half groaned, dragging her hands from her forehead down the sides of her cheeks. "Both. Neither. Ha-ha. Exactly."

"And now for the *Who Wants to Be a Millionaire* question," said Mimi. "Which one do you *want* to hear from?"

Gregory paused with his hand hovering above the doorknob to C 24. Shaking his head, he turned back. Then he stopped in the middle of the hallway, eyeing the door again. "Idiot," he muttered. Turning once more, he yanked open the door to his own suite, C 23.

"Back so soon?" asked Matt from where he was sitting on their big leather couch.

"Yeah," muttered Gregory, sinking down beside him.

"Hey, is it cool if I use your computer to check my—"

"No!" Gregory cried, slamming the screen shut before Matt could discover a certain photograph from the Harvard-Yale tailgate that Gregory was in the habit of leaving open on his browser.

"Geez—sorry," Matt apologized. "I'll go get my own."

When he returned, he found Gregory staring at his cell phone like he was facing down an archrival in a duel. For the moment they had reached a cool détente, but at any second the phone might leap up and start firing.

"Why do you keep checking your phone?" Matt asked.

"What? No reason," said Gregory, dropping the phone like it had burned him.

"No judgment," said Matt, holding up his palms. Gregory sighed and picked up the phone again, scrolling through his messages. Suddenly, Matt began to chuckle.

"What?" snapped Gregory.

Matt continued to laugh, shaking his head. "It's just funny. Last fall you had all these women and now you're kind of . . . acting like one."

For a second Gregory looked murderous. Then he shrugged. "I fail to see the humor in that," he murmured. "In fact, I think it's a bit derogatory toward women."

Matt's eyes grew wide but Gregory didn't notice; instead he was reading, or rather rereading, the unsent drafts in his phone's out-box.

TO ANDREWS, CALLIE: I THINK ABOUT YOU EVERY DAY. IT'S LIKE I'M GOING CRAZY. WHY . . .

TO ANDREWS, CALLIE: REMEMBER THE BALCONY WHEN IT STARTED TO RAIN? THE WAY . . .

TO ANDREWS, CALLIE: I SUPPOSE YOU WANT ME TO LEAVE YOU ALONE UNTIL YOU WORK TH . . .

TO ANDREWS, CALLIE: AS LONG AS I'M NEVER SENDING THESE, I WANT YOU TO KNOW THAT . . .

TO ANDREWS, CALLIE: I KNOW YOU
PROBABLY THINK I COULD NEVER
CHANGE, BUT MAYBE . . .

TO ANDREWS, CALLIE: CLINT
E-MAILED ME AGAIN, WHICH IS WHY
I'M NOT SENDING THES . . .

TO ANDREWS, CALLIE: GREG,
YOU'RE AN IDIOT. YOU KNOW YOU'LL
NEVER SEND THESE.

His fingers, as they had often done in the past few days, hovered over the Delete button. But he just couldn't do it. Shaking his head, he keyed back over to his inbox.

It was still empty. Or at least empty of anything interesting save for the types of messages that had come in from Clint over Thanksgiving break: "ARE YOU SURE THAT I SHOULDN'T AT LEAST E-MAIL HER? NOT TALKING IS KILLING ME . . ."

Gregory's forehead wrinkled guiltily as he reread his own response: "DON'T E-MAIL. YOU GAVE HER AN ULTIMATUM AND YOU NEED TO STAND BY IT. SHE PROBABLY WANTS HER SPACE. I'M SURE SHE WILL CONTACT YOU WHEN, OR IF, SHE'S READY TO TALK."

It was clear that neither of them had spoken to her over Thanksgiving break. Maybe that meant that he and Clint were on an even playing field. That he would have a fighting chance.

"Going somewhere?" Matt asked as Gregory stood up again.

"No," said Gregory, sitting back down. "No I'm not."

❧

"Enough about boys," said Mimi. "What are you going to do about Vanessa?"

"What am *I* going to do? Why should I be the one to *do* anything?" asked Callie.

Mimi shrugged. "I am not sure I am understanding the expression correctly, but I think it is you who should be the bigger person. Even though she is the bigger person this way," Mimi added, gesturing toward her hips.

Callie laughed. "You might not be on her side if you knew what she did to me—"

Mimi cut her off. "I am not taking sides. I do not judge. In fact, I really do not care what happened. I just do not want to spend my reading period being the Berlin Wall."

Am I East or West Germany? Callie wondered.

And so Callie had eventually returned to her desk to pen an apology to the girl who had sold Callie's secrets to Satan in exchange for a "guaranteed" membership in the Hasty Pudding social club. The club, which had rejected Vanessa in favor of Callie, had been the original source of tension in their relationship. (In graphic form it looked like: frenemies → friends → BFFs → frenemies → WWIII.)

It was then that Callie had spotted the "Manifesto" taped to her bedroom window. And so, when she began to write, her words took on a slightly different tone than a traditional apology.

In response to Item 1) *You hooked up with Gregory at Harvard-Yale when you knew how I felt about him*, she wrote:

> What happened at Harvard-Yale was a huge mistake. It was wrong for us to have slept together, and if I could take it back, I would.

In response to Items 2) *You screwed up our entire room dynamic* and 3) *You blew it with Clint*, she couldn't help but agree.

> I messed up the room dynamic, and I probably blew it with Clint.

As for Item 4) *You're an all-out terrible person*, she countered:

> I may be a terrible person, but if I am, then you are just as bad, if not worse.

And now, on to Vanessa's actions regarding Callie's deepest secret, which she had conveniently neglected to include in the Manifesto.

> I cannot believe that I was ever stupid enough to put my trust in someone like you.

Last but not least, in response to Item 5) *There is no hope that I will ever forgive you. We will never be best friends ever again*, she agreed, then amended:

> There is no hope for us in the future. I don't see how we could even just be friends.

"Let alone *best* friends," Callie muttered aloud. And now, for the grand finale:

> There's nothing I can do about the fact that we're living in such close quarters—believe me, if I could, I would—so let's just try to stay as far away from each other as possible.

Setting down her pen, she took a deep breath and read the whole thing over from the beginning. Then, satisfied, she signed her name with a flourish. It wasn't exactly the *best* apology; in fact, it sounded a bit more like a declaration of war. Better not let Mimi proofread it.

"'Lucy, I'm ho-ome!'" a voice yelled from the common room. The sound filled Callie with dread. *The bitch*—to use the bitch's own catchphrase—*was back.*

"Ew, studying already? Reading period doesn't even start until next week!"

"Just trying to get caught up," OK explained.

Callie, note in hand, gritted her teeth. Here goes nothing, she thought. She stepped out of her room.

"Hey. Vanessa."

Vanessa's face froze for an instant, then relaxed. "Do you guys hear something?"

Mimi rolled her eyes. Dana looked up from the calculus, wrinkling her brow. "Yes, Callie just said, 'Hey, Vanessa'!" Apparently *sarcasm* was still missing from the vast lexicon of Dana's brain.

"Oh, my bad," said Vanessa mildly. "I guess I just don't know how to speak *Traitorous Slut*."

Callie's fists clenched at her sides.

"Well, *really*," Dana began, setting aside her book, "if you're going to insist on using that foul language, perhaps we had better take our tutorial elsewhe—"

"Have fun burning a hole in your pocket?" Callie cut in, eyeing the shopping bags in Vanessa's hand. A bag full of overpriced party dresses and her iPhone were Vanessa's favorite accessories. She was rarely seen without them. "Or should we say, *Mommy and Daddy's* pocket?"

Vanessa stiffened. Then she forced a smile. "I have a date tonight," she said, addressing Dana and Mimi. "And no, not with my best friend's boyfriend, or my boyfriend's best friend—it's just not my style."

Callie suddenly felt very tired. She just wanted to lie down and give up. Her response to the Manifesto had crumpled in her fist. It would only add gasoline to the fire; even a true apology note didn't stand a chance of restoring the peace. It was like the Middle East. Not even Jimmy Carter was up to this task.

She exhaled and the note slipped through her fingers. It landed on the arm of the couch before sliding down to join the pile of papers next to OK's textbook.

"All right, Vanessa; you win," she muttered. "I'll try to stay out of your way."

"Thanks, *pal* . . . but wait!" Vanessa called as Callie turned toward her room. "I have a better idea! Why don't you move to Pennypacker? Or somewhere even farther—like Siberia?"

"It's chillier than Siberia in here," OK muttered. Then louder: "Well, ladies, I had better get going back across the hall. Mimi?"

Mimi nodded and started to help OK gather his things.

"I'll come, too," said Dana. Noticing OK's worried expression, she added. "To visit *Adam*. That was enough math for today."

"Yo, Mimi," said OK as she handed him a pile of his papers. "Now I know my calculus: it says you plus me equals us."

"*Eugh,*" Mimi groaned. She stood and followed Dana out the door.

"Hey OK," Callie called suddenly. "Could I talk to you for a second?"

"Sure thing, Blondie," he said, pausing at the door.

"Maybe we should talk in the hall," Callie suggested, feeling Vanessa's eyes burning a hole into the back of her head.

"What's up?" OK asked when they were alone.

"Um . . . well . . . do you think you could do me a favor?" asked Callie.

"Depends on the favor," he said.

"Can you tell Gregory that I need to talk to him?"

"All right."

"And that it's about what happened at Harvard-Yale . . ."

"Got it."

"And can you tell him—um—can you tell him that I missed him?"

"Whoa, whoa, whoa!" said OK, throwing up his hands. "That's kind of a lot to remember."

Callie laughed. "Do you want me to write it down for you?"

"No," said OK, "I'll manage. Callie, talk, Harvard-Yale, missed you—got it."

"Great." She turned back toward her door. "And OK," she added, "thank you."

Inside the common room, Vanessa was admiring her new dress in front of the full-length mirror. She whirled around when Callie walked in. Their eyes locked and Vanessa just stood there clutching the dress, seeming less sure of herself now without an audience. But then Callie turned and, beating Vanessa to the punch, walked into her bedroom and slammed the door.

Eyeing the train wreck that was her room, Callie sighed: she didn't feel like cleaning; preparing for the final week of classes sounded like torture, unpacking would make things messier, and she was probably only one nap away from growing fur and turning into a sloth.

She pulled her running shorts out of her suitcase, along with sweatpants and a sports bra. A long run ought to cure her rage: with every step she pounded she could picture Vanessa's face under her shoe.

"Do not, under any circumstances, go over there right now!" OK cried as he, Dana, and Mimi trouped into the common room across from C 24. Matt looked up questioningly, but Gregory, who had been on his way to the front door again, paused. "Why not?"

"It's colder than the Cold War over there," OK explained.

"Colder than Siberia," Mimi added.

"East and West Berlin circa 1988," said OK.

"Lauren Conrad and Heidi Montag circa 2008," said Mimi.

"Yankees versus Red Sox."

"Harvard versus Yale."

"Harry Potter and Lord Vold—"

"Callie and Vanessa are in a fight," Dana interrupted.

"Still?" asked Matt, looking concerned. "Isn't that a little long—even for girl world?"

Dana shrugged. "I'm staying out of it," she said. Then she walked into Adam's room and closed the door behind her.

"I tried to convince Callie to kiss Vanessa and make up," said Mimi, sinking onto the couch, "but Vanessa does not seem to be in a make-up mood."

"Oh, well," said OK, "guess you'll just have to stay here until the fighting stops." He grinned. "You can sleep in my room . . ."

"Video games, anyone?" Mimi asked, ignoring him and pointing to a shiny new copy of Grand Theft Auto V.

"*Bien sûr, mon amour,*" OK agreed in an abysmal French accent, throwing his calculus notes onto the coffee table and sitting down next to her.

"Sure, why not?" said Matt, picking up a controller.

"Gregory?" asked Mimi.

Gregory looked over his shoulder toward the door, then at the TV screen, and then back at the door. "Just give me one minute. There's something I have to take care of first."

Callie slipped out of C 24. Her feet already felt lighter in her running shoes. Practically jogging down the hallway, she took the stairs two at a time. When she burst out of the entryway, flecks of snow went flying, the freezing late November air nipping at her face. She breathed deeply, letting the frozen air fill her lungs, and then she began to run, leaving the monsters and demons in the dust.

❧

Gregory crossed the hall and walked into C 24. It was empty, the door to Callie's room shut. He took a deep breath and knocked.

No answer.

He looked over his shoulder, then shook his head and opened the door to her bedroom. It was also empty. And a huge mess.

"You're here early!" a voice called from behind him.

"Oh," Vanessa continued, stepping out of her bedroom and blushing when Gregory turned to face her. "Wrong person! I have a date later."

"Uh—cool," said Gregory. "Listen, Vanessa, could you do me a favor? Could you tell Callie that I stopped by?"

Two identical spots of color flared on Vanessa's cheeks. Then she smoothed her face into a smile. "Sure," she said.

Back inside his own common room, Gregory sank onto the leather couch opposite the virtual death match that had manifested in his absence. Mimi whooped when she lit a car on fire and Matt groaned, throwing his Xbox controller on the couch. Shaking his head, Gregory looked down at the stack of papers piled on the coffee table in front of him.

"Calculus?" he asked, rifling through the notes.

"Eh?" said OK, frantically pushing buttons.

But Gregory, who had just picked up a crumpled sheet of paper buried underneath Dana's *Notes on Triangles*, did not reply.

"Oh, that reminds me," said OK, his eyes glued to the television.

"Callie wanted me to give you some sort of a message."

Gregory tore his gaze away from the note he'd been reading and held it up: "So this—this is supposed to be for me, then?"

"What? Oh, she decided to write it down after all," said OK, executing the police officer that he'd been holding at gunpoint. "I'm off the hook—excellent."

Slowly Gregory looked back down at the piece of paper in his hands.

What happened at Harvard-Yale was a huge mistake. It was wrong for us to have slept together, and if I could take it back, I would. I messed up the room dynamic, and I probably blew it with Clint.

I may be a terrible person, but if I am, then you are just as bad, if not worse. I cannot believe that I was ever stupid enough to put my trust in someone like you.

There is no hope for us in the future. I don't see how we could even just be friends.

There's nothing I can do about the fact that we're living in such close quarters—believe me, if I could, I would—so let's just try to stay as far away from each other as possible.

Callie

TWO

YOUR NEW ASSIGNMENTS

From: **Anne Goldberg**
To: **Anne Goldberg**
BCC: **Callie Andrews**
Subject: Dues

Dear Pudding Members,

If you are receiving this e-mail, it is because we have yet to collect your installment of this semester's dues. Just a friendly reminder that we need these before the end of the year should you wish to continue on as an active member of our organization. (Check, cash, or credit by December 31 at the absolute latest, please.) We have many exciting events to look forward to in the coming months, and it would be a shame for you to miss out! I know it's a very busy time for all of us, but please do find a moment between this last week of classes and reading period to drop by the club, or e-mail me to arrange an appointment. I wish you the best of luck with the rest of year!

Cheers,
Anne Goldberg, Secretary

From: **Student Receivables**
To: **Callie Andrews**
Subject: Re: Possible Salary Advancement

Dear Ms. Andrews,
We regret to inform you that our offices are not authorized to grant an advancement of your salary for the position of Reference Desk Assistant at Lamont Library Services at this time. We sympathize with your predicament and suggest that, if the situation is grave, you schedule an immediate appointment with the Harvard College Financial Aid Office at 86 Brattle Street or apply for aid directly online. Raises, also by policy, are not available for students until they have been working at least one semester. We will evaluate your case come February 1, 2011.

Best of luck,
Student Receivables

To: **Theresa Frederickson, Thomas Andrews**
From: **Callie Andrews**
Subject: **[Saved as DRAFT]** I need to borrow one thousand dollars because . . .

~~My roommate's cat is pregnant and needs a~~
~~The textbook for Economics 10b is *really* expensive and~~
~~I am so cold I need at least ten more layers of warm clothing~~
I have developed a gambling problem and the loan sharks are after me

T ap, tap, tap . . .

   Callie moaned and rolled over.

Tap, tap, tap . . .

Her hand flew out from underneath her covers to hit the snooze button on her cell, but the obnoxious noise continued. At some point the alarm had stopped ringing and her phone had figured out how to make a light rapping sound, almost like someone was knocking on her door.

Wait a second. Cell phones can do a lot of things these days, but they can't tuck you in at night, make you breakfast, or say "I love you," and they certainly can't knock. Only humans can do that.

"Come in," she called, sitting up in bed.

"Hey you!" a male voice said. Matt walked into the room with a huge grin on his face and stood hovering over her bed. "Welcome back!"

"Matty!" Callie cried, leaping up and wrapping her arms around him. For a second she felt self-conscious about her pajamas (boy shorts and a tank top). Should I change? she thought.

Nah, she decided. Matt didn't care. Goofy and gangly, it was almost as if he'd been handed a card in the game of life that said, *Go straight to Awkward—do NOT pass Attractive; do NOT collect $200.* He was like the brother she never had. (At least, that's what *she* thought—a clever observer might have reason

30

to believe that Matt would find any "brother" references rather horrifying.)

"Boy, am I glad to see you," she said when Matt finally let go.

"Really?" he asked, a familiar blush creeping into his cheeks. "Then how come you haven't been across the hall? Our door's been open, you know. . . ."

Callie frowned and climbed back onto her bed. "Well, I didn't get back until the middle of the night on Sunday and . . . things are a little crazy at the moment."

"So I heard," said Matt.

"Oh—what'd you hear?" Callie asked, staring him down.

"Not much: Vanessa broke a nail and wants you dead, etcetera, etcetera."

"Yeah. That about sums it up."

"Whatever. You're better off without her. Anyway, we're still on for lunch tomorrow before economics, right?"

"Yep." Callie smiled. Then she groaned. "I can't believe there are only two more classes left until reading period and then we have to take . . . *the exam*. I'm so behind, I'm probably going to fail!"

Matt chuckled. "Stop exaggerating. I'm sure you'll be fine."

"I am *not* exaggerating!" she cried, throwing a pillow at his head. "I got an e-mail from our teaching fellow over the break warning me that I'm in danger of getting a . . ." Her eyes grew wide. Why did it seem like every e-mail she received these days—from Lexi, her econ TF, and now Anne and Student Receivables—was one of the four horsemen of the apocalypse?

"Getting a . . . ?"

"A *C*," she whispered.

"Oh no!" He gasped, his hands flying to his cheeks in mock horror. "The end of the world—it's here!"

"It is!" She moaned. "I've never even gotten a *B* before. It's going to *kill* my dad and he will die of a broken heart or a heart attack and it'll be all my fault—"

She stopped talking when Matt began to laugh. "It's not *that* bad," he said.

She narrowed her eyes. "I'm sure *you're* not getting a C."

"Well, no, but . . . Hey, I could tutor you—if you want."

"That would be amazing!" she cried. Jumping out of bed, she hugged him again.

Averting his eyes from her bare legs, Matt cleared his throat and said, "I also came over to tell you the news: I just found out that I made it past the second round of *Crimson* COMP!"

"You did?" She yelped. Matt was COMPing the *Harvard Crimson*, the university's daily newspaper and parent organization of *Fifteen Minutes* magazine. "Do you think *FM* results are— I mean, uh, congratulations!"

"Thanks." Matt smiled. "And I bet *FM* probably will return your portfolios now if they haven't already. In fact, I think I saw a manila envelope in your drop box on my way in—"

"What?" Callie shrieked, running past him. She flew across the common room and flung open the front door.

A manila envelope was sitting in the box. Her pulse was racing. Callie Andrews was written across the front in big black lettering.

She grabbed the envelope and slipped back inside. Matt was staring at her from across the room. "Well . . . ?" he asked.

She looked at him and then down at the envelope. Her heart slowed to a steady *thrum*, accompanied by a sinking feeling. There was no way she had made it to the final round. Even if Lexi hadn't sabotaged her or—heaven forbid—told the other editors about the tape, she was still competing against so many talented people that—

"Are you going to open it or not?" Matt interrupted her thoughts.

She shook her head. "No. No, I can't."

"Yes you can." Matt walked over and placed his hands on her shoulders. He guided her to the couch and then sat down beside her. "How about you do it on the count of three? One . . . two . . ."

"I can't!" she cried, covering her eyes with one hand and shoving the envelope toward him with the other. "You have to do it."

"You sure?"

Both hands over her eyes now, she nodded.

"All right," he said. Ripping the envelope open, he pulled out the stack of sample articles she had submitted for her second portfolio. Quickly, he skimmed the note on top.

"Well?" she asked, peeking at him through her fingers. "Good news . . . or bad?"

"The bad news is . . . that you've got a lot more work to do over the next coming weeks. But the good news is you made it!"

"What!" she cried. "I—I made it?"

"Yep!" He grinned.

"*Eeeeeeeeeeeyaaaah!*" she shrieked, leaping up and clapping her hands. She'd made it! In spite of Lexi's conspiracies, Vanessa's betrayal, and the destitute states of both her love life and current GPA, *still* she had made it. "Yes!" she cried, jumping up and down. "Thank you, t—" Pausing suddenly, she frowned and said: "'The bad news is'—how could you do that to me?"

"It wasn't me!" he cried. "That's what it says right here."

"Oh," she said, taking the note:

Dear Callie Andrews:
The bad news is that you've got a lot more work to do over the next coming weeks. But the good news is you made it! You are still in the running for the final round. You'll have until winter break to revise these pieces and write some new ones for your last COMP portfolio. Good luck!

The Editors at FM

"Congratulations," Matt said, handing her the other papers he had pulled out of the envelope.

As she took them, another small slip—light pink and what looked like personal stationary—fluttered to the ground. She bent over and picked it up:

Callie,

Please come meet me in the FM offices as soon as you receive this. I will be there today from 10 A.M.—2 P.M..

I would like to offer my heartfelt congratulations and give you your list of assignments for the final round in person.

Cheers to your success,

Lexi

"Heartfelt congratulations"? Since when had *congratulations* become a synonym for *death threats*? Callie glanced at the clock. It was almost 2 P.M. *Shit.* Lexi liked to be kept waiting just about as much as she liked shopping at Walmart or taking public transportation.

Callie looked up. "Matt, I have to—"

"Go?" he finished. "That's fine. Go ahead. I'll see you for lunch tomorrow. And then we can set up our first tutoring session after class."

"Perfect," she said. "Thanks for being the best!"

"You got it," he replied, making his way to the door. By the time it had swung shut, she was yanking on her faded jeans. Hopping around her room with one leg on, one leg off, she grabbed her old soccer sweatshirt, a scarf (the maroon cashmere that Clint had given her), and the one glove she could find. Clothing in tow, she rushed for the door, pulling on her jacket and pocketing the glove as she headed down the stairs and then out into the cold toward the *Crimson* headquarters.

Soon she was climbing the stairs to the second-floor offices in the old brick building where breaking news like "No More Hot Breakfast" and "Widener Library Open Late" was written. The door was shut. Tentatively she knocked.

"Come in," a sweet, clear voice called from inside.

Callie took a deep breath and entered the room. She shivered. Somehow it seemed colder in here than it had been outside.

"Well, if it isn't Callie Andrews," said a girl, spinning around in the black, high-tech ergonomic office chair that, in these parts, was her throne.

Alexis Vivienne Thorndike.

She looked immaculate as usual. Her shampoo-ad-worthy chestnut curls were pinned at the sides with two slim, pearly white barrettes. She wore a deceivingly simple navy dress—plain on the outside, Gucci on the inside label—over sheer tights, and a thin gold belt matched the delicate chain around her neck. The chaos of the messy office around her—with its gray desks, rows of computers, green lamps, and piles of old drafts and newspapers— only threw the perfect order of her appearance into greater relief.

Callie swallowed. No matter how much she hated, or feared, or envied Alexis in her presence one particular feeling took precedence above everything else: inferiority. Suddenly she felt hot and flustered. She pulled off the hood of her sweatshirt, exposing her own shampoo-ad worthy hair—worthy of the "before" section in a "before and after" story, that is—and unwound Clint's scarf from her neck. Remember to breathe, she instructed herself, fiddling with the scarf.

"So lovely to have you back," Lexi cooed.

Translation: *You should have taken my hint and never returned.*

"I was worried that the pressure might be too much for you," she continued.

Translation: *Haven't had enough yet? Well, I can fix that.*

"Do anything fun or *wild* over the break?"

Translation: *Make any more sex tapes I should know about?*

"No," said Callie. "Nothing too exciting other than eating and sleeping and—"

"That's nice," Lexi interrupted. "So," she continued, "you're probably wondering why I called you here today."

To . . . murder me?

"Yes," said Callie, eyes darting around the room looking for a weapon—ahem—reason.

"In addition to congratulating you on defying all of our expectations by making it to the final round, I wanted to give you some advice. From someone older and wiser to someone younger and . . . well, like you. Please—sit," she added, gesturing to a nearby chair.

Callie obeyed. She leaned forward, unaware that she was gripping the edge of her seat so hard that her knuckles were turning white.

"Now, let's see," said Lexi, picking up a pile of papers resting near her computer. "I have a list of your new assignments—for COMP, of course—right here," she said, selecting a sheet from the stack. "Before I give it to you, however, I want to emphasize the importance of completing these assignments without deviating from the instructions."

Callie nodded. So this was it: Lexi was going to keep her off the magazine by forcing her to write on the most ridiculous subject matter possible. These new assignments would probably be even worse than her topics from the previous months, which included *Vaseline: Friend or Foe?* and *Foot Fungus in the Freshman Showers: Alert Level ORANGE*. Callie had tried to make the most of those pieces, tweaking the guidelines to write something more substantial ("while we're on the topic of alert levels, are they really a successful barometer of an imminent threat?") or attempting an ironic spin ("Vaseline is the twenty-first century's cure-all answer to even the toughest problems: Squeaky door? Vaseline. Low on mousse? Vaseline. Out of Mayo? Vaseline!").

Callie sighed. Of course Lexi would never do something so sordid as to release the tape; she was just making sure Callie had an incentive to follow instructions. Still, thought Callie, why bother? *Why not just get rid of me now?*

As if she could read Callie's mind, Lexi, toying a finger through the gold chain around her neck, said, "Now, I know we've had our differences, but your—er—talent is clear, and I've come around to the idea that you could be very *useful*. To the magazine, of course."

Callie gulped.

"It is crucial, however," Lexi continued, "that we, the editors, get a chance to see your commitment, dedication, and above all, obedience. If you should fail or refuse to complete any of these new assignments, I'm afraid that you would be in danger of . . . exposing yourself as someone who has a problem with authority. Is this making sense to you?"

"Yes," said Callie through gritted teeth. "I get it." If I don't write your stupid pieces and make myself look like an idiot, then you'll "expose" the tape. "Are you going to give me the list?" Callie asked, eyeing the paper that Lexi still held just out of arm's reach.

"Silly me—of course," said Lexi, handing it to Callie.

Callie barely glanced at it before looking back up at her. "So are we—" She paused. Slowly her eyes fell back toward the sheet of paper she held in her hands. They grew wide. You can't be serious. "You can't be . . ."

"Can't be what?"

"Um—nothing, sorry, I just . . . I mean . . ."

Lexi gasped suddenly with apparent concern. "Look at the time," she said. "Please forgive me for keeping you; with so much work to do, you must be anxious to get started!"

"Yes," said Callie, clutching her "new assignments" list in her fist. "Lots of work," she muttered, standing and heading toward the door. Her cheeks were on fire, and she knew she was minutes, if not seconds, away from the same helpless hysteria that had set in once during her senior year in high school when an evil soccer referee had given her a yellow card with twenty minutes left in the game. Unable to watch as the opponents clobbered her team, she had locked herself in a bathroom stall, where she had stayed long after the game was over. Too bad the bathrooms at the *Crimson* were all the way down on the first floor.

"Callie?" called Lexi.

Callie froze with her hand poised above the doorknob.

"I have just one more piece of advice."

"Yes?" asked Callie, forcing herself to turn and meet Lexi's eyes.

"Personally I always find that when a girl is truly dedicated to her work, she doesn't have time for boys or a boyfriend—especially not someone older. Upperclassmen can be so distracting, and it would be such a shame to see you lose . . . so much . . . for a fling that never would have lasted until next semester anyway. Am I making myself clear?"

Callie stared, clutching Clint's scarf in her hands. Finally she said in a whisper, "Crystal."

THREE

Are you There, Fairy Godmother?
It's Me, Callie.

COMP ASSIGNMENTS for C. Andrews, December 2010

Prompt: "Where are the best places to go for dry cleaning in Harvard Square?"

Hint: Arrow Street Cleaners is the best, but they close at 5 P.M. Thank you *so* much for volunteering to pick up for A. Thorndike today in time for the Financial Aid benefit this evening!

Prompt: "Massachusetts Drinking Water: Tap vs. Bottled—worth the price?"

Feel free to sample <u>one</u> VOSS water from the prepaid crate that arrives weekly at CVS (under A. Thorndike) on your way between pickup and delivery to Kirkland House, entryway J, room 13.

Prompt: "Top Five Beauty Buys in Harvard Square"

Helpful hints:
1) OPI nail polish in "I'm Not Really a Waitress" from CVS
2) Almost Lipstick in "Black Honey" from the Clinique counter at the Harvard Coop
3) Clinique Happy Heart Perfume Gift Set (also from the Clinique counter)
4) Coconut Body Butter from the Harvard Square Body Shop
5) Gino's Bio-Gel Mousse from the Gino Salon
(Be sure to purchase all of these for research purposes and save receipts to be reimbursed!)

Prompt: "The Underground World of Initiation Tasks for Social Clubs on Campus"

Again for research purposes deliver the items above, wrapped and with a card, as follows:

(1) Anne Goldberg in Kirkland J 13; (2) Brittney Saunders in Cabot B 33; (3) Ashleigh Templeton in Eliot F 16; (4) Madison McLaughlin in Kirkland J 13; (5) Trudy Prince in Winthrop C 44; be sure to ask if there's anything else you can do for your Pudding "big sisters"!

Prompt: "Dining Out: The Best Places to Go for a Light Lunch in Harvard Square"

Wouldn't it be great to get to know each other a little better over lunch? You can drop mine off every Monday through Thursday anytime between 12 P.M.–2 P.M. at the FM Office. Pick up The Vivienne (it's a special salad—they'll know what you mean) and a Diet Coke from the Greenhouse Café at your convenience—wouldn't want you missing any class!

Prompt: "Ten Reasons Why Freshman Girls Should Never Date Upperclassmen"

Nobody likes a hypocrite—live as you preach!

Callie: I hope you'll complete these assignments in a diligent and timely manner! Best of luck, xxx Lexi

Callie paused in front of the big glass window labeled ARROW STREET CLEANERS in gold block lettering, rubbing her arms. Her biceps ached from lugging a gigantic crate of VOSS water—bottled in Norway and made from distilled unicorn and mermaid tears with crushed diamonds instead of minerals (or so you would think, given the price)—from CVS all the way to Kirkland House where Lexi lived in a suite with Anne Goldberg and some of the other Pudding girls. A note on the whiteboard read LEAVE ALL DELIVERIES AT THE DOOR, so she hadn't even been able to sneak a peek into the enemy lair. Even though it had felt like hours, the trip—including four rest breaks—had taken only thirty minutes. Still, she'd barely made it to the cleaners before the 5 P.M. closing.

Like losing her pot-smoking "virginity" or her imminent C in economics, going to the dry cleaners was about to become another College First. After all, since the majority of her clothing ended up with grass stains or in the bottom of her gym bag, she tended to avoid anything sporting a "DRY CLEAN ONLY" label.

The bell above the glass front door tinkled when she stepped inside.

"Hi," she said, smiling at the man sitting behind the counter who had more hair on his face than on his head. "I'm picking up for A. Thorndike?"

The man set down his newspaper and squinted over the thick

frames of his glasses. "You are not Ms. Thorndike," he said, speaking with a Pakistani accent. "Ms. Thorndike will get very, very angry if I give clothing to a stranger!"

"But I'm not a stranger, I'm her—" Callie paused. What was she, exactly? Her maid? Personal assistant? B-I-T-C-H? Blackmailee? Helpless little stepdaughter Cinder-Callie . . .

"Yes?" he prompted.

"I'm doing her a favor. So if you could please just hand over the clothes—"

"No. Absolutely not. You are not doing anybody any favors if Ms. Thorndike's dry cleaning is not here *exactly* the way she likes it. Very good customer—but very, very particular!"

And very, very going to kill me if I don't get this done. "Please . . ." Callie began. The man continued shaking his head. "Please—Wait!" she suddenly cried. "I have a note!" Digging into her book bag, she pulled out the paper detailing her new COMP Assignments, i.e. the lengthy list of personal favors thinly disguised as prompts. "Here," she said, sliding the page across the counter. "That's her handwriting—right there!"

The man made a great show of polishing his lenses before pushing his glasses back up his nose and looking at the sheet of paper. After what felt like forever, he shoved it back toward Callie. "Very well," he said. "Wait here."

"Thank you," she called as he disappeared behind rows of plastic-covered dress shirts.

In a minute he returned wheeling a clothing rack with some fifteen-odd dresses, skirts, and tops, each immaculately ironed, pressed, and individually wrapped. It was incredible: Gucci, Prada, DVF, D&G, Zac Posen, and more: a semester's worth of Harvard tuition all on one little rack in a dingy dry cleaner.

"Which ones belong to Alexis?" Callie asked, sticking her hands in her pockets lest she inadvertently reach out and rip the plastic off to run her fingers over the luscious fabrics. Or grab that cigarette lighter lying on the counter, flick it open, and set the entire rack on fire.

The man gave her a funny look. "All of these belong to Ms. Thorndike."

"All?" Callie asked, her eyes widening. "Everything here?"

"You count," he replied, misunderstanding. "It is all here."

"No, I just meant—"

"You count!" He was agitated. "We make no mistake," he added, pointing to an itemized receipt that was taped to one end of the metal rack. "But you verify, to be certain. We make mistake once: lose dress"—he shuddered—"and Ms. Alexis get very, very angry. She yell, very loud, and my wife—she make her cry. Now my wife, she will not work on Tuesdays."

Callie gulped. She could definitely sympathize with Mrs. Arrow Street Cleaners. "Maybe it is a good idea to check," she said, taking the receipt from the rack, "just to be sure."

The man nodded, returning to his newspaper. Callie began to sift through the clothing on the rack, checking the receipt and then sliding the item from right to left.

She was nearly two-thirds of the way through when suddenly, through the space between a red floor-length gown and a black single-shoulder dress, she spotted a familiar figure through the glass windows making his way down the street: Clint.

He had pulled his scarf up against the cold and his light brown hair was messy and windswept as usual. Even though he was still several dozen feet away, he stood out among the crowd: tall, gorgeous, perfect in every imaginable way and . . .

Slowing down . . . Callie realized with horror. Clint came to a halt in front of the dry cleaner. He glanced at his watch and reached for the door.

Callie grabbed the dresses on either side of her and yanked the hangers toward the center, closing the gap and concealing her—hopefully—from view. She glanced down at her dirty Converses and shuffled to the left behind the red floor-length number.

The bell over the glass door tinkled. "Almost didn't make it!" she heard Clint exclaim, sounding slightly out of breath. She heard footsteps and then his voice coming from near the counter. "How's it going, Hassan?"

"Very well, Mr. Weber. Good to see you, sir." The owner—Hassan—was also blocked from view, and Callie stood still, holding her breath. Were her feet visible? Biting her lip, she tried to concentrate on counting the buttons of a Missoni sweater. She wasn't even sure why exactly she was hiding, only that it was too late to be mature now.

"I will be right back," Hassan continued, and Callie watched, barely daring to breathe, as he disappeared down an aisle and returned with three plastic-wrapped dress shirts.

"Two Oxfords and one tuxedo shirt, Mr. Weber," he said, laying the shirts on the counter.

"Thanks so much. Just in time for the Financial Aid benefit tonight," said Clint, reaching for his wallet. "That'll be . . . ?"

"Seven fifty."

It was silent save for the ding of the cash register. Then—

"You there!" Hassan's voice boomed loudly. Callie cringed. "What are you doing hiding in the corner? Hurry up—the store is about to close!"

Callie did not answer. Instead she continued to count buttons and hold her breath, willing Clint to take his tuxedo shirt and leave: please . . . go . . . now.

"Crazy customer," Hassan muttered. Clint chuckled sympathetically. "I'm sure you've seen it all," she heard him say.

Leave . . . leave . . . leave . . .

There was more rustling and then—thank goodness—footsteps.

Unfortunately they appeared to be heading in the wrong direction. "There's something very familiar about that dress . . . and this one," she heard Clint murmur under his breath. "Hassan, who do these belong to?"

But before Hassan could answer, Clint was reaching out to slide the hangers aside, saying "Lex, is that you back th— *Callie?*"

"Clint!" she managed to choke out, trying to look surprised even though she knew she was redder than the dress Clint was clinging to in amazement.

"Callie?" he said again. "What are you doing?"

"Picking up my dry cleaning," she said with a shrug. And not hiding—definitely not that.

"*Your* dry cleaning?" he repeated incredulously.

"Yep," she lied. "So funny how I didn't see you there! What a coincidence! Isn't it funny how these things sometimes happen? So . . . funny."

"Very funny," he agreed, eyes twinkling and looking—to her horror—like that was exactly what he meant. "So, how have you been? Did you have a nice Thanksgiving?"

When he smiled, tiny crinkles formed around the corners of his eyes: light green, charming, and full of warmth—the kind of glow you could bask in like it was a sunny summer day—

"Ahem." Hassan cleared his throat: a phlegmy, smoker's sound. "The store is closing two minutes ago."

"Right. Sorry, Hassan," Clint said, his eyes never leaving Callie's face. "Why don't you let me carry some of these things home for you," he offered, reaching for a dress.

"No!" Callie cried, intercepting him and throwing the dress over her arm. "I mean, no thank you," she said, piling shirt after dress after skirt on top of it. "I can handle it."

"Okay . . ." said Clint slowly, watching her. "Well, what about later this evening? I have this benefit thing, but maybe after we could go somewhere and talk. I really missed you, you know."

Callie froze. "You—you did?"

"Yes, I did. And I do . . . miss you," he said, smiling and taking a step forward. Leaning in, he propped his arm along the metal rack: no longer a real barrier absent of Lexi's clothing, nothing separating them, save air.

Callie could barely feel the dresses weighing down her left arm. She took a deep breath, and his scent—which smelled sweetly of cinnamon and autumn leaves and still lingered on the scarf she was wearing now and the fuzzy, oversized sweater she had no intention of returning anytime soon—washed over her. She sighed.

Beep beep beep.

"I—I missed a call," she murmured, shifting the clothing in her arms so she could reach for her cell.

MISSED CALL
1 NEW TEXT MESSAGE
FROM ALEXIS THORNDIKE

CALLIE, I HOPE YOU'RE ON YOUR WAY AND THAT THERE WEREN'T ANY PROBLEMS! I'D HATE TO HAVE TO DO SOMETHING DRASTIC JUST BECAUSE I GOT BORED WITH WAITING.

"Crap," Callie muttered. "I have to go."

"Wait," Clint began, reaching out a hand as if to touch her shoulder.

"I'm sorry," she said, ducking around him and heading for the door. "But I'm late—"

"Well, can I at least call you later?" he said, beating her to the door and holding it open for her.

"Uh—I—um—no. Okay? I just have to go," she said. Slipping

past him, she darted out into the cold, hoisting the dry cleaning into both arms and power walking as fast as possible.

Clint watched her round the corner in the direction of the upperclassman river houses, a bemused expression on his face. Then he looked across Massachusetts Avenue at Wigglesworth, her freshman dormitory. Glancing back in the opposite direction where she had just disappeared, he slowly shook his head.

On the plus side, I can cancel my Amazon order for arm weights, Callie thought, trudging up the stairs to the second floor of Wigglesworth. Her arms were really aching now. How it was possible for a bunch of fancy dresses to be heavier than a crate of bottled water was unclear but true nevertheless.

It had grown dark outside in the time it had taken her to finish her COMP assignments for the day. Now, all she had left to do was:

 a) Write response paper about angry philosopher with unpronounceable last name

 b) Get started on *real* COMP assignments

 c) Go to the gym and fight angry 2Ls for a chance to run on the hamster wheels

 d) Eat something, preferably other than basement vending-machine food

 e) Unpack clothing and clean room

 f) Add all of the above to a written schedule of things to do before reading period

 g) Do none of the above and take a nap instead

And the winner is . . . g! Hooray for responsible decision making! (Whoever decided that four-year-olds are the only species deserving of mandatory naptime was seriously misguided.) Then, there was always *h*, aka call Clint and tell him everything.

At the top of the stairs she stopped and unwound Clint's scarf from her neck. He had looked and smelled even better than she'd remembered. This staying-away business was going to be a lot harder than she expected—especially if she could run into him somewhere as random as the dry cleaner.

She was halfway down the hall when she froze.

Gregory had just stepped out of suite C 23, devil-may-care half smile on his face. He saw her a second later, and the smile faded into a grim line. He shut the door quickly behind him but made no move to come closer.

Callie took a deep breath. Fortunately her hands were empty so there was nothing embarrassing to drop (like a box of underwear, for example), no way to humiliate herself as long as her lips remained glued together so she wouldn't say something stupid or impulsively press them to his. . . .

Keeping her feet planted, she forced herself to meet his gaze. His eyes still had the same effect on her, like that of the nightshade flower: blue, beautiful, but deadly poisonous. Symptoms if plucked: paralysis, loss of voice, heart palpitations, respiratory troubles, and probably also death. But possibly also totally worth it. Maybe.

She had obsessively pictured this moment and its endless permutations over the break, lying awake in her bed in California after Thanksgiving and pretending to be incapacitated by a tryptophan-induced food coma so she could avoid the parties where she might run into Evan, or worse, the shadow of her former happy pre-Harvard self. In bed, in the dark, she wondered, What would she say when she saw Gregory? What would she do? What would he do? What would he say? It was a simple set of (1, 2, 3, 4), but it had countless variations: (3, 2, 1, 4,), (2, 4, 1, 3), (3, 4, 2, 1) or even (2, 1, 4) if one of them said nothing or did nothing. On and on and on, until even the mathematics—normally so dependable—seemed useless.

Now the moment was here, so of course she did nothing and said nothing: silent save for her internal monologue, which was yammering a mile a minute—*How was your break? Why haven't you called? Incidentally, I'm kind of obsessed with you, but not in a creepy way.* Still, she forced herself to stay quiet. Hadn't she already made the first move by asking OK to tell Gregory that she missed him and wanted to talk? The ball was in his court now.

But Gregory just stood there, looking, if anything, like he was at a loss for words. Where was the usual arsenal of sarcastic quips and phrases? Searching his face for a hint of that signature smirk, the twisted corners of his mouth that made him seem constantly amused at her expense, she came up blank. He looked serious, which was . . . encouraging? But then why wasn't he saying anything! Was this another game? Was he daring her to break the silence?

If so, she would not take the bait. Instead, she held her breath and counted down from five. Four . . . he was still silent. Three . . . the grim line of his lips was starting to resemble a frown. Two . . .

if he wasn't going to say anything, then why wasn't he moving? One . . . she must not speak.

"Don't you have *anything* to say for yourself?" she blurted, horrified as the words flew out of her mouth.

Gregory shook his head and shrugged.

"Well," she said, completely thrown, "about Harvard-Yale . . . I don't know if you got my message—"

"I got it," he said.

"So, uh . . ." she began, her eyebrows arching, begging him to fill in the rest. Did she really have to spell it out for him? Was he torturing her on purpose?

She took a deep breath. "So, do you—"

A muffled giggle sounded from somewhere inside C 23.

Callie cocked her head, listening, the end of her sentence swallowed into the abyss.

Another giggle—definitely a giggle—cut through the silence, this time from right behind the door.

Gregory shuffled slightly, as if to block the sound. "I should really—"

"Gregory, is that you out there?" the giggler trilled, followed by more giggling.

"Hurry up!" called another female voice—wait, *another* one? "We don't like to be kept waiting."

Gregory stared at Callie, remorseless and, if anything, defiant.

Callie stepped back, her hand fumbling blindly for the doorknob to C 24.

But she wasn't fast enough. As her trembling fingers closed around the handle, the door to C 23 swung open. Two girls, arm in arm, stood framed under the doorway. They were the epitome of a term popularized by none other than Alexis Thorndike: *froshtitutes*.

"Well," said the taller blonde on the left, "some cigarette break."

The shorter one giggled. "Are you coming back inside?"

"I changed my mind," Gregory said abruptly. "Let's get out of here."

"Ooh, where are you taking us?" the shorter one asked.

"It's a surprise," he said, throwing an arm around each girl's shoulders.

"Is *she* coming, too?" the tall one asked, narrowing her eyes and talking as if Callie wasn't even there.

"Nah," said Gregory, starting to turn. "She's just my neighbor."

They retreated down the hall and the giggling faded. Callie, her back against the wall, watched the ménage *à gross* disappear from view. Then, she let her knees give out. Slowly she sank to the floor.

How—*how*—could I have been so *stupid*? she thought, her fingers knotting through her hair. How could she have ever let herself believe that she was special, that she might be the exception that would break the rule? She was disposable, single-serving (but not good enough for the two-for-one special): used and then tossed, just like everybody else.

I should have known better, she thought. Gregory is, was, and always will be officially, unequivocally, and with no exceptions, EVIL.

"Hello-ooh, Gregory . . . and company," a voice said from the stairwell. Callie cringed. She could recognize that simpering trill anywhere, even if it had a bizarre chemical reaction with airborne testosterone that made it two octaves higher. Even if it weren't accompanied by the distinctive stomp and click of dainty high heels bearing the weight of excessive curves and—in this particular case—the jingling of bells and bling that embellished what Vanessa fondly referred to as her "motorcycle boots." (*Motorcycle boots?* Callie had asked last October, before all hell had broken loose. *But you don't drive a motorcycle, do you?* Vanessa had given her that typical what-planet-are-you-from look before saying exasperatedly, *Callie, Christian Lacroix doesn't make motorcycles. These are motorcycle* boots.)

The boots in question were now making their way down the hall. They stopped where Callie sat crumpled on the floor. She probably should have tried to run when she heard them coming, but she lacked the will to move. The velvet bows fluttered, rhinestones (diamonds?) gleamed, golden bells jingled, and black leather crinkled as Vanessa shifted on her feet.

"Sucks, doesn't it?" said Vanessa unsympathetically, digging into her oversized, black Chanel Cambon in search of her keys. "Just another proverbial notch on the old bunk bed post," she muttered as she continued rooting through her bag. "Frankly I'm just glad it wasn't me—"

"It's unlocked," Callie cut in, staring vacantly ahead.

"What? Oh," said Vanessa, slinging her purse back up her shoulder. For some reason her boots weren't moving. Callie could sense Vanessa's gaze lingering on her, but she kept her eyes glued to an invisible spot on the opposite wall.

Vanessa cleared her throat, and when she spoke, her voice sounded softer. "Um . . . are you going to get up anytime soon?"

"Don't have a definite relocation plan for the near future, no," Callie mumbled. She had been aiming for sarcastic but had hit somewhere inside the pathetic-hopeless range instead.

Vanessa still wasn't moving. She was quiet for a moment. "Here," she finally said, leaning down and extending her hand.

Callie looked up and found herself staring into the face of her former friend: a shadow of the old Vanessa before she had transmogrified into her evil, backstabbing, status-obsessed alter ego. Vanessa's fingers fluttered: a white flag ruffling in the breeze.

Callie hesitated. She took a deep breath and started to reach for Vanessa's hand when—

Beep beep beep!

1 NEW TEXT MESSAGE

Gregory writing to say he'd made a gigantic *sex*take and was on his way back.

Or Clint writing to say he knew everything and he forgave her and was on his way over.

Or . . . Reality, which was:

> FROM ALEXIS THORNDIKE
> GREAT JOB TODAY, CALLIE! I HOPE
> YOU'LL KEEP UP THE GOOD WORK.
> LOOKING FORWARD TO LUNCH
> TOMORROW. DOES 1:30 WORK FOR
> YOU? SEE YOU THEN! XXX LEXI

Callie snapped her phone shut and pushed herself to her feet, bypassing Vanessa's hand. Shake and make up with Vanessa? The very girl who had sold her secrets to Lexi in the first place? I don't think so!

"This," she said, pointing emphatically at her phone, "is all your fault."

Vanessa's eyes widened. "Excuse me?" she said indignantly. "You're the one who should have known better! It's not like *I* told him that threesomes were back in vogue or—"

"Not *Gregory*," Callie interrupted, forcing herself to say his name even though it caused a prickling sensation in the corners of her eyes. "Lexi."

"Lexi?" Vanessa echoed, folding her arms across her chest. "What *about* Lexi?"

"Don't play dumb," Callie said, taking a step forward. "The tape! She knows! Because *you* forwarded her a copy!"

Vanessa looked confused. Clearly she was a better actor than she was a dieter. "I did no such thing," said Vanessa, drawing herself up and pretending to look indignant. "You're delusional."

"Oh, *I'm* delusional?" Callie repeated hotly. "*You* were the only person who knew! How else could she have possibly found out if you didn't tell her?"

Vanessa shrugged and reached for the door. "I don't know," she said, stepping through the frame, "but more importantly, I don't care."

Liar, liar, LIAR! Callie had to fight to keep from screaming as the door shut in her face. Wheeling around, she found herself staring at C 23. The hallway wasn't safe. She had to get out before Gregory returned with his Harem. Pressing her ear against C 24, she listened for the telltale slam of Vanessa's bedroom door that would indicate the common room was safe to cross.

It was a shame that Callie's upcoming exam was on the nineteenth and not the twentieth-century novel because she felt like she finally understood what Harvard alum Thomas Wolfe had meant when he wrote, "You can't go home again."

Clearly Wolfe must have had a diabolical roommate just like Vanessa.

FOUR

Sex, Lies, and Videotape

Dear Froshlings:

A lot of you have been writing in to ask me where we here at *Fifteen Minutes* magazine get our information, which FYI we prefer to call "journalism" not "gossip."

So this week, for those of you who are feeling out of the loop, like you live under a rock, like you live in the Quad, or you do actually live in the Quad, I have agreed to share my thoughts on over-sharing and give you all the latest gossip on gossip.

Gossip at Harvard: A History

In the beginning there were monks. They didn't do much gossiping at all, preferring instead to pray, study, and communicate with the higher powers. Those were better times. But then again, there was no plumbing, so maybe things here in the twenty-first century aren't *all* bad.

Several centuries later came the Harvard College Face Book—not to be confused with the popular social networking site. This was a booklet written on actual paper with actual ink that included a portrait (usually a cheesy senior photo) of each incoming freshman and an inspirational quote like "reach for your dreams" or "white men *can* jump."

This booklet (now an ancient relic that you can view at Houghton, our rare books library) was soon replaced by the interwebs, courtesy of Al Gore, who—in addition to the internet—also invented global warming.

People started keeping tabs on one another via Facebook and MySpace and Twitter. New verbs were born: friending, tweeting, and poking; not all of them were good: de-friending, phishing for passwords, and "updating my relationship status to 'looking for' *whatever I can get*."

But truly this is just the tip of the iceberg. Back in the good old days (one or two decades ago), the only people who really had to worry about protecting their privacy were celeb-binaries whose names all started freakishly with the letter *B*, like Brangelina and Bennifer and Billary. At first gossip was limited to the weekly publications, but now, thanks to beloved websites like Gawker, PerezHilton, and Jezebel, we "real" people can enjoy the latest celebrity scandals 24/7, on demand at our convenience.

However, in this modern day and age, it seems like the "real" people are also celebrities: social networking sites, their personal paparazzi. Of course, not everybody chooses to live blog, mingle, or over-share on the web, but while you can control your own online behavior, you cannot control the activities of others—and the thoughts, photos, or videos posted about you that may prove detrimental to your reputation.

In recent years there has been a proliferation of Weblogs dedicated exclusively to gossip in the Ivy and, even more alarmingly, websites that focus specifically on Harvard:

There's **Harvard FML.com**, modeled after the popular FML (Fuck-My-Life) website detailing brief anonymous recaps of peoples' misadventures, as in:

> *Just e-mailed a naked picture of myself to my history
> teaching fellow and my history response paper to
> my girlfriend. FML.*

There's **I Saw You Harvard.com**, modeled after the "Missed Connections" section of Craigslist, as in:

> *I saw you in the library looking like you hadn't showered in days, but you seemed so smart holding that physics textbook. If only I could speak to girls without wetting my pants.*

And then there are the old standbys like Twitter, Facebook, and Bored@Lamont, where you can post your own thoughts—or, more likely, your thoughts on others—for the entire campus to see.

With a click, I could learn far more about you than you might imagine possible from your not-so-private online activities. With another click, that knowlege will be all over school. One final click in an e-mail titled "Tips" to tips@gawker.com and *bam*, you're worldwide news!

In conclusion: be careful! Try to remember that your deepest, darkest secrets are a mere three clicks away from total exposure and that the rest is all just TTMI; that's Totally Too Much Information.

Alexis Thorndike, Advice Columnist
Fifteen Minutes Magazine
Harvard University's Authority on Campus Life since 1873
P.S. Got any tips? Please e-mail us at tips@FM.com or
dial in at 617-555-7293.

"The exam will consist of three parts: multiple choice, short answer, and essay questions," said the teaching fellow, who, standing in front of the blackboard of a small lecture room in Sever Hall, was leading a review session for the Nineteenth-Century Novel. Callie, who had just arrived breathless and late after delivering a certain somebody's lunch to a certain office in a certain newspaper headquarters, slid into a wooden desk chair near the back. She hastened to pull out her spiral-bound notebook and began scribbling down everything that the English PhD student was saying.

"For the essay questions we expect that your answers will be approximately the same length and scope as a typical response paper. While it isn't mandatory that you quote directly from all the material we've covered this semester, you ought to at least be able to cite detailed examples from the text."

Callie's pen hovered over the note she had just made to "cite detailed examples." She swallowed. Not "mandatory" that you quote directly from *all* the material? As in, the students were expected to be able to *quote* from memory most or some of what they had read?

"Some of the other section leaders and I—it's Mary Anne, by the way, for those of you from the Wednesday and Thursday sections—have selected several student response papers for you to refer to as examples." She paused, picked up a large stack of papers from the oak desk in front of the blackboard, and handed them to a guy in the front row. He took one and passed them on.

As the packets made their way around the room, Callie could feel the panic rising in her chest. She'd be fine on the Austen front—after all, Janie was her homegirl—and had also reread *The House of Mirth* over Thanksgiving break (something about Lily Barth's fall from grace into poverty and social exile really hit home). But Hawthorne? She'd barely been able to bring herself to skim *The Scarlet Letter*. And as for *Madame Bovary*, she had interpreted a tad too loosely the professor's suggestion that if they weren't "wholly comfortable with the original, refer to the English translation alongside *la version française*," reading *exclusivement en anglais* and generously gifting her French copy to Mimi. Whoops.

The girl sitting one row in front of Callie on the right turned and handed her the stack of sample essays. She was petite as a pixie and yet there was something imposing about her presence: her black, stick-straight hair hit precisely at her shoulders and framed an angular face. Oversized glasses with square, masculine frames magnified her dark eyes, which lingered on Callie for a moment before she turned to face forward once more.

Seeing that everyone now had a handout, Mary Anne cleared her throat. "I think it would be fruitful to begin with an overview of the major themes, and so, Ms. Lee"—here she nodded at the girl who had just passed Callie the packet—"if you don't mind, could you please start us off by summarizing the main points from your paper reprinted on page one?"

Callie glanced down at the sheet in front of her.

Grace Lee
The Nineteenth-Century Novel
Response Paper

Get Me to the Cemetery on Time:
Sexual Transgression as Death Sentence for the
Nineteenth-Century Heroine

Grace nodded curtly and sat up even straighter—if possible—in her chair. "Certainly," she began. "My main point of issue with the majority of novels required this semester, most notably *Daisy Miller*, *Madame Bovary*, *The House of Mirth*, and *The Mill on the Floss*, is that the only plausible solution—or dare I say 'moral' outcome—for a heroine who has transgressed in the eyes of society—which I define, in the Lacanian sense, as governed by a distinctly male gaze—is death. In *The Scarlet Letter* Hester's metaphorical death in the social sphere supersedes her literal death at the end of the novel; this is, however, the one notable exception to the rule, as all the other heroines—Daisy, Emma, Lily, Maggie—suffer a literal death from their 'crimes' against the Victorian feminine ideal, ranging from innocent flirtation to adultery, from failure to marry in a suitable match, to failure to suppress one's true intellectual and creative spirit."

Callie blinked twice and stared at the back of Grace's head. The size of it hardly hinted at all the big words, intricate analyses, and direct quotes from literary theorists inside.

"Meanwhile," Grace continued, "what reward can the intelligent, free-spirited, and above all, chaste heroine hope to glean for her virtuous behavior? If we take our cues from Austen and Brontë, then we are forced to conclude that, in the world of the Nineteenth-Century novel, the only key to a heteronormative happily-ever-after is the institution of marriage."

Callie's eyes wandered down the page as Grace launched into a more in-depth analysis of examples from the text. There were footnotes—footnotes in a response paper?—detailing hard-to-pronounce names Callie had never heard. She turned the page.

Mary Anne had now opened the discussion to the rest of the students, and the guy in the front row was struggling to form a counterargument. Lee shot him down point by point, and he began to stammer, shrinking into his chair. Callie, impressed as she was, stifled a yawn. She glanced at the clock. Thirty more minutes until two o'clock, when she had to report to her thrilling part-time job at Lamont Library, which paid her a measly twelve dollars an hour to sit behind the front desk and make sure nobody made off with the Guttenberg Bible without first receiving a due-date stamp.

Callie's stomach grumbled. When was the last time she'd had something to eat? Not lunch: she'd been too busy picking up Lexi's; and not breakfast: that time had been used to prep for the review session; so yesterday . . . maybe? Her hands flew to her stomach as it growled angrily in protest, so loud she was certain everyone could hear. The stress of finals (not to mention blackmail) really must be getting to her, because eating was normally high on her list of priorities, right up there with certain other things that had lately, come to think of it, fallen by the wayside, like showering, getting good grades, and happiness.

She willed herself to stare at the TF—instead of obsessively reviewing the long list of things she had to do after her shift at Lamont—and ignore the feeling of dizziness that seemed to be radiating from her stomach. It was no use. Her mind drifted like the snowflakes falling gently on the brick paths outside the classroom window, gathering in banks and frosting the dark brown tree branches. The furnace rumbled—or was it her stomach? She could no longer tell—and she began to feel hot and sleepy. She yawned, overcome by a strange longing to lie in the new fallen snow, fluffy as a white down comforter, and let the fresh flakes quietly bury her.

"Ms. Andrews?" the TF was asking.

Crap. Callie shook herself. Had she fallen asleep without realizing? Had she drooled?

"Is there a Ms. Andrews present? A Ms. Callie Andrews?" Mary Anne repeated.

"Yes?" said Callie cautiously, hands checking the corners of her mouth.

"Oh, good, you're here," said Mary Anne. "I was hoping you could highlight some of the themes touched on in your essay?"

"Um . . . sorry, which essay?" asked Callie.

Mary Anne smiled patiently. "The one reprinted on the last page of our handout."

Confused, Callie thumbed through the packet. She blinked twice.

Callie Andrews
The Nineteenth-Century Novel
Response Paper

Reputation, Reputation, Reputation:

Comparing *Pride and Prejudice* to *The House of Mirth*

Her paper—as an *example*? She flushed and skimmed the page, collecting her thoughts. Then she took a deep breath. "In my essay I compared Austen's treatment of reputation in *Pride and Prejudice* to Wharton's in *The House of Mirth*. I, uh, concluded that even though *Pride and Prejudice* was published nearly a century earlier, Austen's take on reputation is more modern and nuanced than Wharton's, and could even be considered relevant to today's world, in which *reputation* sometimes seems like an antiquated, nineteenth-century concept."

Callie finished, locking eyes with Mary Anne. She gave Callie a sly, you're-not-done-yet sort of a smile.

Callie took another deep breath. "In *The House of Mirth* Wharton depicts reputation as something inextricably linked to status and material wealth: in essence, your good name can be bought. As her material wealth declines throughout the novel, Lily gambles in a series of bets, staking her money and her reputation. Eventually she loses, and subsequently, she dies. Without belonging to the elite upper-class sect of turn-of-the-century Manhattan and without the money it takes to fund said membership, Lily simply cannot go on."

Mary Anne was nodding thoughtfully, and several students, including Grace Lee, had turned in their chairs to face her. Speaking faster, Callie barreled on.

"Austen, in contrast, satirizes reputation with her negative portrayal of characters like Miss Bingley, who look down on people like Elizabeth for her muddy skirts and middle-class roots." Callie paused. "They're snobs—according to Austen. Yet at the same time that she mocks the importance certain characters place on reputation, Austen also captures the gravity of the topic by rendering a situation where the loss of reputation can lead to a woman's downfall—in other words, when Wickham seduces Lydia. So, while Austen implicitly criticizes the snobs who behave condescendingly to a girl simply because she is poor or without the right clothing, family background, or connections, at the same time she also suggests that all a girl like Elizabeth has as a marker of personal value—in addition to her wits—*is* her reputation. So you can see that, uh, Austen's treatment of reputation is more nuanced than Wharton's comparatively one-note conflation of status and material wealth. And, for me at least, it seems more modern since today there are still snobs, and sometimes all you have is your good name, and to lose it would be devastating, though it probably wouldn't, uh, kill you." Time to stop talking. Callie trailed off, looking down at her desk.

"Thank you, Ms. Andrews," said Mary Anne after a beat. People shifted back in their chairs. Grace Lee had bent her head over the essay, and Callie could imagine her eyes flitting across the page, scrutinizing every word. "Several astute points," Mary

Anne continued, "and a good note, I think, on which to end our discussion."

Callie looked at the clock. Sometime during her bumbling analysis that was probably equal parts bullshit and brilliance—she was too light-headed to tell or care at this point—the second hand had mercifully clicked its way to two o'clock. Freedom.

Freedom to go to work, anyway, where she could count the minutes standing between her and food. Quickly she started shoving her papers into her bag, picturing a giant burrito from Felipe's with everything on it: guacamole, sour cream, salsa. . . .

"Don't forget," Mary Anne was saying as people began to stand up and stretch. "Bryce's review session covering close-readings of key quotations is tomorrow at three in Emerson."

Callie stood and ducked into the hall. What about a big slice of pepperoni pizza from Noch's? She hurried down the steps. Or even a huge bowl of cereal from Annenberg. When she reached the bottom she sensed somebody behind her, following closely at her heels.

It was Grace Lee. Callie blinked: for a moment there Grace's head had looked like a sandwich. Grace fell into stride next to her and gave her a hard look. "Freshman, right?" she asked as they stepped out into the freezing December air. Before Callie could answer, she continued: "You write well, if a bit naively."

"Um, thanks," said Callie, deciding that this was high praise coming from someone so scary smart. "My name's Callie—"

"Andrews, right. I know," Grace said, waving the packet that contained her paper. "I wonder: have you ever considered

COMPing the *Crimson*? This semester's COMPers have been a little light on talent so we're looking for new blood in the spring."

"Wow, um, thank you," Callie stammered, her stomach growling again. They had stopped under the trees outside of Sever Hall. Discreetly she glanced over Grace's head—which barely reached Callie's shoulder—to the brick staircase leading up to the courtyard in front of Lamont. "I'm actually still in the running for *FM*, but I have no idea if I'm going to make . . ."

Grace's face changed abruptly. "I see," Grace said. Then she nodded curtly and walked off as suddenly as she had appeared. Callie stood still for a moment, then shrugged and headed toward Lamont.

Her feet dragged as she trudged up the stone steps to the library. She was coming to dread her time at work almost as much as she dreaded running into Vanessa on her way to the bathroom, or worse, into Gregory on her way down the hall. Trapped behind a desk, there was no escape from whoever might decide to frequent Lamont; she was stuck.

She slung her bag over the counter and slipped in front of the reference desk, sinking onto the tall, uncomfortable stool that faced the computer. She stared blankly at the screen for a few minutes, hoping it hid her from whoever might be lurking in the reading room or Lamont Café. She checked her e-mail. Then Facebook, then Twitter, and then *The New York Times*. No major world catastrophes, friend requests, op-eds, or interesting tweets in the past hour or so. She fidgeted. She bit her nails until she realized there was nothing left to chew.

When students arrived at the counter with their books, she stamped the due dates silently, daring them to speak to her. Few tried. Not that she'd been bothering to look in the mirror lately, but she could imagine what she looked like: a zombie. No, worse: a zombie in need of a shower. An ugly, grimy, scary corpse zombie from *Night of the Living Dead* and not the sexy stuff of teenage-girl, undead fantasies—in need of a shower. Did zombies take showers, or did showers make them melt? And was it weird that thinking about zombies was making her hungrier? Or no, it's witches that melt, like in *The Wizard of Oz* . . .

A mobile tweet popped up from @alexisthorndike:

> @FMMAG. SO TIRED OF CELEBRITY
> SCANDALS INVOLVING SEX TAPES!
> GROSS! WHEN WILL THESE PEOPLE
> LEARN THE MEANING OF PRIVACY?

Callie frowned. Slowly she raised her eyes and saw the very thing she'd been dreading staring at her from a table inside Lamont Café.

Alexis Thorndike.

Lexi waved cheerily, phone in hand. She was smiling so widely Callie could have sworn she could see the glint of her teeth from across the room.

Grandmother, what big teeth you have!

The better to eat you with, my dear!

Maybe Lexi would melt if Callie dumped a bucket of water on her perfect chestnut curls. Callie pictured sloshing it all over her newly dry-cleaned dress (free delivery via Cinder-Callie), and watching her disintegrate, green and bubbling like acid. She almost smiled back.

Instead she ducked her head and pulled her worn, ancient copy of *Pride and Prejudice* out of her bag. Skimming through it, she began marking the pages with important quotations that seemed likely to appear on the test. Too bad she'd left Hawthorne at home. What a shame. If only she were in a library . . . Smiling, she gave in and started rereading from the beginning.

"Ahem." Somebody cleared his throat loudly, breaking her reverie. Sighing dramatically, she kept her eyes on *Pride and Prejudice*. She took her time finishing the sentence, then painstakingly pulled a bookmark out of her bag and stuck it between the pages before finally setting the book on the circulation desk. Only then did she look up.

She narrowed her eyes, knowing that the effect might be slightly diminished due to the fact that her heart had started pounding so loudly he could probably hear it, even from two feet away.

"I need a book," said Gregory.

And *I* need a drink. An apology. An explanation. A hug. FOOD! Anything other than *this*. "You've come to the right place," she said, gesturing sarcastically. "Although there's this new invention called the computer—it's really amazing. You type in the name of the book, and then it tells you where to find it. All without ever bothering the person behind the desk."

"Fascinating, but I need a textbook. And last I checked, they keep them behind the desk, though I'm *terribly* sorry to bother you."

Oh. Dammit. "Which one?"

"*Intermediate Microeconomics* by Varian."

Callie narrowed her eyes. "Why do you need *that* textbook?"

"So I can study."

"Study what?"

Gregory rolled his eyes. "Economics."

"But you're not *in* economics."

"Yes, I am."

"Then why haven't I seen you in class?"

There was a flicker of his old smile. "I didn't realize you were looking for me in class . . ."

"I wasn't," she snapped.

"Well," he said, seeming irritated again, "I'm not in your class because I'm in 1010a."

"No you're not. The intermediate level is only open to sophomores and juniors."

"I skipped."

"Right." Because the rules don't apply to you.

"Can I have the textbook?"

"Fine!" she cried, standing. Slipping behind the shelves, she bent down, stopping when she spotted the *V*s. Varian—there it was. So he's in genius-level econ—what do I care? Textbook in tow, she walked back to the counter.

"Hey!" she cried, her face flushing crimson. "Put that down!"

Without an iota of guilt Gregory set her copy of *Pride and Prejudice* on the counter, sliding the bookmark back into place. His blue eyes were bright when he met her gaze. "'She is tolerable, but not handsome enough to tempt me.'" He quoted Darcy's famous line. "Classic. I love that part."

That they both loved the same books—once upon a time that had sent butterflies fluttering from her stomach out to the tips of her fingers and down to her toes. Now it was a twist of the knife. That he could quote from memory just drove the blade in farther, deeper, straight into the left-hand side of her chest. How many other girls had fallen for his tricks? And how could he be so cruel, to deliberately remind her that she had stupidly—oh, so stupidly—fallen, too?

Never again, she vowed. Never—not even if he stood there and recited the entire book from memory—again. Wordlessly she scanned the textbook and slammed the Due Back in One Hour stamp on the front page so hard that it smudged. Then she flipped the front cover shut and shoved the book across the counter.

He made no move to take it.

"Is there something else?" she asked as coldly as she could manage.

He looked at her, his fingers drumming the counter. "The other day . . . in the hall . . . when I . . ." He trailed off. "You seemed—"

She closed her eyes. Thinking about "the other day in the hall" made her sick. She had no idea how he was about to torment her, but she knew if it involved threesomes or her stupid unreturned "I miss you," she simply could not survive. "Just. Go. Away," she said through gritted teeth.

"So . . . that's what you really want, then?" he muttered. For a moment he looked as if she had slapped him. But then he shrugged, and suddenly he was Gregory again. "Fine," he said acidly. "Like you said, 'Let's just stay as far away from each other as possible,' right?" he added, picking up the book. Before she could answer, he turned, heading for the café.

Like I said—when? Just now? Did I . . . The room started to spin, and Callie exhaled, realizing that she had been holding her breath. She inhaled slowly, her eyes darting toward the clock. She had been on duty for . . . only twenty-three minutes and fourteen seconds? How was that possible! Was she really stuck here for another ninety-six minutes and forty-three seconds? Forty-two . . . forty-one . . . forty . . .

Her eyes inadvertently flicked back over to Lamont Café. Her breath caught in her chest. Lexi rose gracefully out of her chair and embraced Gregory, kissing him once on each cheek. He smiled and said something. She laughed and gestured toward the table, taking the textbook he had just offered her and spreading it open between them. Their heads bent together as he pulled out a notebook and pen. Callie couldn't see his face; his back bent indifferently toward her.

Callie closed her eyes, as if doing so could erase the image.

But there was no denying what was clearly unfolding before her:

Gregory and Lexi. On a date, or at least something that strongly resembled a datelike gathering—their second if you counted the night he ditched Lexi to save Vanessa from James "The D-Bag" Hoffmeyer at the Mad Hatter's Ball.

How did they know each other anyway? Was it a secret New York, everyone-knows-everyone-who's-anyone type of thing? Did they have a history? Did he *like* her? Did she like him? Did—

Callie walked over to the cart of books waiting to be re-shelved and started sorting them. Well, started *pretending* to sort them. Her mind was so fuzzy she knew she'd have to re-sort them later, but at least for the time being her hands were occupied, and the watery feeling in the corners of her eyes could be blamed on the dust motes floating off the ancient volumes.

She was just pulling Tennessee Williams's *Cat on a Hot Tin Roof* back from where she had accidentally shelved it as poetry when she heard a voice say quietly,

"Hey there."

She knew from the slightly southern lilt and the sound—like liquid sunshine—who it was without having to look.

"Hi," she said, turning, a smile playing on the corners of her lips in spite of the exhaustion and near starvation.

Clint grinned and let his backpack slide to the floor, then propped his elbows on the reference desk and leaned toward her.

"Do you need—" she began, sitting back on the stool in front of the computer. "I mean, can I help you with something?"

"As a matter of fact," said Clint, smiling even wider, "you can."

"With a book," she asked, flushing and trying to stay professional.

"Yes," he agreed, leaning across the counter even farther. "A book."

"I'll look it up," she said, moving the mouse to tab out of her e-mail and open a new browser. "What's it called?"

"It's called . . . *Come to Lunch with Me.*"

Come to— She stopped typing midway through the word lunch. Her stomach growled. "Lunch?"

"With me," he added, eyes twinkling, not unkindly, with amusement.

"Um, I would love to . . ." The hair on her neck and arms had just crept up like reeds standing to attention in a chilly gust of wind. Someone was staring at her. She looked over Clint's shoulder, and sure enough, there she was.

Alexis.

She was gripping the sides of the *Intermediate Microeconomics* textbook, glowering. Gregory stood in line at the coffee counter, waiting to order drinks. Slowly Lexi shook her head once.

"But I can't. I have to work," Callie whispered.

"That's cool." Clint's smile was unwavering. "What time do you get off?"

"Four," said Callie distractedly, watching Lexi dig into her shoulder bag and pull out her cell phone. Gregory returned to the table with two cups and set one in front of Lexi. He did not glance in the direction of the reference desk.

"A late lunch, then."

"Clint, I—I can't," she said, her eyes darting away from his face and falling blankly on her e-mail.

"You can't or you don't want to?" he asked.

She was silent. Did she *want* to? Was there anything else in the world that she didn't want *more*?

"Look," said Clint, taking her silence as a bad sign, "I had some time to think over break, and I realized I made a mistake, giving you an ultimatum like that. It was wrong: immature, pushy. I got frustrated and was out of line. Of course I want my girlfriend to feel like she can tell me things—anything—but in order for you to feel comfortable about opening up, I have to be a good boyfriend first."

Callie swallowed the lump in her throat. Still she couldn't speak, as if an invisible muzzle were attached to her jaw with an invisible chain stretching across the marble floor into Lamont Café where Lexi held the end of it instead of her phone, her fingers tugging instead of texting furiously.

"I'm not ready to give up on us," Clint continued. "If you don't want me anymore—if you want me to go away and leave you alone, I will. Just say the word."

She shook her head. "No," she murmured, barely audible. "No, I don't want that."

"But—" Clint started to smile—"if there's any chance that I can make things right . . ." He reached across the desk for her hand. She let him take it and twine her fingers through his. "Then I'm not going anywhere."

The computer screen flashed as her inbox refreshed and a new message appeared at the top.

From: **Alexis Vivienne Thorndike**
To: **Callie Andrews**
Subject: FWD: To: tips@gawker.com TIP ALERT! Ivy league girl involved in SEX TAPE SCANDAL!!!

The video features Callie Andrews, a freshman at Harvard University, and Evan Davies of UCLA. A link is included <here> . . .

Callie didn't make it past the first sentence before the room started to spin. She swayed on her stool, gripping the edge of the counter and trying to focus on Clint's face. She was barely conscious of jabbing the Off button on the monitor before dizziness overtook her and she toppled over, smacking her head on the corner of the reference desk. The metal stool made a thunderous clatter when it fell next to her, reverberating through the halls of the library, but she didn't hear it. She was out cold before she hit the ground.

There was blackness everywhere, punctuated by the sound of voices. They faded in and out, like bad reception on a shitty radio. She wished they would just shut up and let her sleep.

"Do you think she hit her head?"

"I'm not sure."

"Should we call UHS?"

"Yeah . . . probably . . ."

"Wait a minute—did you see that? I think her eyelids just fluttered."

A dark green blob hovered over her, and she could feel something—a pair of hands?—cradling her head from behind.

"Yeah, they're moving. Callie . . . *Callie,* can you hear us?"

"Cut it out. . . . Go away. . . ." she heard herself mutter. A hand— it was definitely a hand—gently slapped her cheek.

"What's going on here?" It was a new voice speaking now, coming from a fuzzy-looking giant wearing Bob the security guard's uniform.

"She fainted—"

"Fell right off the stool—"

"Then I hopped the counter—" the green blob continued, and she could feel pressure on her hand, like someone was holding it—

"And we ran over from the café."

There was silence for a moment.

"Did anyone call an ambulance?" the person in Bob's uniform— or maybe it was Bob?—asked.

An ambulance? That would be even louder than all of the annoying voices. NO THANK YOU.

"No. I'm fine. . . ." she muttered, forcing her lids to open. The first thing she noticed was a face: flawless except for the tiny crescent moon-shaped scar on the corner of the chin. It was awfully close to her and upside down. She blinked several times, feeling light-headed all over again.

"Don't try to sit up," Gregory ordered, peering down at her.

"What happened?" she asked, ignoring him and trying to sit up anyway. Bad idea. The dizziness overwhelmed her.

"You fainted," said the green sweater. Clint. "But you're going to be okay," he added, squeezing her hand. His sweater looked so soft and warm up close. She wanted him to take her home and wrap it around her like he used to: cashmere and good-smelling and sleepy. . . .

"For crying out loud, Clint, give her some room to breathe," a girl's voice, musical like wind chimes, floated in. Clint let go of Callie's hand.

French-manicured nails raised a Dixie cup of cool water to

Callie's lips. "Here," the voice said sweetly, placing a gentle yet firm hand behind Callie's head. "Drink up."

"Thank—" Callie choked, spitting the water back into the cup.

Lexi smiled and dabbed at the droplets that had sprayed her Hermes scarf. "Now there's the Callie I know," she said. "You gave us all such a scare!" Concern oozed out of every tiny porcelain pore.

"I've got UHS on the phone—what should I tell them?" a fourth voice—definitely Bob, the security guard—asked Lexi, who had clearly taken charge. Clint was hovering next to Bob over by the phone. Gregory was still crouched by Callie's head, brow furrowed. His hands twitched almost imperceptibly toward her. He jammed them in his pockets.

"I'm fine!" Callie cried, eyes wide, waving away Lexi's arm and pulling herself into a sitting position. "No ambulance! I just need ... some food ..." she muttered.

"You are *not* fine," Gregory spat. "You have a huge bump on your head."

"You have a huge bump on *your* head," she muttered.

Lexi's tinkling laugh pealed like bells. "It can't be *that* bad when her sense of humor's still intact." Clint walked back behind the reference desk and grabbed Callie's hands before she could protest, helping her to her feet. Lexi's smile wavered.

Bob set down the phone. "I told them we don't need an ambulance, but you're taking the rest of the day off, okay?" he said, eyeing Callie in earnest. "Straight home, hydrate, and avoid sleeping for the next few hours, understand?"

She nodded.

"Good," said Bob. "Now which one of you boys is going to take her home?"

"I'll do it," Clint and Gregory said simultaneously.

"Seriously, allow me," said Clint, starting to reach for her book bag.

Gregory beat him to it. "It's no trouble," he said, hoisting the bag over his shoulder. "I was heading back to Wigg anyway."

Gregory and Clint were suddenly standing much too close, jostling and making her claustrophobic.

"I can take myself home, thank you very much," she blurted, grabbing her bag from Gregory.

"Nonsense," Lexi cut in, linking her arm through Callie's. "*I* will walk her back. You two stay here. She's had enough excitement for the day."

Callie froze. She felt paralyzed, yet miraculously, her feet began to move. Lexi propelled her along with remarkable strength for someone so seemingly delicate. They breezed through the double glass doors. Callie's blood turned to ice and not just because it was minus-zero degrees outside.

Was it just her imagination, or could she feel Lexi's perfectly manicured nails digging into her skin like talons, even through her coat? Callie didn't look back as they made their way down the steps. If she had, she would have seen them: Gregory and Clint, still standing there.

When they had cleared the courtyard and were heading down the cement staircase that led to Wigg, Lexi finally loosened her grip. "Overreact much, drama queen?" she asked in a seemingly teasing tone.

Callie felt faint all over again. She struggled to maintain her balance, the stairs slick with black ice and slippery under her feet. "Did you—the tape—how could you—"

"Oh, relax," said Lexi, patting her on the back. "That was just a draft, silly! A reminder to stay focused on *FM* and not let anything distract you!" They had reached the bright green door that led to Wigglesworth, entryway C.

"I would never actually send something like that unless you had done something very, very bad." As she was speaking, Lexi had taken Callie's shoulder bag and was searching through it. Callie watched in a daze. "Aha!" Lexi muttered, pulling Callie's ID key card from the tote and scanning it against the lock. It opened with a click.

"Now you go straight upstairs and hydrate like he said," she instructed, her face a mask of concern. "We need you well rested so you can fulfill your duties for COMP!" Lexi smiled and then turned to leave. Callie leaned against the frame of the door, breathing deeply.

"Feel better!" Lexi called over her shoulder. She pulled out her phone. "And remember," she said, pointing to it, "give me a reason, and I'll give them a headline."

war

From: **Vanessa Von Vorhees**
To: **Callie Andrews, Dana Gray, Marine Aurelie Clément**
Subject: SOMEONE left a HUGE mess in the bathroom

Without pointing any fingers, ladies, someone left a massive, NASTY clump of BLOND hair clogging the shower drain. Could whoever is responsible *please* clean it up? Some of us actually value personal hygiene and like showering without feeling the urge to puke our brains out every time we look at the drain.

xx VVV

From: **Callie Andrews**
To: **Dana Gray, Marine Aurelie Clément, Vanessa Von Vorhees**
Subject: Shower's clean!

Hey, guys,
Today I pulled a big clump of long reddish-looking hair out of the shower drain because, as you know, it was starting

to clog. No need to thank me—I know we're all super busy studying for finals. In fact, Dana: I'm pretty sure I haven't seen you in a week!

Cal

P.S. No more puking, please; it's gross. And if you do feel the urge, at least clean out the toilet bowl after. Please. Thanks!

From: **Vanessa Von Vorhees**
To: **Callie Andrews, Dana Gray, Marine Aurelie Clément**
Subject: Has anyone seen my diamond earrings?

They've gone missing! They were a present from my parents for my sweet sixteen, and they are really special to me. So, whoever borrowed them without asking, I won't get mad: just put them back in the blue Tiffany box on my bureau while I'm in the library today and all will be forgiven.

VVV

P.S. If somebody were trying to imply something, they should just come out and say it to my face. Forgive me for not wanting to live in nauseating filth; have you *seen* the common room lately? Also: has anyone seen my manicure set?

Yes, Vanessa, we've seen it. And as far as I can tell, most of the mess is yours: pizza boxes, candy wrappers, Dunkin Donuts bags. This may come as a shock to you, but we're your roommates, not your personal maids! And while we're on the topic of being more considerate, would you mind keeping the noise level to a minimum every now and then? We hear you when you slam doors. We hear you when you yell for hours at whoever it is you've been yelling at on the phone lately. So, thank you in advance . . . I'm sure the quiet will be much appreciated!

You're calling *me* loud? Did you know that you snore? You snore so loudly, I swear to god I can hear you through the walls! You snore so loudly, I can't even hear the construction crews tearing up the streets on Mass Ave.! And is it really necessary to talk to yourself *out loud* while you edit your oh-so-important COMP assignments?

From: **Callie Andrews**
To: **Dana Gray, Marine Aurelie Clément, Vanessa Von Vorhees**
Subject: Earplugs

Look into it.

From: **Vanessa Von Vorhees**
To: **Callie Andrews, Dana Gray, Marine Aurelie Clément**
Subject: Earrings

BTW, I know you stole them. Put them back on my dresser, or I *will* press charges.

From: **Callie Andrews**
To: **Dana Gray, Marine Aurelie Clément, Vanessa Von Vorhees**
Subject: RE: Earrings

I don't have your stupid earrings! Check my room if you don't believe me.

From: **Dana Gray**

To: **Callie Andrews, Vanessa Von Vorhees, Marine Aurelie Clément**

Subject: RE: Earrings

Can you take me off this e-mail list?
—Dana

From: **Marine Aurelie Clément**

To: **Callie Andrews, Vanessa Von Vorhees**

Subject: RE: Earrings

Leave me on, vous imbeciles. I am "LMFAO."
TTYL bitchezzz—

"FREEZE! Do. Not. Move," Dana's voice yelled from inside the common room of C 24.

Callie stopped walking, one foot in the suite, one foot in the hall.

"You may come in now," Dana instructed, "but tread very lightly."

Callie pushed the front door open a few more inches and poked her head in. She could see Dana crouched on the floor in front of the coffee table, working on an elaborate structure of toothpicks, straws, wax, glue, and multicolored pom-poms. It looked fragile, like a science geek's bizarre house of cards.

Cautiously Callie stepped into the room.

OK and Mimi were near Dana and also on the floor. OK was wearing Bermuda shorts and had his long legs splayed out in front of him, calculus textbook propped on his knees. Mimi lay on her stomach with her head near OK's toes, which, upon closer inspection, were currently separated by a manicurist's pink toe divider. Several bottles of nail polish in different shades were arranged around OK's feet. Mimi frowned as she held up each bottle against OK's ebony skin, considering.

"We are trying to find his shade," Mimi explained.

"I see that," said Callie, taking a few steps farther into the room. The smell was overpowering: not just of nail polish but of stale pizza, coffee grinds, Febreze, whatever mystery scent the Febreze had initially been sprayed to mask, and . . . feet. Boy's feet.

"*We* are trying to *study*," Dana amended.

We who? Callie wondered. Dana's imaginary roommates? Maybe Dana had finally cracked . . . Her brown hair was frazzled and unwashed, and she wore a huge bright turquoise T-shirt with GOOSE CREEK MATH CAMP printed across the front. Callie had seen this shirt once before, during midterms. Dana had left it on for a week. On the back it said something truly incredible, like DO NUMBERS, NOT DRUGS, or NUMBERS AREN'T SEXY AND YOU SHOULDN'T BE EITHER.

Callie crossed the room and cracked open the window. Even though the air that rushed in was teeth-chatteringly cold, she perched on the sill nonetheless, taking stock of the situation. Eventually her eyes settled on Dana, who was Scotch-taping three toothpicks together to make a giant super toothpick. "Dana," she began, "what exactly are you doing?"

"Callie, I am so glad you asked. You see, I couldn't quite picture the mesolimbic dopaminergic pathway—"

"The what, now?" Callie asked.

"The me-so-lim-bic dop-a-min-er-gic path-way—"

"Think of it as a highway to happiness that exists inside your brain," Mimi offered, layering a second coat of polish onto OK's big toe.

"Well, not exactly, but okay, fine," said Dana. "The point is it's definitely going to be on the exam, so I'm building a model."

The elaborate structure looked more confusing than clarifying, but Callie kept her mouth shut.

"Your dopamine transporters seem a bit wonky," Mimi said

dryly. "I personally would have gone with a different color."

Dana's hands froze. "Really?" she whispered in horror.

OK looked up from his calculus. "I thought you said 'peach would provide the perfect ironic contrast'!"

Mimi shook her head and snapped her fingers, pointing back to his textbook.

"But I need to save the blue and green for the monoamine oxidase," Dana muttered, ringing her hands. Leaping up, she began to pace around the coffee table, surveying the model from various angles. "I *can't* use the same colors for MAO-A and MAO-B . . . and I haven't figured out how to make them float yet . . . This is a *disaster.* . . ." Her eyes were wide and she had started to hyperventilate. "If I move the monoamines here and reposition the synapses such that the synaptic cleft contains more realistic levels of dopamine . . . No . . . *no,* that's never going to *work.*"

Mimi shrugged and caught Callie's eye, the tiny hint of a smile playing on her lips.

"Dana," said Callie, coming over to place a firm hand on the shorter girl's shoulders. "Why don't you have a seat, and I'll bring you a glass of water?"

"Water," said Dana, her eyes going glassy as she fell onto the couch. "Two hydrogen molecules bond to one oxygen molecule with bond lengths of 0.096 nanometers and an H-O-H angle of 104.5 degrees, which is actually unique and fascinating, geometrically speaking, because—"

Callie returned from the bathroom with a cup of water and pressed it gently to Dana's lips. "Shhhh . . ." she whispered. "Deep breaths."

Mimi, nail polish brush in hand, made a circular motion near her temple: "She is going hoot-hoot."

Callie frowned. "Cuckoo?"

"Oui," Mimi agreed. "Hoot-hoot."

There was a quiet knock on the door.

"Entrez," Mimi called, turning her attention back to OK's pinkie toe.

A boy from Wigglesworth Entryway B whom Callie hadn't seen since the first week of school stuck his head inside. "I'm here for the study guide," he said. His face was pale, his eyes bloodshot and red. Apparently the exam-induced sickness was catching.

"Yes, yes, come in," said Mimi impatiently, blowing on OK's toes.

The boy shuffled forward, his eyes roving anxiously around the room. "The study guide for . . . you know . . . Drugs and the Brain."

Mimi leaped off the floor and pointed the nail polish brush at his chest. "Were you followed?"

The boy looked terrified. "I—no—I mean, I don't *think* so—"

"Relax, Mike," said OK, flipping a page in his textbook. "She's having you on."

"Oh," said Mike, his body going slack. Mimi disappeared into her bedroom. "Right."

In thirty seconds she was back. "Here you go," she said, handing Mike a packet of papers and a small brown paper bag. "One study guide and five study buddies."

"Thank you," he said, staring at Mimi like she had just saved his life. "Thank you so much."

"You are welcome," said Mimi. "Now get out."

When he had gone, Dana set her glass down on the coffee table with a loud thunk. The dopamine-whatever-it-was rattled ominously. "That's the *third* time today!" she hissed despairingly. "What you're doing is immoral, not to mention *illegal*, and has very adverse long-term effects on your brain, as I've been trying to demonstrate—"

Dana stopped talking abruptly when another knock sounded. "That had better not be—"

"Come in!" Mimi cut her off.

This time it was a girl hovering outside in the hall. "Hey," she said. "I'm here because I heard you might have some extra—"

"Bah-bah-bah!" Mimi placed a finger to her lips and ushered the girl inside. She waited restlessly while Mimi went into her room and returned with a fresh packet of papers and another small brown bag.

"Tell the good citizens of Canaday that I am all out and will not get another refill until Tuesday," Mimi said, waving the girl back through the door.

"Mimi," Callie said slowly, "what exactly is going on here?"

Mimi shrugged. "I am helping people. With the studying."

Callie glanced at OK.

"Don't look at me!" OK cried. "She told me if I let her paint my nails, she would write my French paper."

"*Proofread* your French paper, dearie," Mimi corrected him. "If I actually did it for you, nobody would believe that it was really your work."

Dana made a strangled noise, glaring at Mimi.

"I mean—er—if I do it for you, how will you ever learn?" Mimi tried again.

There was another knock at the door.

"What's happening, dudes," said Matt, strolling into the common room.

"No," Dana murmured, disbelief etched across her face. "Please, God, no. Matt, not you, too—"

"Huh?" said Matt, looking from Dana—hands gripping her cheeks in horror—to Mimi—who had taken a nail file and gone to work on OK's hands. "I just came in to see about the study group—"

"DO YOU HAVE ANY IDEA WHAT DEXTROAM-PHETAMINE DOES TO YOUR BRAIN?" Dana screamed, jumping off the couch. "Of *all* the people—of all the things—I would have expected better from *you*, Matthew!"

"Dextroamphetamine?" Matt echoed. "What, you mean like speed?"

"She means Adderall," Mimi drawled, returning OK's right hand and reaching for his left. "And I have already told her *cent mille fois* that I *have* a prescription. It is for my ADD."

"Adderall doesn't even treat ADD," Dana said weakly, sinking back onto the couch. "It's for attention deficit *hyperactivity* disorder—"

"Eh." Mimi shrugged again.

"—which is irrelevant," Dana continued, "since I *sincerely* doubt that any of the students to whom you're dealing your 'study buddies' are afflicted."

"You have ADHD?" asked Callie, scrutinizing Mimi. It wasn't all that difficult to believe. . . .

"Actually," said Mimi, "the UHS doctor gave it to me because he claims I fell asleep in the waiting room and during the reflex exam. He says I have 'narcoleptic tendencies.' *Ppffft!*" she snorted with a dismissive wave of her hand. "I think *I* would have noticed if I went around falling asleep all over the place."

Callie looked at Matt, Matt looked at OK, and OK looked at Dana. Nobody said anything, though several eyebrows had risen several inches. Mimi didn't seem to notice.

Dana turned her attention back to Matt. "Mathew please, I beg of you: don't do this. There's another way. A legal way. A moral way. God's wa—"

"Dana, relax, I'm not—"

"Look," Dana cut him off. "Just look." She seized a red pom-pom from the coffee table. "*This* is a dextroamphetamine molecule, and *this* is a monoamine transporter where it binds in your brain," she explained, taping the red pom-pom inside a cagelike structure made of toothpicks. "*These*," she continued, casting around and seizing a box of orange Tic Tacs, "are your neurotransmitters: dopamine, norepinephrine, and serotonin. And *this*," she said, shaking the Tic Tacs violently, "is how they start bouncing around in your synaptic space when the amphetamine binds and blocks the transporter. And *this*," she whispered, eyes wide and arms raised, "is what happens when you DO DRUGS!" In one swift move she threw the entire model onto the floor and then jumped on top of it, stomping it with both her feet.

"Huh," said Mimi. "That first part was actually fairly enlightening. I shall make a note of it in the psychostimulants section of my study guide."

Dana froze, toothpicks crunching and colorful pom-poms sticking to her feet. "Glue!" she cried, gasping suddenly. "I need *glue!*" She grabbed her textbook and dashed across the common room. "ADAM! Do you have any—" The door slammed shut behind her.

It was quiet for a beat and then Matt said, "I'm not even going to ask. I don't want to know. I'm going back across the hall now. It'll be like I was never here."

"Econ study group tomorrow," Callie reminded him.

"Right," said Matt, taking one final look at the room. "You would think," he muttered, "that girls would be cleaner." Then he was gone.

"I'm going, too—to my room," Callie said, picking her way through the pizza boxes and stepping over OK's legs.

"Tootles," said Mimi.

"Tootles!" OK echoed, waving his peach-colored nails.

Shaking her head, Callie opened the door to her bedroom.

Nothing could have prepared her for what she saw.

Books had been ripped from their shelves and now littered the floor. Her dresser drawers had been thrown open and clothing overflowed the sides. What little had been hanging in her closet had also been yanked off the hangers. Stepping gingerly over her white down comforter—and noting the distinctive gray footprint of what appeared to be a high-heeled boot stomped across it—Callie approached the desk. A bottle of cherry cough syrup on her dresser had been knocked over: the sticky red liquid oozed over her COMP assignments, dangerously close to her laptop, and trickled over the side of her desk, dripping onto the floor. She grabbed her laptop and set it on her bed. Slowly she sank down next to the stack of papers—sticky with cough syrup—and surveyed the damage in shock.

It looked like she had been robbed. Her desk lamp had also been knocked over; a coffee mug she had "borrowed" from Annenberg had cracked into three pieces, and certain items appeared to be missing.

Taking inventory, she realized what it was: everything that Vanessa had given or lent her last semester: the dresses, the heels, the bags, the sweaters, the jeans—all of it was gone. She had taken her stuff back. Like after a bad breakup. Like an angry ex-wife who throws her husband's clothing out the window singing "You Don't Own Me" while his mistress waits terrified in the car. She had also—by the looks of it—been searching for something: her missing diamond earrings, probably, which she had most likely misplaced herself.

Callie took a deep breath and propped her elbows on her knees, letting her head fall into her hands. Clamping her lips together, she suppressed the urge to scream. It was one thing to have to deal with Vanessa in the hallway, in the common room, on her way to the bathroom, and through the wall—her endless screaming into her iPhone, her catty comments aimed at Callie's room, the dirty looks in the dining hall and in class, her stomping, door slamming, and *her* snoring, but how dare she—how *dare she*—invade the only eight-by-ten-foot patch of space at Harvard that Callie could call her own?

Exhaling, Callie caught sight of a tattered green book cover poking out from under her bed.

That had better not be what I think it is, she thought, bending over to pick it up with a sinking feeling. It was exactly what she thought it was: her copy of *Pride and Prejudice*, now cracked at the spine and split in two. Several loose, yellowed pages fluttered to the floor. Carefully Callie held the two pieces of the book up in front of her. More pages tore free and dangled from the spine. Not even duct tape—which had come to the rescue of Callie's Converses on more than one occasion—had a prayer of fixing it. The book was destroyed.

Callie placed the remains of the book gently on her bookshelf. Then, propping a pillow against the headboard of her tiny twin, she flipped open her laptop and placed it on her knees. She glanced down at her COMP assignments, which were sticking to her sheets, her eyes falling across a particular item on Lexi's latest "Suggested Topics" sheet, "Issues in the Bedroom: What are some of the most common roommate problems that first-year students face?" Callie stared at her screen for a moment. Then she began to type.

Callie Andrews
COMP ASSIGNMENT

The Roommate from Hell

In the olden days monsters could be found in a variety of reliable places: in a cemetery, on the moors, the fens, or in a black lagoon. Today the modern-day monster also hails from a very specific location: a tiny island, population ~1.6 million, known to many as Manhattan. She slinks undetected through her overpriced private school system (where she learns little other than which bags cost the most and how to buy friends and influence people) and somehow bribes her way—no doubt with Daddy's money—into the top university in the country, where she is allowed to live inside the dorms disguised as any other teenage girl.

Oh, but there are signs. Is your roommate really a monster in disguise? Ask yourself the following ten questions:

1. Does she hail from Manhattan? Is it a Park Avenue address, or somewhere else on the Upper East Side? Does her name have some inexplicable Dutch-sounding nonsense or roman numeral suffix or prefix: Van, Von, Jr., the III, the IV, the V?

2. Could she survive a month without wearing the same shoes twice?

3. Does she lose her diamonds as casually as you sometimes misplace your socks?

4. Does she have crazy eating habits: starving herself during the day and eating everything in sight at night—only to purge it later?

5. Is she a slob, content to live in her own filth and blame it on those around her?

6. Does she carry a rope ladder and climb it in social situations? And a knife with which to stab you in the back?

7. Does she sometimes speak in a pitch so high that only dogs

can hear—particularly when screaming into her iPhone?

8. Does she lie to your face? Is she more two-faced than Two-Face?

9. Is she single because she can't even manage to find any real girlfriends, let alone a boyfriend?

10. Does she own any articles of clothing that say PRINCESS or JUICY? How about SPOILED BRAT or MONEY CAN'T BUY GOOD TASTE?

I'm afraid if you answered yes to any of the above questions, you may have a monster roommate situation on your hands. Do not panic, for you are not alone. After all, I wrote the book (so to speak), because the girl who inspired the criteria above is not just *The* Roommate from Hell. She's *my* roommate from hell.

Callie stopped writing abruptly and stared at the page in front of her, breathing heavily.

It was by far the most toxic thing she had ever written, and yet it had been wholly necessary, for the act of writing had been the equivalent of sucking the venom from her veins. Better to spit the poison out onto a Microsoft Word document that would never see the light of day than let it rot her from the inside. Or worse, explode at a random moment and infect those around her or drive her to say something to Vanessa that could never ever be unsaid— though lord knows she deserved it.

And so, thus purged in her own way, Callie saved the piece to the COMP Drafts folder on her desktop: a computer file locked in a vault; another one of her dirty little secrets.

primal scream

Study Tips, aka How to Survive
Your First Reading Period
with Your Sanity Intact

Brought to you by Alexis Thorndike and the Editors at *FM*

Step One: FORTIFICATION. Take this as seriously as an army engaged in medieval warfare would, or as a delusional schizophrenic might in preparation for a nuclear holocaust. Pick a safe study space: your bedroom (inadvisable: too small; the smell will get to you); common room (too public); Lamont (too social; the collective stress does weird things to people—ref: "Primal Scream" below); Widener (pretty good); Cabot (too isolated); Quad library (good, just so far away). Also, bring food. Enough to last the full two weeks of reading period in case you don't change locations. Like, at all. Some people don't. (*Ahem*: science majors who sleep in Cabot Library.)

Step Two: LIBATIONS. Buy your Red Bull, Monster, or canned Starbucks Double Espresso shots early because CVS *will* run out. Take into account how much sleep you plan to skip.
P.S. Polyphasic sleep habits are inadvisable unless your name starts with "Leonardo" and ends with "da Vinci." (Yeah—didn't think so: so don't even try.)

Step Three. Avoid ISOLATION. Now's not the time to be a hero, kid. Ask for help if you need it, and if you don't, then pay it forward to your peers. Sharing study guides is allowed, even encouraged, and is the best way to break up the test material.

Step Four. EDIFACTION. Nothing is as reliable as Old Faithful, i.e. reading the textbook. Dust it off and crack it open, and actually try to learn the good old-fashioned way what you might have missed when you overslept that one . . . month . . . of class.

Step Five. INVITATION. If you get invited to a party at some point during reading period, by all means go! Definitely do *not* go to all of them; instead just choose one or two. Breaks are just as important as studying if not more so: if you don't blow off steam every once in a while, you could burn out faster than you can RSVP *No, thank you. I have to study.*

Step Six. VOCALIZATION. By now you all know that there are supposedly three things you have to do before you graduate: 1) Pee on the John Harvard statue; 2) Have sex in Widener Library; and 3) Run Primal Scream. Reading period will afford you an opportunity to achieve the latter, which, for those of you who didn't already know, is a naked run through Harvard Yard. As unsavory as it sounds, there is evidence to support that this is a legitimate therapeutic activity. Plus, it's tradition! According to the *Crimson*, "Primal Scream is imperative to student body sanity." Just remember: if you decide to participate on whatever TBD night The Scream takes place, its wintertime and frostbite would be a real bummer down *there*!

Step 7. ABDICATION. Accept your limits. You can't learn a semester's worth of material in two weeks' time, so if you were bad this year and worked hard but partied harder, start mentally preparing yourself for the inevitable lump of coal in your report card. And remember: an F can't kill you—it will just ruin your life. Kidding! (Mostly?)

Step 8. CELEBRATION. Whoops! Better postpone this one until you see your grades.

We wish you a happy, healthy Reading Period, and the best of luck on your upcoming exams!

ap tap tap tappity-tap-tap-tap, tap tap tap tappity-tap-tap-tap a pencil eraser rapped rapidly on a desk.

Clack-clack-clackity-clack typed thousands of keys on hundreds of keyboards as fingers flew, scrambling to finish final papers.

Whirrrr . . . whirr . . . beep, beep, beep went the communal printers as they groaned under the strain, spitting out study guides as fast as they could go.

Gnash, gnash, gnash, bubble, bubble, POP! Gnash, gnash, gnash, bubble, bubble, POP! jaws clicked and teeth gnashed nervously as gum expanded into bubbles and then exploded.

Ring, riiing, riiiiiing—oh shit, sorry. Du-du-du-du-DU-du-du-du-DU-DU-DU-du—SORRY, sorry. From the wiiiiinddoooow, to the WALLL, 'till sweat drips down my—FRACK, sorry—get low, get low—where is it?—get low, get low—found it! Sorry.

BE QUIET.

This is a *library*.

We're trying to study.

QUIET, PLEASE.

Badabing!

Gchat from Mimi Clément:

Mimi: What kind of underwear are you wearing?

Callie: Go away, I'm studying. *Badabing!*

Badabing! Mimi: MANDATORY discussion group for our Justice final paper topics, remember? 2nd-floor balcony *allons-y maintenant*! Greggers and OkeeDokee = already there.

Callie: Vanessa? *Badabing!*

Badabing! Mimi: She is in the group. Too late to kick her out.

Callie: Ugghhh. *Badabing!*

Badabing! Mimi: You made your bed. Now if you want to lie in it, you have to unmake it.

Callie: That makes no sense! *Badabing!*

Badabing! Mimi: It makes perfect sense!

Callie: Ha. You've lost it. *Hoot-hoot. Badabing!*

Badabing! Mimi: Stop stalling. *Nous sommes EN RETARD.*

Callie shut the lid of her laptop—which was situated directly across from Mimi's laptop, behind which Mimi was seated at an oak table on the first floor in the main reading room of Lamont Library.

The Justice paper topics discussion group was, unfortunately, like group members Bolton and Von Vorhees, entirely unavoidable. "Fine," Callie spat, glaring at Mimi. "Let's go."

Together, they mounted the stairs to the second-floor balcony: an area reserved for group projects since talking—quietly—was permitted. Like a box seat at the opera, it also afforded an excellent view of the entire main reading room below.

True to Mimi's word, most of the other inhabitants of Wigglesworth Entryway C, second floor, were already there. Dana and Adam sat off to one side, sharing a single study carrel, heads bent together, whispering furiously. Matt, Gregory, and OK were all in a row, crowded around one side of a small rectangular table. Matt hunched over his textbook, his left knee bouncing up and down, keeping time with his pencil, gnawed so thin it could snap at any moment. Callie took the chair opposite him. He sighed as his glasses slid down his nose. He pushed them back up. A moment later they slid down again.

Deliberately avoiding eye contact with Gregory, Callie looked down the table at OK while Mimi sat across from him. He seemed calm—entirely *too* calm in fact, almost as if he'd been dipping into Mimi's little orange prescription bottle and the medication was working as pharmacists had originally intended because—it dawned on Callie—OK might actually have ADHD. He made a mark on the legal pad next to him, looking for all the world like taking notes was something he really did do on a daily basis.

"OK," said Callie, "that textbook looks like you bought it yesterday."

"Correction," he retorted without looking up, "I *opened* it yesterday. Pretty interesting stuff!"

"Sorry it took me so long," a voice said from over Callie's shoulder. There was a loud thunk as Vanessa set five sugar-free Red Bulls on the table next to an enormous Halloween-size bag of mini-Snickers. "Fuel," she explained, sitting. "There's one can for each of my friends . . . and you, Matt."

"Thanks," said Callie, popping open a can before Vanessa could protest and downing it in one gulp. Yeccch—the taste was worse than stale grape medicine.

"That wasn't for you," Vanessa hissed at Callie. "I *said* there were only enough for my *friends*—"

"She can have mine," Gregory cut her off without looking up from his computer screen.

Vanessa snorted, taking an indignant, ladylike sip of her drink. Callie turned, intending to say that a sugar-free Red Bull was the *least* Vanessa could do given the A-bomb she'd dropped on Callie's bedroom, but when she really looked at Vanessa, she completely lost her train of thought. Vanessa appeared even messier—if possible—than the disaster Callie had spent half of the other day cleaning.

After Vanessa had spent months waking up an hour before class to secure every strawberry-blond strand with curlers and mousses and flat irons and god knows what else, her hair had finally defeated her. She had piled it atop her head in a greasy mess. Her skin was breaking out, or perhaps it had always been that way and today she hadn't had time to apply all seven layers of her mineral-based makeup. And if her clothing could be read as a barometer for her nerves, the stress was clearly maxing out at unheard of levels. Vanessa had donned her sweats that said Juicy across the rear and—horror of all horrors—a hooded sweatshirt: two items that had once been declared "illegal outside of the common room" unless one wanted to look, according to Vanessa, like a sloppy eighth grader auditioning for *The Real Housewives of Shady Hills Rehabilitation Center*.

"So . . ." said Mimi, glancing from Vanessa to Callie, "Justice paper topics? Anyone?"

"Remind me what the choices are again?" asked Callie.

"'Is torture ever justified?'" Matt read off a list.

"No," said Callie at the same time that Vanessa said, "Yes."

"Of course *you* would think that it's okay to violate a basic human right," said Callie, "kind of like the right to *privacy*, or *property*—"

"Actually," Matt began, "the Founding Fathers changed Locke's right to property to the pursuit of happiness in the second paragraph of the Decl—"

"Excuse me if I don't see anything wrong with electroshocking a known terrorist every once in a while when it could save the lives of *millions*," Vanessa cut in, "because he has information about an imminent attack!"

Gregory looked up, his frown morphing into a smirk. "Do you think they're going to fight?" he murmured, nudging Matt.

"This is good, no?" Mimi interjected. "This is what we are supposed to be doing—discussing the arguments for and against . . . Next topic?" She looked pointedly at Matt.

"Affirmative action," Matt read. "'Is it true that you can't really claim credit for your upbringing?'"

Vanessa shrugged. "Some people are just born—"

"Born *what*?" Callie interrupted. "Better? Just because they have more money or more diamond earrings to lose—"

"I was going to say 'born with more privileges,'" Vanessa snapped. "But yes, some people *are* better—better friends, for example, or—"

"I think what Vanessa is trying to say," Gregory cut in smoothly, "is that it matters less what advantages you were born with and more what you do with them later."

"You're arguing in favor of a meritocratic approach?" asked Matt, incredulous. "But what about Rawls' veil of ignorance and his claim that things like talent and intelligence are just as much accidents of birth as race or socioeconomic status?"

"I was actually thinking more along the lines of an Aristotelian argument: that people are better suited to places in society based on their specific talents. Or I could take a Kantian stance that—"

Gregory was silenced by a collective groan. Callie yawned. "I yawn"—yawn—"every time"—stretch—"I even *think* about"—she yawned again—"metaphysics."

Gregory smiled.

Callie shook herself and stared back down at her computer.

"Can't . . . Kant." said Matt, laughing. "Get it?"

Mimi looked at him blankly. "*Can't, Kant*," he repeated, his laughter turning silent and slightly hysterical.

"Oh, we get it," said Vanessa. "It just isn't funny."

"You're funny. Funny-*looking*," Matt muttered, cracking up all over again.

"How old are you, twelve?" Vanessa shot back, her hands nonetheless flying to her hair.

"Sorry," Matt muttered, pulling himself together. "So, uh, when confronted with this question about the accident of birth—"

"The answer," OK interrupted, "is one egg, one sperm, and one broken condom."

Matt dissolved, once more, into giggles.

"Speaking of Kant," said Mimi, ignoring Matt and OK and addressing Gregory, "there is another paper topic that seems to pit him against Aristotle: 'Is there a difference between what is right and what is good? Is it ever wrong to tell the truth?'"

"Well," said Gregory, "Aristotle's notion of ethics strikes me as a fundamentally practical one—"

"Practical ethics," Matt interrupted. "Practical ethics, practical ethics, ethical practices . . . Have you guys ever noticed that if you say a word over and over again it loses its meaning?"

Callie stared. "Uh, when was the last time you slept?"

"Day before yesterday," Dana called from her study carrel, snapping to attention.

"Shh . . ." Adam cooed, massaging her back.

Dana picked up her book and resumed her frenetic muttering.

Mimi sighed. "You were saying?" she prompted Gregory. "Kant and Aristotle's central tenets of ethics?"

Gregory nodded. "While Kant believed in a categorical imperative that dictates it is *always* wrong to lie, Aristotle's ethics fundamentally involved finding a way to tell the truth about what is just"—he paused, looking at Callie—"and what is beautiful."

Callie felt the heat rising in her cheeks.

"I can't do it!" Dana burst out suddenly, throwing her head down on the desk.

"Yes you can," Adam reassured her.

"But I have an exam." She moaned.

"Not until late next week," he reminded her, taking her hands. "Now breathe: in and out . . . in . . . and out . . ."

Gregory cleared his throat. "Kant believed in always doing what is best," he continued, "but for Artistole—"

"There was a difference between what is good for us and what is best for us," Callie finished, almost in a whisper. Immediately she wanted to smack herself, having almost said *who* is good for us versus *who* is best for us. Right now, studying was imperative, Kant-style.

"Good versus best?" Matt echoed, scrolling through his notes. "Bentham, Locke, Kant, Aristotle . . . hmm . . . I think I was sick that day. Can I see someone's notes?"

"Sure," said OK, sliding his yellow legal pad in Matt's direction.

"Er, somebody else?" Matt said, clearing his throat and looking at Vanessa, who was marking up her textbook with a pink highlighter.

"If you must," said Vanessa, sliding her MacBook across the table.

"Where—"

"In the folder labeled 'Justice Notes.'"

"Ah, got it," said Matt, clicking the mouse. He was quiet for a moment. "You take your notes on Excel spreadsheets?" he muttered.

"Hmm?"

"Nothing." He stared at the document open before him. "Uh, Vanessa?"

"What!" she cried, throwing the pink highlighter dramatically on the table.

"Why do you have a list of peoples' names, high schools, and home towns?"

Callie's eyes grew wide.

"And what," Matt continued, "is 'Project Fish Farm'? Did I miss an important hypothetical—"

"*Eeeiwehgkadhgghghgggggggg.*" Vanessa let forth a strangled, desperate yelp, throwing herself—torso, arms, and chest—over her laptop.

Callie couldn't help it; she started to giggle.

Vanessa, still prostrate across the table, shielding her stalker-esque list of potential crushes, swiveled her head around to glare.

But when she caught Callie's eye, something cracked; she too started to giggle.

Matt stared. "What's so—"

"It's nothing!" Callie gasped.

"A—uh—hypothetical that you—huh—must have missed!" Vanessa managed to choke out between giggles.

Mimi decided to intervene. "*D'accord*, we came, we did the mandatory discussing bit, and now all that is left is to write our final papers. Due . . . ah, yes, next week."

That sobered everybody up right quick.

Scanning the list of potential topics, Matt asked, "So, what's everybody thinking?"

"I'm going to do the equal rights essay," said Callie, deciding. "It's the last question: the one about same-sex marriage."

"For or against?" OK asked.

"For, obviously; are you nuts?" asked Callie.

"Uh-uh, no way. I am out of here!" Dana cried, standing suddenly. Whether or not she spoke in response to Callie was unclear. "This is simply not the proper environment for studying! I'm going to Cabot!" she said, grabbing her bags. "See you all in two weeks!"

"What about me?" Adam asked.

"I'm sorry," she said, shaking her head. "But it's just not working out. It's not you. It's me. I need my space right now."

Ignoring her, Adam started packing up his things.

"Fine," Dana snapped, starting to walk. "But no more sharing the same study carrel! You are to stay twenty feet away from me at all times, understood?"

Adam shrugged and waved good-bye to everyone and then hurried to follow her down the stairs.

"Whew!" Callie blew air through her lips. She sympathized with Dana: it was nearly impossible to work in this environment. Her eyes darted involuntarily toward Gregory. He was frowning, iPod headphones in his ears, and intent upon his work. Turning quickly, Callie glanced out over the main reading room. Students stole suspicious glances at one another; legs twitched and jiggled. The very air seemed abuzz with a barely contained panic.

And there were still ten days left until the first exam.

Callie's eyes traveled from a boy who lay slumped over a table—passed out and using a thick textbook for a pillow—to a girl who was stretching dramatically, arms saluting the sun like she was in the middle of Bikram yoga.

Callie shook herself and wiggled her fingers over her keyboard. So far all she had managed were her name, the date, and the words *Justice: Final Paper* written underneath. She hit Enter, centered the cursor, and set the font to bold, waiting for a title, and a main argument, to come.

Something flickered in the corner of her visual field. The Bikram yoga girl had abandoned her chair in favor of the table: she now sat on the edge, book on her lap, feet swinging over the side. The other three students sharing the workspace stared, but the girl took no notice, flipping the pages of the giant blue hardback and making notes in the margins.

Callie shrugged and typed *The Case for Same-Sex Marriage* at the top of her page. Too vague, she decided. She needed a Kantian Case or an Aristotelian Argument—something, *anything*, that sounded like she was halfway capable of applying the philosophy she had learned in class to real-life ethical and practical dilemmas.

"Does anybody have a *Justice Reader*?" she asked, looking up across the table.

Nobody answered.

Instead, Matt, Gregory, and even OK were all staring, completely hypnotized, at the reading room below. Vanessa and Mimi had also swiveled around in their chairs. Vanessa had a shocked expression on her face. "What the . . ."

Following Matt's gaze, Callie found herself staring once again at the Bikram yoga girl, who had stood on the table and was twirling around, dancing to music that only she could hear. As she moved, slowly, seductively, her hands pulled at the base of her shirt, lifting it ever so slightly, centimeter by centimeter, to reveal the milky white skin beneath. Nearly everyone in the library was staring now; the whispering and poking and urging others to look began to subside as the fabric of her shirt continued working its way upward.

It was utterly silent by the time she lifted the garment over her head and threw it across the room. A scream erupted, fortified by hundreds of other voices. It was deafening. Primal.

Other students stood up and started ripping off their clothes. Shirts and sweaters rained down in torrents from the second-floor balcony, and people stepped out of their pants. Others cringed and shrank into their chairs, trying to hide behind laptops or the walls of their study carrels. Still yelling, the Bikram yoga girl jumped off the table and ran down the aisle, throwing her stretchy pants behind her and then disappearing from view. A stampede of students followed her; clothing littered the table, armchairs, and floor.

Turning, Callie found herself staring at the retreating backs of OK, Matt, Mimi, and Gregory. They raced for the stairs, laptops and textbooks abandoned on the table. Vanessa was the only one left. Callie looked at her. Her eyes were wide. "Do you think . . ." Vanessa started, slightly speechless. "Is it—?"

"Primal Scream?" Callie finished. "I think so."

"Should we?" Vanessa asked. "I mean, just to . . ."

"Just to check it out?" Callie offered. "Uh, yeah, why not?"

"Well, then, let's go!" said Vanessa, making an *after-you* gesture toward the staircase. Callie started down it, glancing uncertainly over her shoulder. But Vanessa was right behind her. Together they burst into the foyer; ran past Bob, who was ranting hysterically— no doubt about any one of the ten thousand security breaches that had just occurred—and out into the freezing December air.

They could hear screams in the distance. Jogging, they quickly reached the Yard. There were already at least a thousand people lining the outermost cement walkway, which was approximately twice the size of a traditional racing track. Hundreds more, or so it seemed, were arriving by the minute. The spectators outnumbered the runners by an overwhelming ratio, but still Callie could make out the shapes of hundreds of students bare down to their socks and shoes, crowded around the starting line. Not everyone was naked: some wore bathrobes, towels, or trench coats, while others sported scarves, sunglasses, hats, and various accessories to mask their identity. A small contingent had covered their entire bodies with paint: giant Crimson *H*s or Boston Red Sox logos or simply abstract designs. Many had wrapped flags—of America, Kirkland, Canada, Eliot, The Former Soviet Union, Dunster—around their shoulders super-hero-cape style. A few students had simply opted for a paper bag over the head with two holes cut out for eyes; the only way to go, in Callie's opinion, if one planned to run at all.

Harvard flag count: 32.

At-risk frostbite cases: 174.

Students with BA levels of >0.08: 89

"Would you ever . . . ?" Vanessa whispered, touching her arm.

"No way!" said Callie.

"Me neither," Vanessa agreed, sounding thoroughly relieved. "Ohmygosh, look at *that* guy," she cried, pointing at a boy wearing only a tube sock—and not on either of his feet.

Several members of the Harvard band had now arrived. Horns blared and drums pounded as a student carrying a megaphone raised it and cried:

"On your marks . . .

Get set . . .

GO!"

And they were off; a massive whirl of nudity, color, and cathartic screaming. Callie and Vanessa cheered from the sidelines, jumping up and down. Suddenly Mimi zoomed past in boots and her black trench coat, carrying a bundle of boy's clothing tucked under her arm and cackling madly. She spotted Callie and Vanessa and waved. Then she veered off course and continued running back toward Wigg.

"Whatever she's up to—it can't be good," Callie murmured. Vanessa laughed and nodded.

"OHMYGOD! *Eeeeeeeekk. LOOK!*" Vanessa screamed, gripping Callie by the arm. Gregory had just whizzed by in a naked blur, sprinting for all his squash training was worth, followed by OK, who was screaming his head off, and Matt who was missing his glasses and kept bumping into people and apologizing, hopping around, trying to cover himself, and blushing furiously.

Unwittingly Callie had grabbed Vanessa's hand, and the two continued shrieking as they recognized various members of the freshman, sophomore, junior, and senior classes. They saw the girls' hockey team in nothing but their socks, a naked old man who definitely didn't go to Harvard, the wrong half of half their dormitory, and overall, just a whole lot more than anyone would ever want to see . . . ever.

They were still giggling long after the run was over and many students had already left the Yard. Walking side by side, they were halfway down the path between Boylston and Widener when they heard a rustling in the bushes on their right.

"*Pssst,*" a voice hissed. "Callie, Vanessa—over here!"

Exchanging a look, they approached the bushes and peered down into the secluded space behind them. OK, still completely naked, was crouched under the leaves. "That. Mimi!" he exclaimed through chattering teeth, looking completely livid. "Should have known she was up to something!"

Callie and Vanessa tried not to laugh—but it was useless. "Here," said Callie, tossing her scarf to OK. Vanessa, doubled over with laughter, shrugged out of the wool peacoat she wore over her sweatshirt. OK wrapped the scarf around his waist like a skirt and put on the jacket, the sleeves of which barely reached his elbows.

"It's a good look for you," Vanessa managed.

Callie hooted with laughter. "You just . . . can't . . . seem to pass up *any* opportunity to run around naked . . . can you?"

OK ignored them. Emerging from the bushes, he frowned. "I hope you said good-bye to your roommate and told her that you love her," he said. "Because she has only an hour left to live."

"Oh, come on," said Callie, slinging an arm around his waist.

"All in good fun," Vanessa chimed in, looping her arm around him from the other side and holding on to Callie's at the elbow. "But let's get you inside before you get frostbite on the you-know-where."

Pink-cheeked and breathless, they climbed the stairs.

"Thank you kindly, ladies," said OK, bowing to them when they reached his door. "I shall have these laundered and returned to you at my earliest convenience. Now I must retire to my quarters and begin plotting my revenge."

"Sounds good," said Vanessa. "See you later!"

"See ya!" Callie echoed, watching him walk into his room. "Well," she said, turning back to Vanessa. "That was amaz—"

She stopped talking midsentence. Vanessa had picked up two large fancy white envelopes that had been sticking out from under their door. Each was shiny, embossed, and tied with a dark green bow. Vanessa flipped them over, and Callie saw a red wax seal stamped with a familiar crest: The Hasty Pudding Social Club. She also noticed the two names written in ornate calligraphy underneath: Marine Clément and Callie Andrews.

Wordlessly Vanessa handed her the envelopes and opened the door to the common room. She refrained from slamming it, but she didn't hold it open either. Slowly the door swung shut behind her.

Callie stood in the hallway holding the envelopes in her hands and wishing for all the world that she could trade them for what she'd lost.

SEVEN

Limericks

The Hasty Pudding Social Club
Cordially invites its members to the 215th annual dinner:

LIMERICKS
A limerick is a poem in five lines with a rhyme scheme of a-a-b-b-a.
The defining feature of a limerick is humor, sometimes crude or vulgar, and above all,
it is the format we traditionally use for our annual "roast," in which new members
will perform a public presentation of comedic insults, praise, and true (or untrue!)
stories—in verse—in tribute to their elders, and vice versa, in an ancient
bonding ritual dating back to the days of yore.

7-8 P.M.: Cocktail Hour
Upon arrival each roaster will pull a roastee's name from the hat
(neophytes will select a veteran member at random and, again, vice versa).
You will have one hour to socialize and gather as much "dirt" as you can
on your roastee in preparation for the roast.

8-10 P.M.: Dinner
Limericks will be composed at the table while we eat. After
the main course the roast will begin. Everyone will perform out loud
in front of the group. Prizes will be awarded for the most clever, ribald, and lyrical,
(and whatever other categories we invent during dinner) limericks.

10 P.M.: Party
After dinner we'll open the club to your guests.
Please limit guests to one per person.

We look forward to seeing you then.
December 13th, 2010
2 Garden Street
Cocktail Attire
RSVP no later than December 10th

White lace tablecloths covered the long rectangular tables; silver candlesticks flanked flower arrangements in crystal vases, and the silverware had been polished until it shone. Name cards perched on porcelain plates, and next to every cloth napkin at each place setting someone had positioned a thin stack of index cards clipped together by a black ballpoint pen. Candlelight bounced off the wood-paneled walls; bowties were tightened, napkins adjusted, and white gloves donned as the final preparations were made to welcome the members of The Hasting Pudding Social Club to the first annual dinner of the year: Limericks.

"Thank you," said Callie to the man who had just taken her coat. He dipped his head and then disappeared into the coatroom, which looked as if, for once, it was being used for the purpose originally intended rather than for covert activities like smoking indoors, kissing your significant other's roommate while their boy- or girlfriend laughs blissfully ignorant in the next room, or in the words of Mimi, for "powdering your nose."

"Ladies—welcome," came the cool voice of Anne Goldberg. She stood under the archway that led to the main front room and held a black top hat in each hand. The hat in her right hand had been labeled NEOS; the one in her left read VETS. "Please select one name each," she said, extending the hat full of the veterans' names, "and then proceed to the cocktail party." She tilted her head toward the crowd that had already begun congregating.

Everyone looked particularly dressy in the dim glow of the crystal chandelier that was suspended from the ceiling. The soft tinkling sound of champagne flutes clinking together in greetings and in cheers, along with classical music emanating from speakers unseen filled the air. Callie tugged anxiously at the tight, black, strapless dress she had borrowed from Mimi. Even with all the meals she'd been missing lately, she still had difficulty believing that the dress actually fit—unable to shake the feeling that she was a little girl playing dress-up and that all the other guys and girls in suits and cocktail attire were fellow four-year-olds hosting an extravagant tea party so convincing that halfway through they had all forgotten it was only make-believe. Any minute now, however, Mommy would rush in to yell about ruining her lipstick, putting runs in her stockings, or stealing her pearls, and the whole façade would come crashing down.

Or maybe this really was their reality, and Callie was the only one pretending.

She plunged her hand into the hat, trying to avoid Anne's eyes. "Callie," said Anne, "there's a little matter that we need to discuss. Can you drop by sometime next week?"

Callie nodded. (WASPitude Rule Number Six: Never imply that somebody owes you money or directly refer to money in public.) Damn you, dues. This could well be her last Pudding party ever. Her fingers closed around a thin slip of paper. Drawing it out and unfolding it, she read: *Tyler Green*.

Great, she thought, glancing over at the bar where she had spotted Tyler earlier and confirming her biggest fear: that his roommate and best friend, Clint Weber, was right there standing next to him. Just great.

"Who'd you get?" she whispered to Mimi after Anne had shooed them away.

"Brittney Saunders," Mimi muttered with a shrug. "That girl is so dumb she makes the cast members of *Jersey Shore* look like rock scientists."

"Rocket scientists?" Callie asked.

"Non," said Mimi. "Geologists."

Callie giggled. "Maybe you can use that?"

"What I could use," Mimi retorted, "is a drink."

"Amen," said Callie, watching Clint, who was still over by the bar, erupt into laughter and punch Tyler on the arm. "You go; I'll wait here."

"What do you want?" asked Mimi.

"Uh . . . I'll have a dirty martini. No ice, no salt, four olives, and make it a double!"

Mimi raised an eyebrow. "Make it a double?"

Callie blushed. "I thought it sounded good, like in the movies? Shaken not stirred? No?"

"No," Mimi said. Shaking her head, she walked off toward the bar.

"BLONDIE!" a voice suddenly boomed, and Callie jumped as two enormous dark hands landed on her shoulders.

"OK—you scared me!" Callie cried, wheeling around to face him.

"Sorry," he said, patting her on the head. "But I need your help."

"Oh?"

"Yes. I drew"—he paused, making a big show of digging the small slip of paper from his pocket and holding it up for her to see: *Alexis Thorndike*— "you-know-who, and I need some dirt!" he finished.

"Dirt?" asked Callie, biting her lip. "What makes you think I have any dirt on L—you-know-who?"

"Well, she's your COMP director, isn't she? And don't you go out with her ex-boyfriend, what's-his-name, who's always in the sweater vest—"

"*Used* to go out with her ex-b— Clint's his name, and keep it down!" Callie hissed, stealing a glance across the room at the man in question, who was telling what looked to be a hilarious story to a group of sophomores.

"Come on C-money, help a brother out," OK pleaded. "Did I mention you look dashing tonight, neighbor?"

"I really don't know anything!" Callie cried. "And I kind of doubt anyone else does either." Because if they did, they'd probably be dead.

OK's lower lip jutted out.

"Maybe ask one of her roommates?" Callie suggested. "Anne Goldberg, Madison McLaughlin—somebody from the Bee?"

"Good idea!" said OK, clapping her on the shoulders once more. "Which one's Anne again?"

"She's the one who always looks like she has a bad smell under her nose. There," she said, raising her arm to point, "Under the archway holding the h—" Her arm fell to her side. Gregory had just sauntered into the foyer, accompanied by none other than you-know-who herself. Callie watched him wave aside the coatroom attendant and slide Lexi's Andrew Marc trench gently down her pale, delicate shoulders. Her chestnut curls tumbled loose, low down her back, and swayed within an inch of his face. Gregory's eyes flickered toward Callie.

Why the hell is he waving at—oh. She lowered her eyes as OK waved back. Everyone else—or so it seemed—had stopped mid-conversation to stare at the most attractive pair in the room. Or perhaps more accurately, the most attractive *couple* in the room.

"Why don't you ask Gregory if *he* knows anything about Lex—you-know-who?" Callie asked, trying to keep her voice as even as possible. "After all, they seem awfully cozy lately. Almost like they're . . . dating?"

"Eh?" As usual OK was a hundred and ten percent hopeless when it came to taking a hint.

"Those two," Callie said, spelling it out as she watched Lexi try to peer over Gregory's shoulder while he selected a name. "They aren't *dating*, are they?"

"Dating?" OK repeated absentmindedly. "What? No! Gregory doesn't *date*. I think they know each other from back home—she may be friends with his cousin at Princeton?"

"Really?" asked Callie, openly staring now at Gregory, who was whispering something in Alexis's ear. "Because it *looks* like—"

"MIMI!" OK boomed, leaping forward to embrace Mimi—who had just returned from the bar—and squeezing her so tightly that she almost spilled their drinks. "Where have you been all my life?" he added, finally letting her push him away after a few failed attempts.

"Hiding, mostly," Mimi said, trying not to smile and handing Callie her martini.

"Thanks," said Callie, trying not to let any of the clear liquid slosh over the rim. Tentatively she raised the glass to her lips. In the meantime OK had appropriated Mimi's drink and taken a sip. "This tastes like plain tonic water," he remarked, handing it back to her, confused.

"So?" Mimi said, daring him to say more.

"Here—*ugh*—take mine," said Callie. Like so many other "grown-up" things she'd been yearning to try in college, the martini was another disappointment: sounds cool in theory, tastes terrible in practice. Just one salty, burning sip and the room had gone immediately—and alarmingly—blurry around the edges.

OK took a long drink and then stared at them over the rim of the glass. "'The name is Bond. James Bond,'" he said. "The mission," he continued, speaking into an imaginary Bluetooth device in the cuff of his sleeve, "is to acquire intel on target you-know-who; Perpetual Sweater Vest and Bad Smell Under the Nose are possible suspects for interrogation." He turned to Mimi, cupping her chin in his hand. "I will return for you later." Then both girls watched as he darted through the crowd and over to the wall, along which he began to creep covert-ops style.

Mimi shook her head. Callie laughed. "Should we be finding 'dirt' for our limericks, too?" she asked, looking around the room.

"I wish we could skip the dinner and get to the party," Mimi said with a sigh.

"*I* wish we could skip the party and get back to the studying," Callie commented morosely.

"*Arrête, tu es ridicule,*" said Mimi. "You promised we could have a break after we finished our Justice papers. And as we say back home: sometimes the only work that needs doing is on your sanity. Otherwise you will end up like Dana—completely hoot-hoot."

"Where *is* Dana, anyway?" asked Callie. "Last time I saw her was two days ago—she said she was going to camp out in Cabot Science Library."

"Ah," said Mimi. "So that explains the missing sleeping bag and toothbrush."

"Oh dear," said Callie, furrowing her brow. She had heard that science majors sometimes camped out in Cabot Library, which was open a dangerous twenty-four hours a day during the week leading up to finals, but she hadn't seriously thought that people actually slept there—until now, that is. Poor Dana.

"If she's not in the room when we get back," Callie began, "we should go check on her in the morning. What about Vanessa?"

"What *about* Vanessa?"

"Did you invite her tonight?"

"I did." Mimi shrugged. "But she said she already had an invite and did not need me to 'do her any favors.'"

"*Hmpf,*" Callie snorted noncommittally. "If you ask me—"

"Excuse me," said a senior girl Callie had only spoken to once during punch, "but are you two roommates?"

"Er . . . *oui*?" said Mimi.

"And you're Callie Andrews?" said the girl.

Callie nodded.

The girl turned to Mimi. "Great, I need to borrow you," she said, ushering Mimi away toward the bar. Callie gulped, praying that Mimi would stick to tonic water and thus select her embarrassing Callie stories wisely. So, so many to choose from, Callie thought with a sigh. And one absolutely mortifying secret.

Callie's eyes fell on Lexi, who had made her way over to Tyler and Clint. Gregory was nowhere to be seen—not that Callie was looking. Her eyes narrowed as she watched Lexi lean in with her hands raised as if to adjust Clint's gray-green tie. Clint smiled but smoothly beat her to it, tightening the knot himself. Lexi's hands fell to her sides.

Turning suddenly, Clint caught her eye. Callie flushed and looked away, casting around for Mimi or someone else to talk to so she could avoid—

"Hi," said Clint, having crossed the room at lightning speed.

"Hey," Callie replied, her heart thundering in her chest. Why was he leaning so close to her? And why were his lips moving toward her—

"*Agh!* Sorry!" she cried as their noses collided. He had been aiming for her cheek, and she had tilted her head to avoid what she had stupidly (wishfully?) assumed was an imminent kiss on the lips—only she had gone the wrong way and it had come close to the real thing. *Dangerously* close, she chided herself, angling her body to avoid Lexi's glare. It's not my fault he's talking to me! she thought. Not my fault, not my fau—

"So . . . are you ever going to tell me why you're avoiding me?" Clint said, his playful smile almost masking the serious note.

Because your ex-girlfriend has been blackmailing me with a secret that no one can ever know? Especially not impossibly perfect you—

"You know, finals," she said, waving her hand dismissively. She could still sense Lexi's eyes on her. "I should really check on Mimi."

"Wait," he said, catching her arm. He paused, seeming to search for something to detain her. Her elbow tingled under his touch, his hand so warm and—

"Callie!" said Lexi, interceding gracefully and leaning in to air-kiss the space next to Callie's cheeks. Clint's arm fell to his side. Callie's elbow still felt warm where his hand had rested not a second earlier. "And how's my favorite mentee this evening?" Lexi cooed. "Doesn't she look lovely tonight?" she breezed on before Callie could answer. "I can see why you liked her." Lexi let the past tense hang, a proclamation undisputed, in the air.

"You're in a good mood tonight!" Clint said, permitting himself a tentative smile.

"I am," Lexi agreed airily. "And I think you know why," she said, leaning in. "It's Limericks! I *love* Limericks." She smiled at Callie. "Everyone's dirty little secrets laid bare . . . to roast!"

Callie swallowed.

"Who did you draw?" Lexi pressed her. "Don't be shy now . . . Go on, tell us and we can probably help you!"

"Tyler, actually," Callie admitted, glancing at Clint.

"Tyler!" Lexi clapped her hands together, the very picture of delight. "Well, as Clint can certainly attest, the question there is not a matter of uncovering *what* terrible things Tyler's done but rather where to start!"

Clint laughed. Even through her claustrophobic feelings of dread, Callie had to admire how swiftly and totally Lexi could take control of a conversation.

"Remember freshman year when Tyler and Bryan were in a fight and Tyler peed in Bryan's dresser drawer?" Lexi asked with an uncharacteristic giggle.

Clint's eyes twinkled. "To be fair, Bryan had thrown all of Tyler's underwear out the window into that huge tree in front of their dorm the day before."

"Why?" asked Callie, suddenly struck by the thought that Clint and Lexi had once been freshmen. Obvious as it was, the idea took her by surprise: confident, always-knows-the-right-thing-to-say Clint as a freshman? She just couldn't picture it. Nor, for that matter, could she really picture Clint dating Lexi, though that had obviously happened, too. Suddenly she found herself wanting to know everything: how did they meet and where, what was their first date like, were they in love, and what had happened after to change Clint's tastes so dramatically that he could possibly be looking at Callie the way he was right now, even with Lexi standing next to her.

"I think it was just your typical roommate drama," Lexi said with a shrug. "They lived in a double that those PETA people would probably consider inhumane for a pair of chickens."

An image of Vanessa trashing her room flitted through Callie's mind. But then she pictured Vanessa returning from the library or wherever else she had gone to avoid the getting-ready festivities that evening and sitting in C 24 all alone. Callie frowned.

"Speaking of freshman year, remember that time in Justice when Sandel cold-called Tyler and made him stand up and take the microphone?"

"Yes!" said Lexi with a smile. Callie tugged at her dress. "Sandel asked him if he had anything he'd like to share with the class and he said—"

"'Cindy, I think I'm in love with you and would very much like to take you to dinner this Friday night!'" Clint finished, erupting into laughter.

"Cindy?" asked Callie, looking back and forth between them.

"Cindy was Tyler's TF," Lexi explained, shaking her head. "More than one freshman boy was in love with her. . . ."

"But Tyler was the only one who was crazy enough to announce it in front of the entire class," said Clint. "Classic Tyler. Overconfident to a fault. Reminds me of sophomore year when we had to dress up as Catholic school-girls for Fly Initiation and perform a Britney Spears song on the steps of Memorial Church at noon, only Tyler got the time wrong. He showed up at eleven, but he turned on his stereo and sang 'Baby One More Time' by himself anyway, belly shirt and blond wig and all."

Despite Lexi's continuing, spine-chilling proximity, Callie cracked a smile.

"Somebody caught the whole thing on their Flip cam and that was the end of his presidential campaign," Clint said with a wink.

"He means for the United States, not the Pudding," Lexi added, smirking at Callie's half-horrified, half-confused expression.

"Right," said Callie. How silly of me.

Clint had reached the bottom of his scotch. He rattled the ice cubes in his glass. "I think I might be due for another one of these—then the *real* secrets will start to come out!"

Lexi caught Callie's eye.

"Can I get you anything?" Clint asked, touching Callie's arm.

"I'll have a white wine," said Lexi.

"Callie?" said Clint.

"I'll . . . have the same."

"What kind?"

What do you mean "what kind"? Uh, white!

"Chardonnay for both of us," Lexi said.

Oh.

"Be right back," said Clint.

Callie took a deep breath. Lexi turned to face her. "I think you got all the information about Tyler that you'll need," she said pointedly.

"People," Anne Goldberg suddenly called, clapping her hands. "The staff has just informed me that dinner is almost ready. Please draw your present conversations to a close and begin making your way to the dining room."

Thank you, God, and thank you, Anne! Excusing herself with no more than a tight smile, Callie headed straight into the dining room. She exhaled with relief when she spotted her name card in the middle of the second of four long banquet tables, next to Marine Clément on the left, and OK Zeyna on the right. Taking her seat, she marveled at the decadence—even her senior prom hadn't seemed nearly this fancy. She closed her eyes, determined not to let thoughts of prom take her on a perilous trip down memory lane. . . .

"*Oh-la-la*, have *I* got the dirt on *you!*" Mimi sang, sliding into the chair next to Callie.

"Me?" squeaked Callie, sitting up in her chair.

"No, not *you* silly—Brittney!" said Mimi, grabbing the index cards near her plate and uncapping the pen next to her knife with delight. "Brittney, Brittney . . . *oh*, Brittney." Mimi hummed happily, scribbling down a few lines. "Where to start . . . Get anything good on Tyler?" she added.

"Yes, actually," said Callie, picking up her own pen and staring at the card in front of her.

"I'll give you a hundred dollars to switch seats with me," a BBC British-accented voice suddenly whispered in her right ear.

Callie smiled and leaned over to read the name next to OK's plate: Anne Goldberg.

"Maybe for a thousand," she whispered back, yanking OK down by his sleeve. *Exactly the price for my Pudding membership.*

"Will you take a check?"

Callie rolled her eyes. She was about to whisper that a thousand dollars couldn't buy Mimi's love when she spotted Clint making his way around the table. Callie watched him take the seat across from her several people down, just out of earshot. He smiled at Callie, then held up his index cards and mimed writing on them with a pen. *"How's it going?"* he mouthed.

She looked down, a tiny smile playing on the corners of her lips. Writing in bold capital letters, she quickly scribbled on a note card and held it up: HAVEN'T STARTED YET!

Clint grinned. As the people next to him began to take their seats, he uncapped his pen and wrote back: NEED ANY HELP?

Callie reached for a fresh index card, but before she could think how to reply, she spotted Lexi rounding the other side of the table with Gregory at her heels. Seeing Callie, Lexi gave her a cheerful wave. Callie frowned. Looking back toward Clint, she shook her head no and stared at the tablecloth, waiting for the salad course to arrive.

Two appetizers, one main course, and some indeterminate number of wine refills later (since the amount in the glass optimistically never seemed to dip below half full), Anne Goldberg was in the midst of summoning the room to attention, dinging her champagne glass with a fork and looking a little wobbly on her feet. "Attention! Attention!" she called, the noise in the room gradually dying. "It is almost time to begin! I will now read the order from my list— my list!" she cried, stopping and searching the pockets of her dress. "Where is it?" She continued searching, taking another sip of champagne. "Oh, hell," she muttered. "Who wants to go first?"

There was silence for a moment, but then a steady chant began to build: "Neos, neos, neos, NEOS, NEOS, NEOS!"

"*C'est moi!*" yelled Mimi, leaping to her feet.

The room burst into applause.

"Ahem," Mimi lifted her glass in a toast:

> "Let me tell you a little story about Brittney,
> Took Modern African Politics and called the continent
>> a country,
> But she made friends with her TF,
> And you can guess what comes next—
> She aced her oral exams and scraped by with a B!"

Raucous laughter rang out across the room, followed by hooting and more clapping. "Bravo!" a boy yelled from the table closest to the kitchen. "Encore!"

Even Brittney was laughing good-naturedly. "What—I don't get it!" she yelled. "Just kidding. Africa has, like, lots of countries. I earned that B!"

Triumphantly Mimi took her seat. "Wow," said Callie, tearing her latest index card into ten little pieces. "That was . . ."

"Incredible." OK beamed at Mimi.

Anne Goldberg was back on her feet. "Will the veteran who has Mimi please stand!"

"Ah, *merde,*" Mimi muttered. "Shit, shit, shit."

"You deserve whatever's coming," OK said, leaning across Callie, who had begun frantically scribbling on a fresh card, trying to think what rhymed with *drawer.*

A sophomore girl Callie knew very vaguely stood and waited for the noise to subside.

"Is it true that Marine got kicked out of boarding school?
Stole a car, robbed a bank, got caught naked in the prime
    minister's pool?
Is a ho? Likes the snow?
Are they rumors? We don't know—
And in truth, we don't care, because she's just too damn cool."

"Hmm," Mimi murmured over the cacophony that followed. "Could have been far worse."

The neophyte who had drawn the veteran girl's name—a sophomore boy Callie had never spoken to—stood and began to deliver his limerick. Then the next person, and the next, until the waiter was setting a plate of dark chocolate torte drizzled with raspberry sauce in front of Callie. She barely glanced at it, frowning at her half-finished limerick and crossing out the second line.

"Er, miss?" said the waiter.

"Yes?" asked Callie, realizing that he was still hovering over her.

"I have a note for you," he murmured, sliding a folded index card halfway under her plate, "from the gentleman."

"What gentle—" But before she could finish, he was gone, refilling OK's champagne flute.

Her eyes flitted around the room, and then Callie plucked the card out from beneath her plate and unfolded it under the table: *You look cute when you're concentrating.*

She read it twice, an enormous smile spreading across her face.

When she looked up, Clint was grinning back at her, which would have been confirmation enough even if she hadn't recognized his handwriting.

"NEXT!" Anne's voice boomed above the crowd.

A girl who Callie thought might be one of Lexi's roommates stood up on the other side of the room.

> "Okechu-however-you-say-it, I can't pronounce your name,
> But I've heard it a lot through your several claims to fame:
> Like the fact that you're royalty,
> Or your ex-girlfriend had a problem with loyalty,
> But don't worry—we all agree—that Sexy Hansel is lame."

"Not me!" a girl yelled from the table closest to the door. "Sexy Hansel forever!"

"Take it back!" OK yelled, leaping to his feet. "Er—kidding," he called quickly. "My turn, is it?" He picked his index card off the table and held it out in front of him.

> "I searched high and low for tales that were mean,
> But about Ms. Thorndike, not a dirty detail could I glean,
> For when a bad thing is said,
> Why, it's 'Off with your head—'
> Because that's—and I quote—'what it means to be Queen.'"

The sound of Lexi's tinkling laughter rang out above the slightly subdued applause. Her pearly white teeth gleamed in the candlelight. "I love it," she said, standing and half curtsying as if she personally had done something to elicit their praise.

"I want you to save it for me so I can have it framed." She lifted her limerick from the table. "I actually picked Gregory," she said.

"Uh-oh," he called, rolling his eyes.

"Don't worry," she reassured him, her hand resting briefly on his shoulder. Callie took a big sip of her wine, unable to tear her eyes away as Lexi began:

> "Tales of his womanizing have long been told,
> But I've known Gregory since he was two years old.
> His charms make girls faint,
> And a saint he sure ain't,
> But his darkest secret is his heart of gold."

"Stop," drawled Gregory. "You're making me blush. All lies, ladies, all lies," he added, smiling across the table at Elizabeth, who lived above them on the third floor of Wigg. Elizabeth, to Callie's horror, smiled back, seeming to have developed total amnesia for Gregory's total amnesia regarding her name after they had presumably spent the night together at the beginning of the year.

Then—even more horrifying—Callie watched Gregory pluck a rose from the vase nearest him and present it to Lexi. Callie couldn't hear what he was saying, but Lexi accepted the flower with a smile and let him lean in to kiss her cheek. Callie had to bite the inside of her own cheek to keep from asking OK, again, whether or not they were dating. Because it was really, really, *really* starting to look—

"My turn," Gregory said standing. He cleared his throat.

"I think you all know my man Clint Weber.
His squash racket's faster than a light saber.
Robbed the cradle this semester,
So I propose the nickname: 'freshman molester'
In the hopes that from now on he'll be on better behavior."

Everyone burst into thunderous applause: several of the female members, including Elizabeth, *wahooed* with particular gusto, and the guy sitting next to Clint punched him on the arm. Clint winked at Callie. She tried to smile back, but her gaze was soon drawn as if by an electromagnetic force field back to the other end of the table, where Lexi was looking less than amused. That makes two of us, thought Callie. Wait—no—make that three, she added, noting that Gregory's grin was more of a grimace.

Now it was Clint's time to perform: he stood and delivered something altogether too polite about Elizabeth, who then roasted a veteran girl—the senior who had stolen Mimi away during the cocktail hour and was now looking at Callie in a manner that could mean only one thing.

"When it comes to Callie Andrews, I think we're still
    very curious,
Though the secret to her Pudding membership is less
    than mysterious,
Bewitched Clint Weber's eye,
One tipsy evening at the Fly,
And since then they say he's been quite delirious."

So . . . clearly the majority of members thought that Callie had kissed her way into the Pudding; big whoop—she'd been having nightmare flash-forwards about what rhymed with sex tape. Callie nudged Mimi and gave her a thumbs-up under the table, grateful that her roommate had neglected to mention the dining hall flash/fall incident or the not-remembering-who-Clint-was-when-I-spilled-on-his-sweater moment; Mimi nodded and raised an index finger to her lips. I like sober Mimi, thought Callie, making a mental note to tell her when they were alone.

"Your turn," Mimi whispered, poking her in the side.

"Oh, right," said Callie, climbing reluctantly to her feet. "Um . . ." She raised her champagne glass and drained it. The bubbles made her feel worse, not better. She took a deep breath.

> "With regard to his antics, some say his political career
>   can't survive:
> After Spice Girls greatest hits Britney is his favorite jive,
> In a drawer he did urinate,
> And asked his TF on a date,
> But so what? I say we'll be inaugurating Tyler as President
>   in 2025."

The room erupted into a roar. Tyler's shrill wolf whistle broke through the crowd as people catcalled him or wiped the laughter-induced tears from their eyes. Callie sank back into her chair with a sigh.

"Miss?" said the waiter, who had returned under the same pretext of refilling her glass. As he leaned in, he slipped her another folded index card.

"Thank you," she said, opening it under the table.

> Brilliant roast! And she was right: I <u>am</u> delirious.
>
> Enough so to write this:
>
> Callie Andrews is completely sublime.
>
> She's the type of girl that makes a guy rhyme.
>
> Shortly after I met her.
>
> She spilled coffee on my sweater.
>
> But I didn't care because I knew that one day she'd
>
>   be mine.

Callie's breath caught in her chest—and not just because her dress had grown a few shades tighter over the course of the meal. With all the stress spiking her cortisol levels to dangerous heights, she had almost forgotten how nice something as simple as a single compliment could feel. Her eyes slightly blurry, she stole a glance down the table at Lexi and Gregory, who were giggling over discarded drafts of their limericks. Their heads were bent close: whispering, laughing, touching. . . .

Something snapped, and in an instant, Callie made her decision. Turning the poem over, she scribbled on the back of the card: *What are you doing later?*

Motioning over the waiter, she pressed the card into his hand. Then she watched him make his way to Clint. Clint's entire face lit up while he read, and the glow felt infectious, wrapping around her from the other side of the table. Lexi could *have* Gregory; what she couldn't have was both.

The dinner was drawing to a close: people were getting out of their seats to say hi to members at other tables, exchange copies of limericks, or pose for photos. Anne looked as if she was trying to make another announcement, but she soon threw her hands in the air and then walked into the kitchen. A minute later she returned lugging an enormous set of speakers. Callie checked her phone. 10:02 P.M.: party time.

She waited in her chair, watching the area empty as people trickled out into the main room, where the lights were quickly dimmed and the speakers plugged in. Only when the wait staff had begun to clear the tables did she stand.

"Hey," said a voice as a pair of arms wrapped around her from behind.

Since Lexi was nowhere in sight, Callie allowed herself a full three seconds before she slid out of Clint's grasp.

"The reason I've been avoiding you," she said, turning and thinking quickly, "is because of . . . *FM* COMP."

"I understand that you're a very busy girl with lots of goals—that's part of why I like you," said Clint. The flecks in his gray-green eyes were the same golden color as the candlelight filtering through the bubbles in the leftover champagne.

"Well, yes, I've been very busy," she agreed, "but I'm also worried that talking to you—*seeing* you—could jeopardize my chances of making the magazine."

"Oh? Why's that?"

"Because Lexi . . ." Callie paused, casting around for the right way to phrase it.

"I don't think you need to worry about *that*," Clint cut in with a smile. "True, we have a complicated history, and she's sometimes been . . . possessive, but based on the way she was acting tonight . . . Well, you heard her: she called you her favorite!"

Uh, emphasis on the word *acting*. Subtext: so lost on most boys.

"I'm sure she's moved on by now," he added.

Right. With *my* neighbor.

"So *we* don't have anything to worry about—"

His hands reached for hers, but Callie recoiled. He looked at her questioningly. "I know we have a lot that we still need to talk about, but I thought—I mean, did I misinterpret?"

"Oh—no, not that," she said quickly. "Just, look: I'm sorry if it seems like I'm being paranoid, but getting on the magazine means everything to me right now, so do you mind if when we're in public we keep whatever's going on here a . . . secret?"

So many secrets . . . It seemed to be the trend these days. She looked at him pleadingly.

"Sure," he said, smiling his eye-crinkling grin. "Anything you want."

"Okay," she said, breathing deeply. This could work. It had to. She was done staying away from him. "Maybe later we could meet up and talk?"

"You could come over to my place," he volunteered.

"*Just* to talk," she clarified. "Like you said, we still have a lot to talk about."

"Talk . . . yes," he said, staring into her eyes. "Just talk. Sure. Like I said, whatever you want."

"*If* I come over, do you *promise* that'll be it—just talk, nothing else?"

"I promise."

"So . . . to the party, then?"

"Yes, where I will do my best to ignore you. Which will be difficult, incidentally," he said, leaning in to whisper in her ear, "because you look beautiful tonight."

And so they parted ways.

For the rest of the evening nothing could diminish the glow illuminating her from the inside—that special kind particular to a happy secret. Not even Vanessa's arrival at close to midnight could dampen her mood—in fact, Callie probably would have overlooked her roommate altogether if Vanessa hadn't stopped to talk to Tyler and Clint, whom Callie kept stealing covert glances at through the duration of the party.

At five minutes to one her phone beeped.

> HEY, GORGEOUS, I'M READY TO
> TAKE OFF.
> SEE YOU AT ADAMS IN 15 OR SO?

Smiling, she texted back:

> I'LL BE THERE IN 10. CAN'T WAIT!

EIGHT

THe MorninG After

My dear little Froshtitutes:

Finals may be right around the corner, but as we near the end of reading period, the student body's study focus starts to slip. You decide to go out for just *one* hour, have no more than *one* drink, be back at Lamont by *one* A.M., and before you know it, you're waking up in an unfamiliar room with one hangover, one strange bedfellow, and it's one in the afternoon. There's no way to turn back the clock, but you can attempt to exit the situation as gracefully as possible.

THE MORNING AFTER:
Rules, Etiquette, and Helpful Hints

THE NIGHT BEFORE: No matter how crazy things get, any clothing that comes off in the course of the evening must be located, folded neatly, and placed within reach of the bed *before* you pass out in it. Tossing your undergarments all around his common room the night before in a "fit of passion" *may* seem like a good idea at 3 A.M., but it will be a whole different story in the morning when you wake up without them. You've all heard of Emily Post's guide to dressing–please consider *this* rule your Guide to *Un*dressing.

THE WHAT'S-HIS-NAME: Never, no matter what, under any circumstances, even CIA interrogation, reveal that you are unable to remember the name of the person lying next to you. Either a) perform a quick visual scan of the room for identifying objects—term papers, awards, discarded nametags, whatever; or b) invent a pet name—if you can't think of one, rely on the old (and surprisingly gender-neutral) standbys: grandpa, killer, or son.

WHAT'S IN YOUR PURSE: Of course, since you were going out for only *one* hour and *one* drink, you've forgotten to wear waterproof mascara and carry the other bare necessities one might need to conceal—like, say, concealer—your nighttime romp the next morning when you inevitably wake up looking like a raccoon who stepped into a bathtub holding an electrical appliance (Urban Dictionary: *sex hair*). So when you wake up—and you'd better pray you wake up first—grab your clothes (next to the bed where you put them) and your purse (stocked with makeup essentials and a hairbrush) and make a beeline for the nearest bathroom to fix your face!

CUDDLE A DELICATE BALANCE & MAKE AN ACCEPTABLE EXCUSE: Do not over-cuddle and do not under-cuddle, but rather try to channel Goldilocks and get the amount of cuddling just right. When it is time to leave, instead of inventing a specific lie on the fly (bound to be too vague or too specific 95 percent of the time) simply use the Twenty Minutes Rule: "Thank you for your hospitality. I would love to stay, but I have to be somewhere in twenty minutes."

WHAT TO TAKE/WHAT TO LEAVE BEHIND:
TAKE: While you should obviously never steal anything, you may want to *borrow* some item of clothing, depending on the length of your walk home and what you were wearing the night before. A little

black dress or miniskirt may have seemed socially acceptable at a Final Club the night before (though, freshmen, you will be hard-pressed to spot an upperclassman without a scarf and sweater)—but in the morning you're bound to get some judging glares. So please do borrow some kind of cover-up: not only will you look classier on the walk home, but you'll have an excuse to bring it back—or a nice new sweater (I swear, my lips are sealed).

LEAVE: If, and only *if* your mistake might not be a mistake and you want to see him/her again but aren't sure how to broach the topic between fixing your face and making your meeting in twenty minutes, slip an item of jewelry onto the nightstand. Either he/she will be in touch to let you know you lost it, or you'll have an excuse to drop by and see if you left it there. Conniving? Yes. Effective? Yes.

NEVER TAKE OFF YOUR SHOES: When you walked out the door with high heels on the night before, you made a choice, and you have to honor it: think of it as a social contract. I don't care how intoxicated you get, or how much your feet hurt from dancing, or how silly your heels look the morning after—DO NOT REMOVE THE SHOES. If you do, I have no words but *Oh, for shame, for shame*.

My final piece of advice is that you avoid engaging in the sequence of stupid decisions that will lead you to find yourself in this situation in the first place. But I'm an idealist and a dreamer, and I know that sadly I have to prepare myself, and you, for the harsh realities of this college life.

Seriously, whatever you do, don't take off the shoes,
Alexis Thorndike, Advice Columnist
Fifteen Minutes Magazine
Harvard University's Authority on Campus Life since 1873

allie's eyelids fluttered open and a low moan escaped her lips. Her entire body felt heavy in that deliciously well-rested way; the weight of a feathery down comforter above her and pillows below to match caressed her in a warm embrace, like she was sleeping in a fluffy, heated cloud. She stretched, and the bed seemed to span for miles—in contrast to her tiny twin, in which one wrong roll sent you over the edge and onto the floor.

On this particular morning—or rather, early afternoon—after Limericks she had the entire thing to herself, because Clint, in honor of his "promise," had slept on the couch.

"You said just talking!" he cried at four in the morning when she indicated that she might be interested in more than cuddling. "You made me promise, remember?"

"No, I forget. . . ."

"Really? Because you were quite emphatic earlier that I promise—"

"I know what I said!" she cried, whacking him with a feather pillow. "And I hereby officially release you from said promise!"

"Nope," he said, shaking his head. "I'm sleeping on the couch."

"Uggh," she groaned, throwing the pillow over her own head. Why, why was he so good all the time?

"What would my promises be worth if I didn't keep them?" he teased, lifting the pillow off her head and kissing her forehead.

"Fine," she said. "Get out."

Rolling over, Callie buried her face in the pillows and smiled. Clint's bedroom in Adams House, where he lived in a suite with Tyler and a couple of other junior guys, had always been her safe haven, even before the problems with Vanessa had started. It was the Vanessa-free zone. And now it was also the site of Callie and Clint's reconciliation, which had been far less traumatic than she had expected. When it came time to address the reason for the split (or "break" or whatever it had been), which had been Callie's freak-out when they were on the verge of sex, she had miraculously, accidentally, gotten herself off the hook with almost no explanation at all. . . .

In the early hours of the morning, with no light save for the soft glow emanating from the lamp on his desk, they had lain on Clint's bed: stomachs down, elbows bent, chins propped in their hands, and faces only a few inches apart. In that moment Callie had contemplated telling him the truth about what had happened with Evan. She had been wrestling with the dilemma all night. On the one hand, telling him would not only alleviate the enormous weight on her shoulders from worrying about what would happen if he found out, but it would also diminish some of Lexi's power over her. Maybe Clint could even help by convincing Lexi to destroy the file instead of showing it to the entire school. On the other hand, if he knew—if he saw it—he may never look at her the same way again. That way he had been looking at her all night, and was looking at her now as he tucked a loose strand of hair behind her ear and whispered that she could tell him anything.

"At the end of high school," she began, "my ex-boyfriend . . ."

She paused. This was it: do or die. She stared at him, wanting to memorize everything about his face: his smile, the crinkles around his eyes, the way he let his light brown hair grow too long and fall into them, and particularly, the expression. She wished there were some means to capture the way he saw her now: not necessarily for what she was but rather for what she wanted to be. She had been aching for someone to look at her that way ever since Clint had broken it off and then Gregory had abandoned her the morning after Harvard-Yale. Could she really risk losing that feeling again now after she'd already had a taste? And—if she told Clint about Evan—shouldn't she also tell him about Gregory?

She took a deep breath, her fingernails digging into the sides of her cheeks. "My ex-boyfriend once . . . did something . . . without my consent—"

Clint's brows drew together in alarm. "Oh, Callie," he whispered softly.

"I—uh—" she stumbled, realizing what she had implied yet unsure how to correct herself.

"Don't say anything more," Clint said, sitting up and wrapping his arms around her. "Is this—is this all right?" he asked gently, sitting cross-legged and guiding her head into his lap.

She nodded and he stroked her hair.

"It wasn't—I mean, the way it happened isn't exactly what—"

"Shhh," he said, stroking her arm and bending to kiss her cheek. "You really don't need to explain any further. I understand." He was silent for a moment. "I just can't believe *I* was such an asshole!"

he exclaimed suddenly, running his hands through his hair. "The way I pressured you . . ."

"You didn't pressure me at all!" she cried, sitting up to face him.

"I did," he said, gripping his head at the temples. "I tried to force you to talk about it when you clearly weren't ready. I didn't—I mean, I should have guessed it was something awful."

Callie started to reach for him, but her hands froze midway through the air. This was *not* the way things were supposed to go: Clint feeling guilty while she got away without confessing any of her sins by staying silent.

"Clint," she said. "There's something else I need to tell you."

He looked at her in earnest. "Okay. But before you do, can I just say something?"

She nodded.

"I feel like such an asshole," he muttered, "and I think I need to explain why *I* freaked out when you shut down and wouldn't talk to me." He took a deep breath. "The reason is Lexi."

"Lexi?" Callie echoed. What *about* Lexi?

"One of the main problems in our relationship, and part of what eventually led me to end it, was that she always had some hidden agenda. She would keep things from me or shut down with no explanation—like you did that night—only she did it to introduce drama. She was constantly playing games or trying to make me jealous. She even implied that she had cheated on me once, just to see how I would react."

And how would you? Callie bit her lip to keep herself from asking it aloud.

"It was all about power for her, you know? It was like we were constantly struggling to see who had the upper hand in the relationship. I'm not saying she's a bad person or anything—"

Agree to disagree, thought Callie.

"But she did do a lot of messed-up things to make sure that she had the control." Clint paused. "When it ended, I kind of promised myself that I wouldn't ever put up with anything like that again. And that's when you come along," he said, smiling at Callie.

"You're so different in every way," he continued, taking her hands. "Things with you come so easily. And not because you're shallow or uncomplicated or anything like that but because you're down to earth and straightforward, and clumsy in a way that's innocent and cute—"

"Stop!" she cried, blushing.

He laughed. "What I'm trying to say, basically, is that I think you're amazing."

Callie worried that if her smile grew any wider, her face would probably explode.

"Now what did you want to tell me?"

She blinked. "Nothing!" she cried a little too hastily. "I mean, just that . . . I think you're amazing, too!" And with that, she leaned in and kissed him on the lips.

A few seconds later he broke away. "I'm pretty sure kissing was against your rules."

She thought for a moment. "True," she agreed. "But cuddling is permissible!" she cried, pushing him over playfully and snuggling into the crook in his arm. She sighed, staring at the ceiling. "You know what your room needs?"

"What?"

"Those glow-in-the-dark solar system things you can stick on the walls!"

"So third grade," Clint said, laughing.

"No, no, you'll see. I'm going to buy you some! Then it'll be like we're up on the top floor of the science center looking at the stars all the time."

"So, you're planning on spending a lot of time here in bed with me, huh?"

"Yep. I'm never leaving, so get used to it!"

"I definitely could," he said, kissing the top of her head.

She lay there quietly for a moment. "So . . . boyfriend and girlfriend again, then?"

"Yes."

"But for now can we keep that between the two of us?" she asked.

He was silent.

"Just until COMP's over!" And the tape is destroyed. Somehow.

"If that's what you really want . . . then it'll be our secret."

She smiled. "Our secret."

They couldn't have been apart for more than six hours—at least five and a half of which had been spent sleeping—but already she missed him. Yawning, she climbed out of bed and pulled on her favorite of his sweaters over the T-shirt and pajama bottoms he had lent her. Flinging open the door to his bedroom, she walked out planning to jump onto the couch—only it was empty. The extra sheets, blanket, and pillow were still there but no Clint.

She frowned. Where could he have gone? Suddenly it felt difficult to breathe. She remembered waking in a strange room, the sheets scratchy and unfamiliar, and rolling over to find that the space next to her was empty. Exhaling sharply, she shook her head. No, Clint was *nothing* like Gregory. Wherever Clint had gone, he would be back. And probably soon. Sighing, she turned, heading for the bathroom.

The door was unlocked; the knob gave way under her hand. Opening it, she stepped inside.

"WHAT ARE YOU DOING?" a familiar voice cried. Alarmed, Callie started to retreat. "Are you insane? SHUT THE DOOR!"

Callie leaped back and slammed it, clicking the lock into place. Breathing heavily, she turned. "What the hell are *you* doing here?"

"Baking a cake, what the hell does it look like?" Vanessa snapped. The bathroom was long and narrow like a hall: with the bathtub down on the end behind Callie, closest to the door, and the mirror and sink on the other. Vanessa was currently perched on the windowsill behind the sink, a pair of black stockings yanked halfway up her knees.

"Look what you made me do!" Vanessa cried, gesturing at the enormous run that had torn down the length of her calf. She looked— Well, let's just say that she had seen better days. Sometime during the night she must have suffered a serious mascara malfunction, and her eyes now looked like a raccoon that had been punched in the face—twice—in a bar fight and was now sporting two black eyes. Her hair was knotted and matted in all the wrong places; Callie wondered why they called it "sex hair" in the first place since there was really nothing sexy about the way Vanessa's was frizzing out right now.

"I didn't *make* you do anything," Callie countered. "Now, if you'll excuse me, I'll just be going—"

"Wait," Vanessa said. "I need . . ."

"You need?" Callie echoed.

"My purse," said Vanessa. "I forgot to grab it on my way in here, and now . . ." She gestured toward her face and hair. "I can't possibly go out looking like this!"

It took all the strength Callie had not to smirk or remind Vanessa that she *could* do it and the results probably wouldn't be fatal. Possibly highly amusing, too.

"So, will you help me? Yes or no?"

"Sure. You want me to, what, go back out there and grab your purse?"

Vanessa nodded.

"Well, where is it?"

Vanessa stared at the floor. "It's in . . . s'room."

"*Which* room?" Callie prodded, starting to enjoy herself.

"Tyler's."

"Tyler's!"

"Keep it down!"

"Okay—jeez—I'll go," said Callie, reaching for the door.

"Wait."

"What is it this time?"

"I'm also missing . . . my—" Vanessa's arms flew to her face, the last word muffled by her hands.

"Your underwear?"

"Not—so—loud," Vanessa hissed in a strangled whisper.

"Sorry!" Callie hissed back. "Well . . . where do you think you left it?"

"In Tyler's room, where else?" Vanessa's eyes were wide. "I was just going to make do with my stockings but . . ." She motioned at the gaping run before tearing them off in frustration and tossing them in the trash. "Plus, it's not really—"

"The type of thing you'd want to leave behind?" Callie finished.

"Yeah. Exactly."

"So you want me to . . ." Callie trailed off, realizing. "What do they look like?"

"Pink . . . thong."

Thong? Ewww . . . But Vanessa having to walk home without underwear = *Ewwwwww,* which, with twice as many *W*s, was indisputably a greater evil. The numbers just didn't lie.

"All right," Callie said with a sigh.

"Thank you," Vanessa whispered, closing her eyes.

A minute later Callie was standing in front of Tyler's door implementing Lesson Number One of the day: knock, knock, knock.

The door flew open. "I was wondering what was taking y— Oh! Callie?"

"Hi, Tyler," she said.

"What are you doing here?" he asked.

"Clint," she said shortly, tilting her head and trying to spot Vanessa's bag. Ah, there it was, the Chanel Chambon, inconveniently located on the other side of the room.

"Oh? *Oh* . . ." Tyler said, nodding. Callie nodded back absentmindedly, trying to think of a way to get to the purse. "When I saw him on the couch earlier this morning, I thought . . ."

"You thought what?" Callie asked, snapping back to attention.

"Nothing!" Tyler said, shoving his hands in his pockets guiltily.

"What?" Callie asked.

Tyler sighed. "Just, in the olden days, Clint used to get into a lot of fights with a certain someone and she would make him sleep on the c—"

"Say no more," Callie cut in, holding up her hand and trying not to let the image of Lexi anywhere near Clint's bed—which was Callie's safe space—pollute her mind.

"You got it." Tyler winked. "And between the two of us, I like you better."

Callie beamed. "Thanks!"

Tyler smiled back. "So . . . was there something you wanted?"

"Uh, yes . . ." said Callie slowly, glancing around. "Clint asked me to tell you . . ." She paused, looking down to her left, and then smiled. "Clint asked me to tell you that it's your turn to take out the trash!" she cried, tying the ends of the bag together and lifting it out of the bin that was sitting against the wall on her left. "Here you go!" she said, thrusting it into his arms.

"Um—thanks?"

"No problem!" she said. "Better go quickly now. He'll be back any minute and you know how these things can sometimes escalate between roommates: one day he's asking politely, then he calls upon his lady friend for reinforcement, and then the next thing you know, he's dumping the trash on your bed and you're throwing his underwear out the window and Bryan's peeing in your drawer!"

Tyler shook his head, laughing a little. "You're an odd one, Callie Andrews. Look, I'm leaving now," he added, stepping into his slippers and heading for the door. "If Vanessa asks, tell her—"

"I will!" Callie nodded, ushering him out.

Whew, she breathed. Rushing into his bedroom, she threw the Chanel bag over her arm. Now, where the heck is . . .

Leaning, she checked under the bed and the floor over by the desk and even peeked into the hamper full of dirty laundry in Tyler's closet. If I were a pink thong, where would I be? Wrinkling her nose, she threw back the sheets on Tyler's bed.

One black dress sock.

One—was that . . . a gum wrapper?

But no pink thong.

I give up, she thought, nevertheless lifting the pillows in despair. Standing in the middle of the room, she covered her forehead with her hands. Tyler would be back any moment now and—

Looking up suddenly, she smiled.

There, poking out over the edge of the top of the standing halogen lamp by the window, was a tiny stripe of pink.

"Got you!" she muttered out loud, standing on her tippy toes and gingerly plucking the underwear from the top of the light. Quickly she shoved it into Vanessa's purse, vowing never to ask the owner how it had come to be there in the first place.

Vanessa, Vanessa, Vanessa, you *so* owe me, she thought, heading back to the bathroom.

"Found it!" she called after she had shut the door behind her.

"Ohmygod—thank you *so* much!" Vanessa cried, leaping off the windowsill and running to Callie. She leaned in for a hug—but then caught herself at the very last moment. An awkward pause ensued.

"Uh—well—you're welcome," said Callie, handing her the purse and then turning around to give her some privacy. "So . . . Tyler, huh?" she said, staring at the colorful fish on the shower curtain. Were he and Vanessa a good match? They were both pretty hilarious in their own ways. "I guess that kind of makes sense," Callie mused.

"And what's that supposed to mean?" Vanessa asked, an edge creeping into her voice.

"Nothing," said Callie. "I can just see why you like him." Turning, she glanced at Vanessa, who, having restored her underwear to its proper place, had gone to work on her hair. She had wiped the excess mascara from under her eyes and reapplied a fresh coat, and even though her frilly purple party dress was out of place for the middle of the day, she was starting to look more like her normal, put-together self.

"So, is Tyler the one who invited you last night?" Callie asked, anxious to reinforce the beginnings of the bridge that had sprung up between them.

"Yes," Vanessa said shortly, pulling a tube of concealer from her bag and dabbing some under her eyes.

"Seems like a good strategy," Callie teased. Vanessa was silent. "You know: if you still wanted to get into the Pudding, who better to date than the president?"

Vanessa set her compact on the sink with a clatter. "You do know that the only reason they chose you is because of Clint, right? A lot of people think that's why you were dating him in the first place."

"That's not true and you know it," Callie said quietly, looking Vanessa in the eye. It had been one thing to hear a similar accusation last night during Limericks, but somehow coming from Vanessa, it hurt a whole lot more.

"Looks like he took you back, anyway," Vanessa said coldly, leaning toward the mirror and applying a coat of gloss to her lips. "I'm guessing that means you haven't told him about what happened with Gregory?"

Gregory. Even hearing the name made Callie wince.

A cruel smile played on Vanessa's lips. "Didn't think so," she said, blotting them with a tissue. "After all, why would you? You didn't tell *me* about the Pudding and you didn't tell me about Gregory either."

In the silence that followed, Callie heard the front door to the common room open and then shut with a thunk. Someone had just come home: probably Tyler but possibly Clint.

"I'm . . . I'm sorry," Callie whispered, her eyes wide and pleading. "I'd been trying—I mean, I *have* been trying to find a way to tell you that I liked him, a lot and since the beginning of the year, and that the whole thing was a mistake . . . a huge, gigantic mistake."

Vanessa just stared at her.

"If it makes you feel any better, afterward he basically abandoned me and left me for dead. And when I tried to tell him how I felt, he ignored me and then . . . Well, you know: you saw those two girls. What an asshole."

Vanessa stayed silent.

"You're not going to say anything to Clint, are you?" Callie asked, still speaking barely above a whisper.

Vanessa snorted. "Please," she muttered, rolling her eyes. "As if I cared enough about your stupid problems to do something like that."

Callie was suddenly overcome by the urge to slap her. Forcing her hands to stay by her sides, she snapped through clenched teeth, "Just like you didn't care when you decided to tell Lexi about the tape? Did you know she's" —Callie caught herself just before her voice rose too high— "*blackmailing* me?"

Vanessa kept her eyes trained on the mirror. "For the millionth time, I did not tell Lexi about that tape." She threw her makeup back into her purse and brushed past Callie, pausing with her hand on the door. "And I'm not going to say anything to Clint either because, unlike you, I'm actually a good friend."

With that she walked out into the common room. "Oh, hi, Clint!" Callie heard her say. Counting to ten, Callie checked her face in the mirror and then left the bathroom.

"Girls!" Tyler exclaimed from over where he was sitting on the couch. "Always going to the bathroom in pairs! What on earth do you get up to in there?"

"Oh, we just braid each other's hair and tell secrets," Vanessa said lightly.

"Where were you?" Callie asked Clint, searching his face for any indication that he had overheard what had transpired in the bathroom. She must have appeared particularly anxious because he took one look at her and rushed over to wrap her in an enormous hug. "Aw, did you miss me?" he teased, kissing the top of her head. "Silly girl, I was gone less than twenty minutes! And I only went out so I could pick up some breakfast," he explained, pointing to the white Au Bon Pain bag that was resting on the coffee table. "I figured you'd still be in bed by the time I got back."

"I'm leaving," Vanessa announced.

"Okay, bye!" said Tyler. Clint, still holding Callie, shot him a look. "I mean, I'll walk you out," Tyler amended, climbing to his feet.

"So," said Clint. "Back to bed and I'll bring you breakfast?"

Before Callie could answer, her cell phone beeped. "Hang on," she said, running into Clint's bedroom. She flipped it open.

1 New Text Message
From Alexis Thorndike

Callie, dear, there's a bit of a mess in the *FM* offices this morning—would you mind terribly if I asked you to swing by and clean it up? Thanks so much in advance; you're the best!
xx Lex

Callie breathed an angry sigh. All she wanted to do was climb back into bed with Clint, but with her final exam for the Nineteenth-Century Novel tomorrow at noon, she should have been at the library hours ago—plus, there was no telling how long a "bit of a mess" might take to clean up.

"I'm so sorry," she said, emerging from Clint's room with her dress and her cell phone in tow, "but do you mind if I take my breakfast to go? I have to get to . . . the library."

"Not at all," Clint said. "And hey, if you give me a minute, I'll grab my bags and come with you!"

"No! Er—I mean, maybe that's not the best idea. I should really run home and change, and I just remembered I have to stop by the *Crimson* and since my first exam's tomorrow, I need to concentrate completely on studying because, let's face it, when you're around, I tend to get a little . . . distracted," she said, leaning in to kiss him lightly on the lips.

"Mmm . . . point taken," he said, kissing her back. "So, when's the next time I can see you?"

"Tomorrow after five?"

"It's a date."

NINE

Game Theory

Modeling Game Theory
w/ Real-Life Examples—Notes, C. Andrews

The Prisoner's Dilemma:

	Player G Admits Feelings	Player G Stays Silent
Player C Admits Feelings	Each lives happily ever after	Player C: loses face Player G: gloats
Player C Stays Silent	Player C: gloats Player G: loses face	Each dies alone

"It's. Just. No. Use!" Callie cried, throwing her pen across the room. "If I don't understand it now, there's no way I'm going to get it in time for the test on Wednesday!"

Matt sighed and stood to retrieve her pen. It had landed over by the potted plant in the corner of his common room in suite C 23, where they were sitting on the floor and studying. Or trying, anyhow. Every available surface was covered with economics-related material: textbooks, old problem sets, papers, and the diagrams Matt had been drawing all morning in his attempt to tutor Callie prior to the exam, their last of the semester.

"Your problem here is not a question of intelligence," Matt said, handing her the pen. "It's patience. I get the feeling that in high school everything came so easily to you that it's made you lazy—"

"Hey!" she cried, whacking him on the arm.

"Well, it's true! If you can't grasp a concept within five minutes of reading about it, you get angry—"

"I don't get *angry*—"

"Yes, you do. You get angry and then you throw things."

"I don't thr—Oh." She looked at her pen. Setting it gently on the table, she ran her hands through her hair in despair. "I'm. Going. To. Faaaaaaiiiiiil," she wailed.

"With that attitude, yes you are."

"Matt, I love you, but sometimes you sound like a *Sesame Street* special."

Ignoring her, he pulled the textbook toward them and spread it across the table. "Okay, you've got a solid foundation in theory of the consumer—"

"Yes, thanks to living with Vanessa I do—"

"And you understand monopoly and monopsony?"

"Monopoly: a child's board game that is fun when you're five."

"Callie—"

"Monopoly: a circumstance when one seller faces many buyers." Example: what Alexis Thorndike has on the Harvard social scene.

"And monopsony?"

"Monopsony, opposite of monopoly: when one buyer faces many sellers." Example: Gregory on Friday night at Wellesley.

"Good," said Matt, flipping a few pages ahead. "Now explain the fundamental principles of game theory."

Callie chewed on her lower lip. "Game theory: a convoluted, nonsensical concept that our professors invented out of thin air for the specific purposes of tormenting me."

"I think we should take five," Matt said.

"I'm sorry," Callie started. "I'll be better, I swear!" She pulled the textbook toward her. "Look, see, I'm concen—"

The front door swung open, and Gregory strolled into the room, squash racket and gym bag tossed over his shoulder. His hair was sticky with sweat and peppered with little flecks of snow.

"—trating . . ." Callie absentmindedly bit the end of her pen.

"'Sup?" said Gregory, nodding at the pair of them.

"'Sup?" Who said "'sup" anymore? Could you possibly be any more annoying!

"Do you mind?" Callie said, angrily flipping the page. "We're trying to study here."

Gregory smirked and headed for his room.

"Some people!" Callie muttered. "Anyway . . . what? Why are you looking at me like that?"

Matt held up his hands. "Nothing, no reason. So—game theory. Essentially game theory attempts to mathematically model behavior in strategic situations— Callie? Callie! Are you listening to me?"

She wasn't. Instead she was staring at Gregory, who had emerged from his bedroom wearing only a towel wrapped low around his waist.

"And what exactly do you think you're doing?" she called as he sauntered across the room.

"Taking a shower," Gregory answered slowly, "which I intend to do in my bathroom, off of my common room, where I live. If that's all right with you, of course."

"Yeah. Yeah, whatever," she muttered, staring at the coffee table. He must have come straight from squash practice, because his muscles were still taut, his body glistening slightly with sweat.

Callie breathed deeply and let it out through pursed lips. "Game theory: where you use strategy to solve mathematical situations?"

"Almost," said Matt. "Other way around."

"Dammit!"

"Language!" Dana's voice called from Adam's bedroom, followed shortly by Dana's head, which poked out around the corner.

"Dana," said Matt. "I didn't realize you were here."

She gave him a funny look. "Well, why shouldn't I be? It's *my* room after all."

Callie stared at her. Dana seemed to have just woken from a lengthy slumber—probably her first time really sleeping in a week, if not more—and now occupied that strange mental state between dreaming and waking. "This is Matt's room," Callie said.

"Is it?" Dana asked with a yawn. She surveyed the room with confusion. "I remember being in Cabot, and I remember finishing my exams, and then I went to the Coop to buy books for next semester so I could get an early start, but after that"—she yawned again—"it's all a blur."

"You're done with exams?" Callie asked, hoping the envy wasn't too obvious in her voice. "That's great!"

"You should celebrate!" Matt said.

"Celebrate?" Dana muttered. "I think I will. Good night!" she said, shutting the door.

"Sleep does sound fun, doesn't it?" asked Callie.

"Yeah, I miss it," Matt said nostalgically. "So much that we take for granted . . ." Rousing himself, he tapped his fingers on the textbook. "I think you should reread these first couple of pages on the fundamental principles of game theory just to jog your memory."

"Okay," Callie said with a sigh. "What'll you do in the meantime?"

"Edit these," he said, reaching into his book bag and pulling out a stack of article drafts he had written for *Crimson* COMP.

"Ugh, COMP—don't remind me," she groaned. "Is your final portfolio due the day after the ec exam, too?"

"Yep." He nodded.

"I can't even begin to think about that right now," she muttered. "Game theory, okay . . . 'Game theory was initially developed to understand economic behaviors, particularly those of firms, markets, and consumers—'"

"Can you read *silently*?" Matt asked, scribbling on his paper with red pen.

"*Yes,*" she said. Fine, fine. Be nice, she told herself. Patience! You have only two friends right now—maybe two and a half—and Matt is one of them.

The bathroom door popped open, and Gregory walked out, still wearing only a towel. Little droplets of water trickled down his abs, down to the ridges right above his hip bones—

Firms, markets, and consumers! Firms, markets and consumers. OH MY! Firms, markets, and whhaaaaat—

Gregory's bedroom door shut behind him.

Matt shook his head irritably. "Show-off," he muttered.

"Wha . . ." said Callie, still staring at the door to Gregory's room.

"Oooh, Gregory, isn't he so dreamy?" Matt cooed in a high falsetto.

"Stop! Shut up!" Callie cried, throwing her head back against the lower couch cushions from where she sat on the floor and placing the textbook over her eyes.

Matt chuckled, making a note in the margin of his piece.

Callie stayed hidden under her textbook for a full minute before uncovering her eyes and once again starting to read: "firms, markets, and consumers, and is now used to study a wide range of economic phenomenon including—"

"So, when's the test?" Gregory asked, emerging from his bedroom—fully clothed, *finally*—and rubbing his wet hair with a towel.

GET OUT! Callie wanted to yell—but she didn't; it was, after all, his room.

"Wednesday," said Matt.

"You ready?" Gregory asked, plopping on the couch quite close to where Callie had just been resting her head. Leaning forward, he peered at the textbook over her shoulder.

"No," said Callie through clenched teeth. "And it's a little hard to focus with all these interrupt—"

Buzz buzz buzz. Matt's phone vibrated on the coffee table. "Ah, crap," he said, reaching for it. Reading the text message, his eyes lit up. "Oh no," he whispered, the fear tinged with an odd note that sounded rather like excitement. "It's my COMP director. I didn't even know she had my phone number."

"Grace Lee?" Callie asked absentmindedly, flipping the page even though she hadn't processed a single word. Gregory's left leg was very close to her right arm. She wanted to smack it away.

"You know her?" Matt asked. "Isn't she just . . . terrifying?" He said "terrifying" in the same tone someone else might use with "wonderful."

"Yes," said Callie. "Very frightening for someone who stands no higher than four foot eleven."

"I should go change!" Matt cried suddenly, leaping off the floor.

"Change? What—why? Where are you going?" Callie demanded, lowering her textbook in alarm.

"To the *Crimson*! I have to leave right now!" Matt yelled over his shoulder, racing toward his room. "She said"—he poked his head out from around the door—"that she *needs* me."

Gregory snorted.

"But . . . what . . ." Callie gaped. "Who's going to help me study?"

"I can help you," Gregory commented from over her shoulder.

"Yes, Greg can help you!" Matt repeated, rushing from his bedroom to the bathroom. Callie watched him grab a comb and attempt to flatten his hair.

"Does this shirt make me look too skinny?" he asked them, returning to the common room.

Callie just stared.

"I knew it!" he wailed, running back to his room. "Knew it, knew it, knew it. Should have done laundry last week before all my quarters disappeared." Callie heard him muttering over the sounds of drawers opening and closing.

"So," said Gregory, "what're you working on? Game theory?" he added, reading over her shoulder.

Turning, she looked up at him. You're not *seriously* going to pretend to be helpful, are you? "I've—uh—thanks, but I've got it under contr—"

She stopped talking as he slid down next to her on the floor, gently taking the textbook from her hands and spreading it open between them on the coffee table.

"It's not as complicated as it initially sounds," he said, picking up her pen and pulling a blank sheet of paper in front of him. "At the end of the day it's really just a matter of applied mathematics— and you're good at math, right?"

"Uh . . . sure." Right. At least I used to be, once upon a time.

"I think it will help if you stop thinking of a game as an abstract theoretical concept and start thinking about it like a math problem. A game is just a well-defined mathematical object with three components: a set of players, a set of strategies available to those players, and a specified set of payoffs for each combination of strategies." As he spoke, he wrote everything down under headings: 1) *Players;* 2) *Strategies;* 3) *Payoffs.* "Does that make sense?"

"Yes." Callie nodded. Actually, it sort of did. "And there are different types of games, right? Like cooperative versus noncooperative?"

"Correct," said Gregory, rewarding her with a smile. "Here, write them in," he added, handing her the pen so she could scribble the various subcategories under the heading *Games*.

"There's also symmetric and asymmetric, zero-sum and non-zero-sum, simultaneous and sequential . . ." Matt walked out of their bedroom. Picking up his book bag, Matt shoved his COMP pieces inside and then slung it over his shoulder.

"Does this shirt look okay?" he blurted, stopping in front of the door. It was a *little* wrinkled, but given that Matt seemed a *lot* frazzled, Callie smiled and said, "Yep! You look great."

"I'm really sorry to leave you like this," Matt apologized. "But at least you're in good hands?"

Callie glanced at the notes Gregory had made so far and decided that, for once, she agreed. "It's totally fine—go!"

"Okay," said Gregory when he had left, all business, "now that we've identified the 'math problem,' can you explain the idea of a solution concept?"

"You mean the equilibria?" asked Callie.

"Without looking at the textbook," Gregory said, covering it with his hand. "Let's start with the Nash equilibrium."

Callie closed her eyes.

"Write it down if that'll help," he said, handing her the pen.

Opening her eyes, she scribbled a few things on the sheet of paper. She looked at him.

"Okay, I see you've memorized the equations," he said with a small smile. "But what does it *mean*?"

"Well, strategy is an assumed constant, and each player is going to adopt a strategy to maximize utility, so . . . the game can be said to constitute a Nash equilibrium if, when all strategies are known, no individual player has an incentive to change his or hers?"

"And is the strategy adopted necessarily the *most* beneficial for each individual player?"

"No, but that's because when analyzing decisions made by multiple 'players' you want to take into account the decisions of everyone involved. Player A's decisions influence Player B's and vice versa. What's best for the group may not be what's individually best for the players. So Player A might initially be tending toward one choice, but she may change her mind once Player B makes his or her strategy known."

"Good," said Gregory. "Now give me a real-world example."

"Can I draw?"

"Yes, you can draw," he said, suppressing a smile.

An hour and a half later they had reviewed the most common types of games and their solution concepts.

"I still don't really understand *why* anyone would want to use game theory in economics. I mean, besides the fact that it's boring, a lot of the time it just doesn't work!" said Callie.

Gregory laughed. "You're not the first person to wonder why or if game theory is actually useful," he said. "Some economists assert that it can be used to describe or predict how populations will behave—but, like you say, there are counterarguments—while others think that equilibria prescribe how we ought to behave. But that falls apart at times, too, as in the case of the Prisoner's Dilemma, when . . . ?"

"'Sometimes two people don't cooperate even if it's in their best interests to do so,'" Callie recited. "I remember that one because it's my favorite," she said, setting her pen down and stretching.

Gregory smirked. "Glad we cleared that up. I'm sure there's going to be a test question on 'what is your personal favorite fundamental problem with game theory and why?'"

She wasn't sure if he was teasing or ridiculing—or both—but she smiled anyway. "It's one of the only strategies or solutions or whatever that takes actual human motives into account. People don't just 'play games' to 'maximize utility'—there are other factors involved. Plus, it's so poetic: two prisoners alone in their interrogation rooms. If neither talks, both go free, but the threat of the other's betrayal inevitably drives both of them to crack—every—single—time."

"Maybe you *should* major in English," Gregory said.

Her head snapped up in his direction, but she quickly saw he didn't mean it unkindly. "Maybe I will!"

"Well, I'm sure you'll be good at whatever you decide to do." He hesitated for a moment, staring at the papers in front of him. "Except drawing."

"Or economics," she added ruefully. "How come you're so good at this stuff, anyway?"

"My dad worked on Wall Street for a long time and now he has his own hedge fund, so I kind of just grew up knowing it." Gregory shrugged. "You're not terrible. You'll pass the test," he said, stating it like it was a fact. "You *are* good with the numbers; it's the real-world applications that seem to trip you up."

"So what am I? Some autistic mathematician who's good in theory but bad in practice and doomed to be poor forever?"

"You forgot to include the term 'reasonably attractive' in between 'autistic' and 'mathematician.' But otherwise, yes, that sounds fairly accurate."

Blushing, she giggled. "Oh . . . why is it so hard to stay mad at you?"

"Maybe because I just spent the last two hours of my life saving yours . . . though it could be because you saw me in a towel?"

"Hey!" she cried, picking up the nearest stack of papers and hurling it at him.

"Hey yourself!" he retorted, reaching in to tickle her sides. Laughing uncontrollably, she grabbed a pillow off the couch and started whacking him on the head. He let her get away with it twice before he grabbed the pillow in one hand and her wrists in the other, slowly lowering them back to her sides. Her resistance and her laughter faded abruptly as he looked at her, his hand steady on her wrists, their faces only a few inches apart—

"*What* is going on out here? Why are you being so *loud*?" a voice grumbled from the doorway to Adam's room. Gregory dropped Callie's hands immediately.

"Dana—" Callie gasped, reaching to gather her papers off the floor. "We were just studying."

"Studying? Harrrumff," Dana snorted. "Gregory, your phone," she added as it started to ring.

"I should take this," he said, checking the caller ID. "Hey!" He stood and walked over to the window. "How are you?"

Callie ran her fingers through her hair and tried to smile at Dana. But even with all the notes, textbooks, and pens, Dana did not seem convinced.

"Good, just studying for exams . . . Lexi? Yeah, she's great." Gregory said to whoever was on the other line.

Callie's fingers froze. She cocked her head, straining to hear every word without making it obvious that she was listening.

"Limericks, and then I took her to lunch just the other day. . . . Yes, she said to send you her love as well."

Quickly Callie began to gather her papers and shove them

between the pages of her textbook. Gregory looked over. "You leaving?" he mouthed, covering the receiver with one hand.

She nodded.

He looked like he might be about to say something else, but the person on the other line must have still been talking because he said, "What? Yes, I'm listening." He watched Callie gather her things. "Actually, now's not the best time. But I'll see you over the break?"

Callie shook her head, motioning that he should continue his conversation.

"Actually, I was already planning to drop Lex in Connecticut when I drive down next week so we can get together then," he said. "Perfect. I'll tell her you said so."

Callie had reached the door. Without looking back at him, she pulled it shut behind her.

TEN

Final Exam
FRIENDSHIP 10A

http://www.harvardfml.com

For all those beautiful Harvard moments where you just want to throw your hands up and say, FML.

> Showed up to take my Life Sciences 1a final on Thursday. Not only was the final on Tuesday, but I've spent the entire semester attending lectures for Life Sciences 1b without realizing. FML.

> I hate my roommate, and I hate his pet fish. It smells. Was it so wrong to put rat poison in the fish food? And is it my fault that the freakazoid eats his fish food? Sitting in the UHS toxicology center . . . FML.

> I don't even go to Harvard and I'm still reading this website. FML.

> Been here three years now and have yet to receive a single party invite. But I have gotten five invitations for jury duty. WTF? FML.

> I'm one C- away from getting kicked out of Harvard . . . again. Second time's so NOT a charm. FML.

" Told my dad I expect straight As this semester, then found out they mail freshman report cards home after break. It wasn't a *total* lie: doesn't my A in Tribal Basket Weaving count for anything, Dad? FML.

" My boyfriend's parents hate me. So much so that his mom has posted profiles for him on eHarmony, match.com and JDate. He's not even Jewish. FML.

" I thought I had proved the Riemann hypothesis. I e-mailed my Math 55 professor and even the Clay Institute to announce that I'd soon be collecting my million dollars in prize money. Turns out I was wrong. I should really stop smoking pot while I do my math homework. FML.

" I'm having a hard time breaking up with my girlfriend. Just filed a transfer app to Stanford. FML.

" I have only 203 Facebook friends, but my two real-life friends say that it's your real-life friends who matter. Too bad both of my real-life friends are imaginary. FML.

" I gained so much weight this year that my parents told me they no longer consider me an Asian. FML.

" I slept through my final exam, and I slept through my doctor's appointment in which I intended to secure a note about my "life-threatening illness" that was "responsible." FML.

"Are you ready?" Matt asked. He and Callie were in Annenberg waiting to bus their breakfast trays.

"Uh-huh, yep, totally, ready-set-go," Callie rattled off, her foot tapping up and down. Maybe that fifth cup of coffee had been a bad idea after all. Then again, if she hadn't stayed up all night studying in Lamont, her answer might have been more along the lines of: *Non-uh, maybe a little bit but really no-not-at-all.* But she *had* stayed up and she *was* ready. Sort of. And if she wasn't, at least—

"It'll all be over soon," Matt said, reading her mind. "Just three hours and fifteen minutes of economics and pain and then . . . we're free."

"COMP," Callie reminded him, shoving her tray full of only partially eaten food onto the conveyer belt.

"Shhh," said Matt, throwing an arm around her shoulders and walking her toward the dining hall's exit. "Don't think about that now."

They left Annenberg and headed down the cement walkway toward the Science Center, where, in lecture hall C at 9:15— exactly fifteen minutes from now—their Economics 10a exam was slated to begin.

"I feel sick," Callie muttered as they stepped through the double glass doors of the building.

"Bathrooms are downstairs if you need to puke," Matt replied, looking a little nauseous himself.

Perversely Callie wondered if Vanessa was already down there undoing the damage—real or imaginary—done by all the stress eating she'd been doing lately, if the empty wrappers littering the floor of the common room were any indication. No, thought Callie, suddenly remembering that Vanessa had been absent at breakfast. Maybe she had the right idea in skipping it, Callie mused, her stomach rolling over when they entered lecture hall C. The walls were a bright, almost mockingly cheerful green. The room itself was a huge amphitheater with seating for at least five hundred rising high above the small patch of floor in front of the blackboard. A proctor stood down there now: she was old and wrinkled, a dragon lady guarding the exams.

Following Matt's example, Callie took a seat in the back, clasping and unclasping her hands to keep from tapping them on her desk chair. "We're too early," she said, glaring at Matt for no good reason.

"Would you rather be too late?" he shot back.

"QUIET PLEASE!" the proctor croaked. Slowly she stood up and walked over to the blackboard. The chalk scratched as she dragged it to form the words NO TALKING IN THE EXAM ROOM.

Callie's foot bounced up and down as the room filled with students. She recognized many of the other first-years and even waved to a few, but Vanessa—not that she had any reason to be checking—had yet to arrive.

"Did you see Vanessa on your way out this morning?" Callie asked Matt, leaning in to whisper.

"No," he said. "Didn't you?"

"No." Callie shook her head. "Library all night, remember?"

"Right," said Matt, looking around. "Well, there are still a couple of minutes left. . . ."

"Right," Callie agreed. "Nothing to worry about." But in the meantime her foot had begun to tap just a little bit faster.

"If students could please settle down in their seats," said the proctor, speaking into a microphone, "I can start reading the rules."

Callie turned around anxiously in her desk chair.

"Rule Number One: no talking."

Callie looked up at the clock.

"Rule Number Two: there must be at least one empty seat between you and the person next to you."

Leaning forward, Callie scanned the room, searching for that telltale flash of strawberry blond.

"Rule Number Three: when I say 'pencils down,' you stop writing."

Vanessa was nowhere to be seen. Callie pulled out her phone and drafted a text: SOS—WHERE ARE YOU? EXAM STARTS IN THREE MINUTES!

"Rules Number Four, Five, and Six: No gum. No cell phones. No bathroom breaks except one at a time and with my permission."

"What should I do?" Callie hissed at Matt. A teaching fellow who was patrolling the aisles coughed pointedly, indicating that Callie should put away her phone. The screen was still dishearteningly blank.

"About what?" Matt asked, digging in his book bag for an extra pen.

"About Vanessa!"

"She really isn't here yet?" He was finally starting to look concerned.

"Rule Number Seven: if you leave without a pass once the exam has started, you will not be readmitted to the room."

Shit, thought Callie. Shit, shit, shit. She didn't know where Vanessa was, but she certainly wasn't here.

"Rule Number Eight: no calculators."

"I have to go," Callie said, standing without stopping to think.

"What?" cried Matt. "Wait!"

But she had already jumped over his feet. "I'll be right back," she called over her shoulder, apologizing as she nearly tripped over two other students in her race for the aisle. "Explain what happened if I don't make it—"

And then she was off, bursting out of lecture hall C, through the double glass doors, and into the cold, sprinting for all she was worth.

She traversed the Yard in what had to be a record ninety seconds, gasping as she leaped up the stairs in Wigglesworth entryway C three at a time. Exploding into their common room she screamed, "VANESSA!" Then, racing toward the door decorated with the giant Marilyn Monroe poster, she flung it open.

Vanessa was in bed and fast asleep: her signature Princess eye mask blocking the light, a pair of hot pink earplugs stopping any sounds. "Vanessa!" Callie cried, shaking her. "Wake up!"

"Wha . . ." Vanessa groaned, swatting Callie and rolling over.

"VANESSA, WAKE UP!" Callie screamed, pulling an ear-plug out of her ear.

Vanessa sat up straight and yanked off the eye mask. "Callie, *what* the *fu*—"

Registering the expression on Callie's face, she stopped talking.

"Oh my god!" she cried, her eyes going wide. Her lower lip trembled. "What time—"

"Late. It's about to start. Here," said Callie, grabbing the first pair of stretchy pants her fingers touched in Vanessa's dresser drawer and tossing them to her.

"How—is there—can we still make it?" Vanessa stammered.

"Yes. Now stop talking and get dressed," said Callie, pulling out socks and a sweater and shoving them into Vanessa's hands. "Pens?" she asked while Vanessa yanked the sweater on—over her silky negligee—and pulled the pants up under it.

"My desk—second drawer," Vanessa cried. "Shit! My iPhone. It didn't go off—"

"Let's go," Callie cut her off, sticking the pens in her pocket.

Vanessa stood frozen, staring at the bottom of her closet. "I . . . what shoes . . .?"

Callie turned to her in disbelief when, looking down, she realized that every pair of shoes in Vanessa's closet had at least a two-inch heel. "Here," said Callie, kicking off her dirty Converses. Barefoot, she ran into her bedroom and jammed her feet into her running shoes, trying to ignore the clock on her nightstand, which read 9:17.

"Thanks," Vanessa whispered, still moving slowly as if in a trance.

"No time—come on," Callie said, grabbing her hand and pulling her out the door.

Red-faced and panting, they arrived outside the Science Center. Callie ushered Vanessa inside. Jogging up the ramp, they reached the entrance to lecture hall C.

Both doors were sealed shut, and a TF sat on a folding chair in front of them, blocking any entry.

"Sorry we're late," Callie gasped between breaths. Vanessa, her face tomato red, had yet to regain her powers of speech.

"I'm sorry, too," he said, lowering his magazine. "But you know the rules: I can't let you in."

"What!" Callie shrieked. "We're like three minutes late! They probably haven't even started passing out the exam yet!"

"Rules are rules." He shrugged. "And you're four minutes late," he added after checking his watch.

"Please," Vanessa managed to sputter, tears streaming from her eyes. "S'all—my—fault."

"I really am sorry, but we can't make any exceptions—even for freshmen," he said, since their age was clearly obvious. "The university does not accept any excuses for missing an exam unless you are gravely ill and have a doctor's note from UHS. You'll have to appeal to the administrative board next semester. Hopefully, they'll let you make it up sometime over the summer. Otherwise . . . well, you won't be the first to fail Ec 10, and you won't be the last either."

"That's—completely—ridiculous!" Vanessa choked out. "We're here now. Let. Us. In!"

He shook his head, turning, infuriatingly, back to his magazine.

"Do you"—Vanessa began as Callie placed a restraining hand on her arm—"have *any* idea"—Callie tugged Vanessa's arm—"who my father—"

"We're going now!" Callie interrupted. "Straight to the registrar's office. We'll see what they have to say about this."

"Good idea," muttered the TF, now thoroughly engrossed in his magazine.

Vanessa's feet stayed planted on the ground. "Callie—what—no! What are y—"

"Shhh," hissed Callie, dragging Vanessa toward the exit. "We are *going* to the *Registrar's Office*," she called loudly, aiming the words over her shoulder.

"This is insane!" Vanessa exclaimed as soon as they were outside. "What a dick! He can't—we can't just—you know the registrar won't do anything—"

"I know," said Callie, her eyes bright. "That's why we're not really going to the registrar."

"We're not?"

"No," said Callie, starting to circle back around the Science Center. "Come on," she added, motioning that Vanessa should follow. Soon they stood facing the back entrance. Callie pushed open the door, and they slipped inside.

Vanessa hesitated. "Where are we—"

Callie clapped a hand over her mouth and placed an index finger over her own lips. Quietly they walked down the hall and turned left into an empty corridor. Callie stopped walking. "Aha," she said.

Vanessa's eyes were wide. "You're not seriously thinking about—"

"Uh-huh." Callie nodded absentmindedly, flicking open the little glass door nestled at shoulder height in the wall.

"Callie, I don't think this is a good idea—"

But before Vanessa could finish her sentence—and she could change her mind—Callie *yanked* the small red lever as hard as she could.

BREEEP, BREEEP, BREEEP, the fire alarm shrieked. *BREEEP, BREEEP, BREEEP.* Lights started flashing in the halls.

"RUN!" Callie yelled, grabbing Vanessa's hand and dashing down the hall. "Other way!" she cried as Vanessa started to turn left. They sprinted down the hall and burst out through the back door. "Stop!" Callie hissed in a strangled whisper, flattening herself against the side wall. "Okay, come on," she said after a beat, ducking and creeping forward under the cover of some bushes that lined the wall. When they were almost to the front of the building, Callie held up her hand, motioning that they should stop. From where they were, they could see the courtyard in front of the Science Center starting to fill with students. Frantic TFs were issuing instructions, crying in vain that the students should remain silent and refrain from discussing the test.

A proctor from a different exam had gotten hold of a megaphone. "Please stand still and do not speak," he boomed. "We have reason to believe that this was a false alarm, but they are checking the building now to be sure. Barring any fire, the exams will resume momentarily."

Almost as soon as he stopped speaking, the alarm ceased.

"Should we go—" Vanessa started, pointing toward the crowd.

"No." Callie shook her head. "Back this way," she said. "Now," she added, seeing Vanessa's hesitant expression. Reentering through the back door, they headed for the stairs. Callie glanced over her shoulder—there were a few people traversing the halls, but nobody paid them any attention—and then she and Vanessa took the stairs two at a time. At the bottom Callie paused. "This way," she said, deciding. Vanessa, too shell-shocked for words, numbly followed. They weaved through another long narrow hallway until Callie found what she was looking for: a door, the same bright green color as the walls of lecture hall C. Ignoring the sign that said FACULTY ENTRANCE ONLY, Callie pushed it open and peered inside.

The empty lecture hall—but for how much longer, she couldn't say. There on the table in front of the blackboard were the sign-in slips, extra blue books, and a few leftover exams. The rest, Callie noted looking at the desks, had already been passed out. "You stay here and watch the hall," she said. Vanessa nodded: she looked horrified, but she propped the door open nevertheless. Callie darted inside.

Whipping out one of the pens she had taken from Vanessa's desk, she filled in two blank sign-in slips—one for each of them—and then slid the written records that they had, in fact, arrived for the exam on time, into the middle of the pile. Then she tucked two tests and two blue books under her arm. Barely breathing, she started walking toward Vanessa.

"Someone's coming," Vanessa hissed. "I can hear footsteps—"

F@%#^$@. Callie turned around and looked up. The doors at the top of the stairs were swinging open. We are so dead, she thought. Her eyes met Vanessa's.

"Come on," Vanessa said suddenly, grabbing Callie by the wrist and slamming the Faculty Only door shut behind her. Several students were trickling through the front entrance, but nobody seemed to have noticed the two girls standing at the bottom of the room. Without hesitating, Vanessa pulled Callie up the far left-hand aisle and pushed her into one of two empty desk chairs in a row somewhere in the middle of the auditorium.

"*Don't* turn around," Vanessa spat. Callie sat completely still, listening to the chatter of other students who had begun making their way to their seats. She slipped an exam and a blue book over to Vanessa, who smoothed it out across her desk like this was exactly where she had left it before the fire alarm sounded. Together they watched the old dragon lady of a proctor hobble through the Faculty Entrance Only door and take her seat in front of the table without pausing to check if any of the papers had been disturbed.

Callie's pulse thundered in her ears, nearly masking the clamor of the hundreds of students who had now returned to claim their desks. The dragon lady adjusted her microphone. "We will resume the exam once everyone has returned to their seats. Quickly and quietly please."

"LADIES!" a severe-sounding voice suddenly barked. The color drained from Callie's face. Turning, she found herself staring at a female teaching fellow. Vanessa released an almost inaudible whimper. Busted.

"There needs to be at least one empty seat between the two of you," the TF said. Callie stared. You mean, we're not—

"You, just move over one to your left," she instructed, pointing at Callie. Quickly Callie obliged her. Satisfied, the TF continued to make her way down the aisle.

"*Ohmygod,*" Vanessa breathed through her lips. "I can't believe you just did that," she muttered, keeping her eyes facing forward.

"Yeah, well, I busted my ass studying for this test," Callie whispered. "Plus, there's no way I'm going to remember any of it by next week."

"No, I mean what you did for m—"

"Quiet please, ladies," the TF admonished, frowning at them as she made her way back up the aisle.

"Well, hopefully that's everyone," said the dragon lady proctor as she surveyed the room, half to her microphone, half to herself. She cleared her throat. "Due to the interruption, we are adding an extra fifteen minutes to the clock."

"Good luck," Vanessa whispered. "And thank you."

"Pencils up—*begin!*"

ELEVEN

WHEN CLINT MET CALLIE

For all the Harvard couples out there:

Perhaps it was in anticipation of the early nineties romantic comedy revival happening at the Brattle Theatre this month that I asked you to write in with your picks for the Top 5 Romantic Clichés seen in movies, books, or life from the past few decades. Why I decided to balance that list with another Top Fiver—The Top 5 Breakup Clichés—is beyond me; maybe it's that seminar I'm taking on cliché or maybe I'm just down on love? Regardless, here they are:

The Top 5 (Worst) Romantic Clichés

1. **The driven career girl grows a heart:** *So*, so tired. You all know the story about the girl who chooses work over love every time—only to meet the perfect guy, who thaws her heart and teaches her a life lesson about love and balance, etc. Oh, please. For once, I'd like to see the girl stick to her guns and pick career, because really, you *can't* have it all.

2. **Undercover journalist on an assignment:** Insert obligatory scenes where her friends and new boyfriend (whom she fell for on said assignment) are deeply upset about the article she has written *here, here,* and *here.* Also, obligatory makeup scene *here.*

3. **I am hopelessly in love with my best friend but do not realize/am too afraid to say something until the stakes are dire:** I'm actually okay with this particular trope if and *only if* the idiot who fell in love with their best friend in the first place makes an even bigger idiot out of themselves throughout the course of the story and in the end, instead of breaking up their best friend's wedding/engagement (ref: "until the stakes are dire"), learns a lesson: that only an idiot falls in love with their best friend in the first place.

4. **The reform of the irresistible bad boy:** Unless your name is James Dean, please don't park your motorcycle on my front lawn and don't smoke your smelly cigarette in my face. Have you ever just read a story and wanted to slap the heroine for falling for the wrong guy? And then he reforms and you want to slap him, too, and get your money back?

5. **Fish out of water/Let's all root for the quirky girl:** There's a difference between good quirky (think: Audrey Hepburn circa *Breakfast at Tiffany's*) and bad quirky (think: any "neurotic" blond, Meg Ryan-esque character who frequently bumps into things—but oh, isn't it so adorable?—in any Nora Ephron movie). I simply fail to see the appeal in a story about a girl who doesn't fit in because she's *different* until somebody falls for those *differences* and suddenly validates her quirky, fringe existence, letting everyone out there know that they too can knock things over and ramble in a manner only appropriate to a psychiatrist's office but still find social success with a cute little giggle and a hair-flip.

Now let's say you find yourself living one of the above mostly-seen-in-movies clichés: what better way to exit the situation than with one of these:

The Top 5 Breakup Clichés

1. It's not you, it's me . . . but really it is you.

2. I love you, but I'm not in love with you . . . This may as well be my interior monologue when I'm cleaning out my closet and deciding which dresses to keep.

3. I think we're better as friends . . . and I'll call you so we can hang out and enjoy all those things we have in common. . . . Oh, wait . . .

4. You want more than I'm prepared to give . . . you high-maintenance, demanding freak!

5. I'm just not ready for a relationship right now . . . because first I have to wash my hair and stay in to feed my cat. Oh, and I'm busy and important.

Dumper: please spare us (and your significant other) by coming up with something more original than these!

Dumpee: If you hear one of these: a) add *with you* to the appropriate place in that sentence for the truth about why things are ending, or, the old fortune cookie favorite, *in bed* at the end for a laugh; b) slap them. Hard. Then go watch a Nora Ephron movie and cry your eyes out, whether you love Meg Ryan or think she's the most annoying thing since— Well, really it's not her, it's me: I like her, but I'm not *in* like with her—if y'know what I'm sayin'.

Alexis Thorndike, Advice Columnist
Fifteen Minutes Magazine
Harvard University's Authority on Campus Life since 1873

"I'm doooone," Callie called, opening the door to C 24. She had meant it to sound enthusiastic, but it had manifested as more of a groan.

"Weeeeeeeeeeeeeeeeeeeeeeeeeeeeeeeeeee!" Mimi screamed, running over from where she had been sitting on the floor with OK and wrapping Callie in an enormous hug. *"Merci Dieu, maintenant on se saoule!"*

"Whoa," said Callie, catching a whiff of her breath. Apparently sober Mimi was a thing of the pre-finals past, and pre-pre-finals Mimi a thing of the pre-afternoon present. "What're you guys up to?"

"Quarters," OK muttered, attempting, and failing, to flip a coin into a shot glass on their coffee table. "She's killing me."

"Je vais te tuer!" Mimi echoed happily, jabbing at him with an imaginary sword.

"Care to join, Blondie?" asked OK after he had downed the contents of his shot glass. "I've got a whole sock full of these things," he added, holding up a yellow-toed sock filled with coins. Someone—probably Matt's mom—had sewn a little label printed with M ROBINSON along the top. Oops.

"Callie!" someone cried, pushing open the front door. Turning, she saw Matt looking panicked.

"What the hell happened to you?" he asked. "One minute you're running out of the exam and then I didn't see you—and the fire alarm—I mean, did you come back? Did you take the test?"

"I did." She sighed happily. "I looked for you afterward, but I was just so"—she yawned—"exhausted that when I couldn't find you, I came home."

"What about Vanessa?" asked Matt.

"*What* about a fire alarm?" OK added.

"Vanessa overslept. I woke her up and we ran over as fast as we could, but we were late and they weren't going to let us in until—uh—luckily the fire alarm went off for some reason, so we were able to sneak in, you know, in the confusion."

"Luckily . . . the fire alarm went off . . . for *some* reason . . . and you were able to sneak in?" Mimi repeated slowly, her eyes dancing.

"What?" said Callie sharply.

Mimi shrugged. "*Bravo! C'est une bonne décision.* Saving Vanessa, I mean. *Où est-elle maintenant?*"

"She has another exam at two fifteen, so she went back to the library," said Callie, making her way over to the couch. "I feel so bad for her—I seriously don't think I could survive another one."

"You feel bad for her—this is good, no?" Mimi commented, expertly flicking a quarter into a shot glass. OK moaned, picking it up. "Things are good—better?" Mimi ventured.

"They are . . . or I think they will be," said Callie. Then, for the first time quite possibly in three days, she smiled.

"Getting her was really cool of you," Matt said, collapsing next to Callie on the couch. "Man, but wasn't that fire alarm thing so crazy! I wonder how it happened. My guess is maybe a Bunsen burner in one of the— Hey, is that my sock?"

"Er, no?" said OK. His eyes fell on M ROBINSON. "I mean, yes, found it!" he amended, holding it up.

"Relax. I'm too tired to care." Matt moaned, rubbing his face with his hands.

"Here," said Mimi, pouring him a shot.

To Callie's surprise, he accepted it. "Oh, what the hell," he muttered. "I can take a few hours off before final edits." He downed the liquor and made a face, trying not to choke.

"Callie?" asked Mimi.

"Bed," she answered, standing. "Bed, shower, dinner, Clint, edit, edit, edit."

"Quite a to-do list," OK said. "Ha-ha, to *do* get it? Clint? Get it?"

"Oh, do this!" Callie cried, flipping him off. Then she walked into her room and dove headfirst onto her bed.

When she came to several hours later, it was dark outside and difficult to tell whether the clock meant 6:30 A.M. or P.M.. P.M.—*duh*—she realized, lifting up her cell. She wished she hadn't checked, because there was a new text message from Lexi waiting for her.

> CAN YOU PICK UP SOME COFFEE
> FILTERS AND CUPS AND BRING
> THEM TO THE *CRIMSON* NEXT TIME
> YOU STOP BY? I'LL BE HERE LATE
> TONIGHT AND EARLY TOMORROW

MORNING, AND YOU SHOULD
HAVE PLENTY OF TIME TO RUN TO
CVS BEFORE YOUR 2:00 FINAL
PORTFOLIO DEADLINE. SEE YOU
THEN! AND THANKS! XX LEX

Callie groaned. Can't Lexi once—just this once—ask another COMPer to do the b-i-t-c-h work? I'm already pressed for time as it is, she thought, glancing at her laptop and trying not to think about all the pieces that still needed editing. She hadn't the faintest clue at this point whether or not she'd make *FM,* and moreover, she was finding it difficult to muster the strength to *care.* She'd done everything Lexi had asked. (Well, minus staying away from Clint, but she needed to worry about keeping that secret for only the next forty-eight hours—then she'd be home safe for winter break). She'd also done everything she could with the topics she'd been assigned. Nothing left to do but a final read-through, print, and pray. Oh yeah, and buy coffee filters.

But that would all have to wait. Right now she had just enough time to hop in the shower, run to dinner, and then head off to her Super Top Secret Done with Exams Date with Clint. Or as most normal, non-subject-to-blackmail-by-psychotic-ex-girlfriend people probably called it, "going to the movies." The Brattle Theatre was having a Nora Ephron marathon, so Clint was taking her to see her very first screening of the classic *When Harry Met Sally.* Should she stay in and work on her COMP portfolio instead? Maybe. But was Mimi right when she said that some-times you ought to work on maintaining your sanity? Definitely.

❧

Twenty minutes later Callie was emerging from the service area of Annenberg with a tray full of food, scouting for a place to sit. At a table near the back she spotted OK, Matt, and—even though he was facing away, she could still recognize him—Gregory. She hesitated. Eh, whatever, she decided, making her way over.

"Hey, guys," she said, setting down her tray.

"Hey."

"Yo."

"'Sup?"

Matt giggled. Wait. Matt giggled? Why in the heck . . . *Oh.*

"You guys forgot the crucial step between day drinking and night drinking, didn't you?" Callie asked.

"Cuddling?" Matt volunteered.

"Peeing!" cried OK.

"Napping," said Gregory.

"Oh, you read Lexi's article last week then, too?" Callie asked.

"Yup," said Gregory.

Callie frowned, nibbling on the edge of her sandwich.

"So," said OK, "what are you going *to do*—ha, get it?—on your *date* later?"

Callie dropped her sandwich and whacked OK on the arm. "Shhh . . ." she hissed. "That is *supposed* to be a *secret*."

"Then *why* did you broadcast it to all of us earlier this afternoon?" Matt asked, munching on a green bean.

"I didn't— Oh." Damn. So much for top secret.

"I must have missed the announcement," Gregory said, sounding bored. "Who do you have a date with later?"

"Well, I really shouldn't sa—"

"It's with that Perpetual Sweater Vest character," OK offered helpfully. "Though really, Blondie, we don't know *what* you see in him."

"Nuh-uh," said Matt, taking a swig of his drink and shaking his head. Callie peered into the cup, beginning to suspect that they were "pulling a Mimi," i.e. had smuggled alcohol into the dining hall.

"I mean, he's always—wearing—a sweater vest!" said OK. "Yes, we get it. Cute, stylish, appropriate for the major seasons. But all the time? That's a big fashion no-no."

Matt cocked his hand to his mouth and whispered, "Mimi's been reading him her ladies' magazines."

Gregory started laughing loudly. "Perpetual Sweater Vest is Clint?" he roared as if it were the most amusing thing he'd ever heard. "Don't get me wrong, I like the guy, but it's kind of true."

Callie glared at the three of them.

"Plus," Gregory added, "he's too old for you." His face had a similar expression to the one he'd worn right after he'd delivered his limerick. "You should stick with someone closer to your own age." Matt nodded in agreement.

Callie, electing to ignore them, took a big bite of her sandwich and chewed. "Doesn't that go both ways?" she blurted suddenly.

"What d'ya mean?" asked Gregory.

"I mean, what about Lexi: isn't *she* too old for *you*?"

"Well, no, because I'm not dating her," Gregory said slowly, staring at Callie like she had just asked him how to spell *stupid*.

"But—yes you are!" Callie cried. She couldn't believe that even he would sink into such a low level of sketchdom as to deny the relationship outright.

Gregory lifted one incredulous eyebrow. "Now, where'd you go getting a crazy idea like that?"

"Blondie," OK added sternly, "we've been over this before: Gregory does not date!"

Gregory grinned, offering his hand to OK for a high-five. Callie tried to keep herself from rolling her eyes as their palms smacked together.

"Well, I don't care *what* you call it," Callie interrupted their bro-fest: "Dating, hooking up, seeing each other, smushing—together is together no matter how hard you try to deny it for the sake of getting into other girls' pants."

Uh-oh. That had come out a tad too angry.

But Gregory just smiled. "Smushing?" he repeated. Matt giggled again. "I'm not sure what that is, but I'm pretty sure I haven't been doing it with Lexi. She's my cousin's best friend; she's like a sister to me. I've known her since I was two."

"Told you so," said OK, looking triumphantly at Callie.

"Told you so . . . when?" asked Gregory, his eyes narrowing. "You were asking about—what? Whether or not I was dating someone?"

"No," said Callie, facing down OK with an expression she prayed would paralyze his mouth. "I don't care who you date."

"Well, you do care a little," OK teased. "Otherwise you

wouldn't have cornered me after Thanksgiving break and asked me to tell h—"

Finally registering the look on Callie's face, he stopped talking.

"Tell me what?" asked Gregory, his eyes darting back and forth between OK and Callie.

"Nevermind," OK muttered, staring guilty into his soup. "Just drop it."

"I have to go," Callie said, standing abruptly. Without looking back, she headed straight for the line to bus her tray.

"Wait," said Gregory. He had followed her. "Is he talking about . . . what I think he's talking about?"

Callie set her tray on the conveyer belt. "Look," she said turning. "Whatever I might have said right after Thanksgiving break . . . I don't mean it anymore."

"You don't mean it anymore?"

"No."

"Well, then—"

"I have to go. I'm late." And with that she left the dining hall, trying not to dwell on the way his expression had suddenly, mysteriously, lit up or the nagging sensation—which she couldn't seem to shake— that somehow, for some reason, there was something she had missed.

"Ooh," said Callie, her hand entwined with Clint's, their arms swinging as they made their way down Brattle Street, "and what about the part where she wails, 'I'm going to be forty!' and he asks when, and she cries 'Someday!'?"

"Yes," Clint agreed. "That part's good, too."

"And what about all those sweet older couples talking about how they met and fell in lo—" Clint twirled her around and stopped her mouth with his lips. For the moment reminiscing about *When Harry Met Sally* gave way to kissing.

"And how about that restaurant scene!" Callie cried when Clint finally let her up for air. "'I'll have what she's having!'"

Clint laughed, shaking his head with a tolerant smile. This line of conversation had begun when they exited the theater; lasted over two mugs of steaming hot chocolate piled high with luscious whipped cream at Burdick, the famous Harvard Square chocolatier; and was now—apparently—compelling enough to carry them all the way home. "I can't believe that was your first time seeing it," he said.

"I can't either!" she exclaimed. "I loved it. Loved-it," she added, standing on her tippy toes to kiss him again. She knew she should be more careful in public, but it was dark out and she didn't recognize anybody on practically deserted Mt. Auburn Street. Plus, sometimes kissing Clint was just too impossible to resist.

"What other surprises do you have in store for me?" she asked when they had started walking again.

"Actually, there is something that I could use your help with," said Clint. "If you're willing to stop by Adams for a few minutes."

"This isn't a trick to get me to spend the night, is it? Because like I said earlier, I'd love to but I have—"

"Have to go home and edit your final COMP portfolio and then get up at the crack of dawn so you can run errands and turn it in," he recited. "I know. But this won't take more than thirty minutes and it'll be fun—I promise."

"Oh-kaay," said Callie.

A few minutes later Clint was unlatching the gate that led to Adams courtyard: a secluded area full of cement benches tucked away under towering trees, sequestered from the hustle and bustle of the neighboring streets by the various wings of Adams house. Tonight the usually grassy ground was covered in a powdery layer of new-fallen snow, gleaming white as the moonbeams bounced off it. Callie relished the soft crunching feeling her feet made when they sank into the snow, leaving tracks behind as they walked. The courtyard was lit by nothing but two black gas lamps and the moonlight. No one else was around; they were all alone, and it was beautiful.

"Hey—what's that over there?" Callie asked, pointing to a cluster of what looked like . . .

"Snowmen!" Clint exclaimed. "That's what I wanted to show you. Come on," he said, taking her hand. Together they crossed the courtyard. Snowmen—about fifteen of them—in various shapes and sizes had been erected under a giant oak tree.

"Adams House has a competition every year to see who can build the best snowman," Clint explained.

"Wow," said Callie, looking around. Some of the snowmen were just your average top-hat-and-scarf-wearing-with-a-carrot-for-a-nose variety, but others were cleverer or downright creative, decked out in wild accessories: a khaki vest and a fishing pole; a pipe, a pair of horn-rimmed glasses, and a bowtie; a cowboy hat and a bandanna; an apron and a chef's hat; and more. "So cool!" Callie exclaimed. "What do you get if you win?"

"Besides infinite glory?" Clint chuckled. "Gift certificates. This is ours," he continued, pointing to two lumps of snow. "Our blocking groups' snowman, I mean. Tyler and Bryan have been working on him all morning."

"Where's its head?" Callie asked. Given that this was the first year she had even seen snow, let alone a snowman, she wasn't exactly an expert, but all of the other snow people seemed to be constructed of three giant snow balls.

"That is why I want your help!" Clint said. "Frosty needs a head. And a stylist."

"Head first," said Callie, stepping back to assess the situation. "But how do you . . . ?"

"It's easy—I'll show you."

Following his lead, she sat cross-legged in the snow and started helping him pack the powder together. When it was about twice the size of a tennis ball, they stood and started to roll it along the ground.

"I can't believe this actually works!" Callie cried, watching the ball of snow grow bigger and bigger with each roll. She knew she probably sounded like a five-year-old, but she didn't care.

Clint smiled. "I think that's big enough," he said. "Shall we?"

She nodded and they hoisted the head on top of the base.

"Perfect!" said Callie, clapping her hands together. "Now, how do we accessorize?"

"Ah," said Clint. "Wait here." He ducked into the bike entrance of Adams and disappeared, returning moments later carrying a giant plastic bin.

"Where did you get all of this?" Callie asked in amazement,

pulling out a rubber chicken, some flippers, and a turquoise sequin vest.

"Every year my house throws together all the stuff lying around in the Lost and Found, and people drop off old outfits from theme parties or clothes that they were planning to donate to Goodwill. Sometimes Adams Pool Theater contributes worn-out costumes or extra props, too."

Callie pulled out a big electric blue feather boa and threw it around her neck. "Do you think I can keep this?" she asked.

"But what about poor Frosty?" Clint exclaimed. "He's so cold and . . . naked."

"Naked, hmm. I see your point." Callie unwound the boa and wrapped it around Frosty's neck.

"Nice," said Clint. "So, we're going for a sort of, like, diva theme?"

"Yes!" Callie agreed. "I like it!"

Rifling through the bin, they selected:

1. a truly awful yellow wig
2. a shiny rhinestone tiara
3. one set of hot pink lips (somewhere a mute Mrs. Potato was probably weeping silently)
4. three strands of Mardi Gras beads
5. a set of sparkly false eyelashes
6. a light pink double-D bra that Callie refused to touch and made Clint grab instead.

Callie arranged the wig and placed the tiara on top while Clint walked over to the bushes in search of some twigs to use for arms.

By the time she had stuck the false eyelashes and lips into the snow to make a face, he had returned. She selected two of the sticks, and he broke them down to size. Then Callie stuck them in the snow and wrapped the Mardi Gras beads around at the wrist. Picking up a discarded stick, she prodded the humongous bra. "Can you . . . ?"

"Yes." Clint laughed, reaching for the bra and draping it so it hung across the arms and covered the "chest." Stepping back, they surveyed their handiwork.

"Something's not quite right . . ." Callie began.

"He needs some pants," said Clint.

"He?" Callie echoed incredulously.

"She?" Clint stared at their creation. "You're right. Our snow lady is a SheMan, a . . . Shenoman."

"A Tranny Man!" Callie yelled. "Who is definitely, definitely in need of some pants." She rooted around in the bin. "Aha!" she cried, lifting out a yellow sarong printed with hideous orange suns. She tied it around at the waist. "There," she said, sighing happily.

"What'll we name her?" Clint asked, wrapping his hands around Callie's waist and nuzzling her ear.

Callie thought for a moment. "LaRhonda."

"LaRhonda the SnowSheMan," Clint said. He was silent for a minute, holding Callie tight. "We should sign our work!" he suddenly announced. Grabbing a spare twig, he leaned over and wrote in the snow: *Callie & Clint, December 2010.*

He stepped back. Callie stared at the ground. Turning to him, she said: "You're so swee—"

The end of her sentence was lost in a face full of snow.

"How dare you!" she shrieked, wiping the snow from her eyes. Scooping up a fistful, she hurled it at him. Was this it—her first snowball fight?

He dodged, bending to pack more snow in his hands.

Before he could throw it at her, however, she rushed over and tackled him. She screamed and they toppled over, their fall broken by the snow. Landing half on top of him, she clamored to restrain his arms with one hand and gather some snow in the other. Her hand closed around an icy clump, but before she could rub it in his face, he sat up and kissed her.

They were both too covered in wet flakes already to realize that it had started to snow: tiny little dots no bigger than confetti or particles of dust, sprinkling unnoticed over their hair and eyelashes.

"I'm really going to miss you," Clint said, leaning away to look at her.

"It's only ten days!" Callie cried. "Then you'll be back for squash—"

"And you'll be back for *FM*—"

"Maaaybe."

"But still . . . ten days is a long time."

"Will you wait for me?" Callie said melodramatically, kissing his nose. It felt cold underneath her lips.

"I *guess. . . .*"

Callie narrowed her eyes, her hand closing around the loose snow next to her knee. Then, gently, ever so gently, she smashed it in his face.

"Waaaah!" she cried, darting away as he tried to catch her. The snowball he had hurled after her broke across the tree she had dived behind for cover. Sneaking up to the trunk, Clint feigned left and she ran right, ending up back in his arms.

She was at his mercy. Her eyes opened wide, pleading, and his hand went slack. The snow fell back to the ground. Wrapping his arms around her, he twined his fingers through her hair and pulled her to him. It would be a while before they broke away.

Across the street a single light burned brightly in the second-floor offices of the *Harvard Crimson*. The building loomed just high enough that, if one were on the second floor near the western window—which happened to be the window situated directly above the desk reserved for the current *FM* COMP director— that person would have an excellent vantage point from which to spy on whatever might be transpiring in Adams courtyard.

As she watched her ex-boyfriend and her "favorite mentee" wrestle in the snow, the girl who was working alone in the offices whispered words that fell on empty ears, "Callie Andrews: you are so dead."

TWELVE

D-DaY

FM Homepage ~ Advice ~ Topics: Freshman Year ~ Blogspace

Dear Alexis:

What the heck is this J-term thing, anyway? Is break really only ten days long? What do they mean when they say that returning to campus in January is "optional"? Is that Harvardspeak for mandatory? Do we get extra credit for coming back early?? Help!

—Stoughton Resident, Class of 2014

Dear Still Clueless Even After a Whole Semester:

J-term, i.e. January term, is the optional—yes, *optional*—three-week period between the official ten-day winter break (which starts tomorrow) and the beginning of second semester. You have the freedom to choose—yes, choose, like an actual real-live adult—what to do with this time, though for some students, like those who have been COMPing this semester or who play on a sports team, return to campus *is* mandatory. There are also a variety of short seminars in which you can enroll if you haven't completely burned out after your first final exams and are still thirsty to learn (read: "don't have any friends or anything better to do at home"). Will you get extra credit just for showing up? Will anybody even notice or care? I don't know. Is there such a thing as Santa Claus? Happy holidays!

—Alexis

Dear Alexis,

I only want to know one thing and that is: WHEN DO WE GET OUR FINAL GRADES?!?

—Holworthy Resident, Class of 2014

Dear Quintessential Harvard Student:

Correct: there *is* only one thing and one thing alone in this world that matters and as such you *should* allow it to define you, control your mood, and validate your very existence on Earth—your GRADES (?!?). No matter whom you bribe or beg, your grades will be available only after we return from break. You can check them online over the Harvard network and arrange to do the necessary damage control then. Or celebrate. But probably damage control.

Best of luck!

—Alexis

Dear Alexis:

Why do all COMPers have to come back for J-term when we won't even find out if we've made it until we arrive on campus? What about the people who don't get on? What are we supposed to do—sit around and cry for three weeks?

—Strauss Resident, Class of 2014

Dear Mr. or Mrs. Plagued-by-Self-Doubt:

Yes, because we are just that cruel.

Grow a pair,

Alexis

Dear Alexis,

Is there anything that we should be doing over break?

—Weld Resident, Class of 2014

Dear Future Ulcer Victim:

You mean besides curing cancer, alleviating world hunger, and fixing that hole in the ozone layer? Oh, I don't know, maybe eat some ice cream, take a nap, watch a movie, and tell your parents you love them? Or how about—*gasp*—nothing? Relax! You earned it ;)

—Alexis

allie raced up the stairs to the *Harvard Crimson* two at a time, her heart pounding in her chest. It was 1:59. She felt like the living embodiment of Finagle's Law of Dynamic Negatives: Anything that can go wrong will—and at the worst possible moment.

Not one but two printers in Lamont Library had jammed while Callie had hastened to print her final pieces—and that was only after she'd had to open every single file in her folder entitled COMP Drafts because she'd forgotten to separate the finals from the earlier versions and discards. Earlier that morning she'd purchased the wrong coffee filters—cone shaped rather than square—and had been ordered back to CVS by an irritable, under-caffeinated senior. Then, on top of everything else, she'd forgotten her hat, scarf, and gloves, and so her fingers and ears felt like they were about to fall off.

The warm air that rushed over her as she pushed open the doors to the *Crimson* and headed down the hall hardly offered any relief: instead of the chill ebbing away she experienced what she imagined—based on her mother's description—must be similar to the hot flashes normally associated with menopause. Sweat dripped down her back by the time she reached the second floor. Wiping her brow, she opened the door a crack. The clock on the wall read 2:01, but the offices were—mercifully—empty. A wooden box stacked high with manila folders and labeled FINAL COMP PORTFOLIOS rested on the table.

Slipping inside, she pulled off her coat and slid her final portfolio into the middle of the pile. No need to give Lexi any extra excuses like "you were sixty seconds too late" to disqualify her. Then, yawning widely, Callie walked over to Lexi's ergonomic "throne." Glancing over her shoulder to verify that no one was there, she sank onto the plush black material. She twirled around and bounced up and down, yelping out loud when she pulled a lever on the side and the seat shot into the air.

Huh, she thought. From this vantage point she could see over the top of entryway A in Adams House and into the courtyard. In fact, if she leaned in and peered over the computer screen, she could definitely make out the bright yellow color of LaRhonda's wig, the tiara winking in the pale end-of-December sunlight. Yawning again, she smiled. So this was what it felt like to be done: done with finals, done with COMP, and best of all, done with staying away from Clint. Soon she'd be done with secrets, too— how exactly, she wasn't sure, but she had ten whole days to devise a strategy to deal with the one tiny little tape of a problem standing between her and a stress-free—dare she say—normal?—existence.

Leaning back, she closed her eyes. She barely heard the door as it clicked open behind her. But the sweet, tinkling voice that sounded a moment later acted like twelve volts of electricity to the spine.

"Callie, dear," said Lexi, shutting the door. "We need to talk."

"Callie!" Vanessa called, knocking on her bedroom door. "Are you in there?" She waited a moment and then entered, nudging the door open with her hip because her hands were full with an enormous gift basket. The wicker handle was topped with a big bright red bow; the basket itself was stuffed with cookies, mixed nuts, crackers, cheeses, two bottles of wine and a wine glass, gourmet coffees and teas, jellies and jams, a festive holiday mug, bath salts, eau de toilette, and a Princess eye mask identical to the one Vanessa slept in every night.

There was also a card tucked underneath the bow. On the front was a picture of a hairy butt, and on the inside it said, *Thank you for saving mine!* Underneath Vanessa had written:

> Sorry for everything.
> I was wrong about you:
> You are a good friend.
> Here's to a new semester and a new start!
> Love,
> V

Callie's room was, as usual, kind of a mess. There were stacks of papers everywhere, mostly with the heading *FM* COMP piece draft # XX, heavily marked with different colored pens. Vanessa peered at the organizer that lay open on Callie's desk. Under today, December 21st, she had written in all caps and underlined twice: 2 P.M. – FINAL COMP PORTFOLIO DUE. Vanessa checked her watch.

It was 2:10. "Hmm . . ." she mused aloud. Setting the basket on Callie's bed, she pulled out her roommate's desk chair and sat down.

Glancing around the room, she blew a gust of air through pursed lips. Then, her eyes fell across the computer screen. A folder called COMP Drafts had been left open. She read through some of the titles, giggling: "Pop Culture Words for 'Hooking Up' and What They Really Mean," "Dry-Cleaners in Harvard Square: An Ode to Arrow Street," and "Top Ten Beauty Buys That Will Certainly, if Nothing Else, Drain Your Wallet." She clicked the last one open and scanned through the list, nodding approvingly and humming to herself. Minimizing the window, another heading caught her eye, "The Roommate from Hell."

Chewing on the end of her hair, she clicked open the file and started to read. A few sentences in, she started to frown. Midway down the page her face fell. Looking at the sidebar, she reread the folder title, COMP Drafts. Her eyes darted over to where Callie had written 2 P.M. – FINAL COMP PORTFOLIO DUE. Then she pulled the article back up and read it until the end. Two spots of color almost the same shade as the reddish strands in her hair flamed on either cheek. Breathing heavily, she stood and slammed the laptop shut.

She whirled around, reaching for the basket, and then stopped—

"Gregory?" she blurted in surprise. He was standing in Callie's doorway.

"Hey," he said. "Is Callie here?"

"No," said Vanessa through gritted teeth.

"Something wrong?" he asked.

"Nope," she said. Suddenly seizing the basket, she thrust it into his arms. "Here, take this, would you? Holiday present from me to your room," she explained, ripping off the card and shoving it into her pocket.

"Uhh . . . thanks?" he said.

"You're welcome." She paused. "Well, I'd love to stay and chat, but I've got a plane to catch."

"Oh. You're flying back?"

"Yep. You driving?"

"Yes. I have to leave in twenty minutes to pick up my car from the garage."

"Cool. Well, maybe I'll see you at a party sometime over break," said Vanessa, sliding past him.

"Uh, Vanessa?" he called when she had almost reached her room.

"Yes?" she said, turning.

"Can I ask you something?"

"Yes?" she repeated, her cheeks still flush.

"Uh, well. I was wondering . . ." He looked extremely uncomfortable. "Has Callie ever said anything to you about me?" His brow furrowed in disbelief, almost as if he couldn't believe he had just uttered the previous sentence aloud. "I mean, *recently*. Has she said anything about me recently?"

"Mmm . . . yeah!" said Vanessa, her eyes oddly bright, her voice sounding just a tad too cheerful. "As a matter of fact, she has. Just the other day in the bathroom at Clint's she called you an asshole, said that Harvard-Yale was a huge mistake, and that you're a womanizing whore."

"She said all that—just the other day?"

"Maybe that's not exactly a direct quote, but you get the gist," said Vanessa, opening the door to her room. Looking at his face, her expression softened ever so slightly. "I wouldn't take it *too* personally," she said. "That's practically a compliment in comparison to some of the things she has to say about me."

Gregory didn't seem to have heard a word. He appeared confused, his eyebrows knit together. But then his face went slack. "Cool, thanks," he said. "That's really all I needed to know."

"She'll probably be home any minute now—if you want to hear her say it to your face."

"Nope," he said. "Have a good break. And thanks again for the—uh—this?"

"You're welcome again."

"Need to talk about what?" Callie said, jumping out of the chair.

Lexi hadn't bothered to plaster on her usual mask of kindness—today she just looked livid.

Callie had to remind herself to breathe.

"Oh, I think you already know," said Lexi, making her way over to the box of COMP portfolios. "I gave you a very simple set of instructions, which you failed to follow."

"I don't know what you're . . ." Callie started, giving up halfway through. Lexi, who was sifting through the stack of portfolios, clearly wasn't listening.

"You disappointed me, Callie," she said, reading the name on top of each portfolio before setting it aside. "And I had such high hopes for you. . . . Ah." Her hand closed around the manila envelope that Callie had slid into the center of the stack. "Such a shame," she said softly, flipping through the pages. "So much work . . . and all of it . . . gone to waste."

Callie tried to speak but found that she couldn't; nor, for that matter, could she move: her feet seemed to have frozen in place. "I . . ." she finally managed to sputter. "I—"

"Save it," Lexi snapped. "I know you've been seeing Clint. Honestly I thought you would have been smarter—that maybe you would have figured out by now that nothing escapes me. I know everything about everybody, and pretty soon, everybody is going to know everything about you!" Callie's COMP portfolio landed on the table between them with a loud *thwack*. Some of the papers scattered, fanning out across the wood.

"Please," Callie whispered. "I'll do anything."

"I'm afraid it's too late for that," said Lexi. Crossing over to the computer on her desk, Lexi stepped around Callie and turned it on. Callie stood helplessly, watching her take her chair.

"It's kind of poetic, isn't it?" said Lexi, her eyes fixed on the monitor as the machine whirred to life. "The same computer on which you so stupidly left your e-mail open could be the origin of your on-screen debut. . . ."

Callie had a wild fleeting fantasy of shoving the entire computer—monitor, keyboard, and all—or Lexi, along with her chair, through the second-floor window. She shook her head. No way. There was *no way* Lexi would release the tape while she was standing right there. "You wouldn't dare..." Wait a second. "My e-mail? You found the tape—because I left my e-mail open?"

"Like I said, I don't see why some of the editors think you're smart." Lexi snorted. "Now let's see. Facebook? YouTube? Maybe a simple e-mail to cweber at fas will do—"

"You wouldn't!" Callie cried, finally finding her voice.

"Well," said Lexi, pretending to stop and think, "maybe there is one thing you could do."

Callie bit her lip so hard she was almost certain she drew blood. *Do I really have to say it again?* She looked at Lexi: the corners of her lips were twisted up in a tiny smile, waiting. *Okay, fine.* "I'll do anything. Anything you want," Callie muttered, determined not to cry.

"Now, there's the attitude I've been looking for!" Lexi chirped. "I think . . . perhaps . . ." She was drawing it out on purpose. Callie wanted to slap her. Thirty more seconds and she probably would. "Perhaps if you could think of a way to really prove to me, once and for all, that you are dedicated to this magazine, to your and our reputation, and to the future of your career, I might reconsider."

Callie waited.

"In fact, I see no reason why any of your work has to go to waste," Lexi said, gesturing toward Callie's pieces that were still fanned out across the table. "If you can show me that your priorities are in order."

"How?" Callie asked.

"What was one of the last things that I said to you when we

returned from Thanksgiving break?" Lexi asked, spinning ninety degrees in the chair to face her.

"Don't—I mean—that I shouldn't let myself get distracted by upperclassmen."

"So, you *do* remember," said Lexi.

Callie breathed a tiny sigh. "You want me to break up with Clint."

"Callie, you're thinking about this all wrong. You see, it's not about what *I* want; it's about what *you* want. Do you want to make *FM* and preserve your reputation? Or do you want to sacrifice it all for a fling with someone I promise isn't right for you?"

Callie was silent. "I'll do it," she finally whispered. "As soon as we get back from break, I'll do it."

Lexi shook her head. "Not good enough."

"Now, then," Callie said. "I'll go over there and—"

"I see no reason for you to go all the way over there," Lexi said, standing. Gesturing toward her chair, she said, "Sit. I think it would be best—easiest—if you wrote it down and sent him an e-mail."

Callie was all too familiar with the break-up e-mail. Was she really about to end things with Clint the way Evan had with her? Were there any other options?

Silently she pulled up a browser and logged into her e-mail, clicking on Compose New Mail. The screen had gone slightly blurry, but she forced her eyes to focus while her fingers formed the words.

She cycled through the usual string of clichés. It's not you—you're great—it's me. I'm just juggling too many things right now.

I need to focus on my work; I don't have time for a relationship. Maybe we can still be friends.

Reading over her shoulder, Lexi shook her head. "You and I both know that the first thing he's going to do when he reads that is call you and ask for an explanation."

Callie *did* know that, actually, and she had been banking on getting away with it. No such luck. Her fingers trembling, she deleted a few lines and typed: *I think it would be best if we didn't talk for a while. Please don't try to contact me. It will just make everything harder.*

Silent tears were leaking out of her eyes when she finally reached the end of the e-mail.

"Looks okay," said Lexi, skimming over her shoulder. Suddenly she placed a pale hand on Callie's back. "You're making the right decision. I know you probably hate me now, but one day maybe you'll thank me. I have known Clint since the beginning of our freshman year, and you two do not belong together. Even though you can't see it yet, I'm actually saving you the heartache and trouble of finding that out the hard way."

Callie jerked out from under Lexi's hand.

Lexi sighed. "I guess that's it, then. Send it, and you're home free."

"No," said Callie, spinning to face her. "I'm not sending this until I have assurances that you won't release the tape—not today and not ever."

Lexi narrowed her eyes. Then she smiled. "I see you're finally catching on to the way things work around here. Maybe you're not so dumb after all." She nodded thoughtfully. "Fine: you have my word not to release the tape—"

Callie shook her head. "Not good enough. It needs to be destroyed. So either hand it over, or delete it in front of me right now."

Lexi fixed her with a hard stare. "Are you sure you wouldn't rather have me guarantee you a spot on the magazine?"

Callie looked at her. "You could—you could do that? But what about the selection process—all the work that everybody else put in?"

Lexi shrugged. "A couple of the editors owe me favors. . . . And most of them already like you. Or your work, anyway."

My work, thought Callie. My work can—and, more important, *should*—speak for itself. Anything I get will be because I earned it. That's one of the differences between you and me, she thought, meeting Lexi's eyes. "No."

"Suit yourself," said Lexi. Then, reaching into her purse, she pulled out a set of keys. Bending, she unlocked the bottom drawer of her desk. Callie caught a glimpse of the items inside but barely had time to wonder how many other peoples' potentially life-ruining secrets were kept locked away in that drawer before Lexi was slamming it shut and handing her a small, white USB flash drive. Her initials, C.A., were printed across it.

Her hands shaking, Callie stuck the flash drive into the side of the computer. The removable storage device window immediately materialized. A single file titled Captain's_Practice.avi was inside. Breathing deeply, she opened it. Five seconds later she hit Close and, sensing Lexi's smirk over her shoulder, yanked the flash drive out of the USB port.

Suddenly Lexi leaned in over the keyboard and, before Callie could react, tabbed into her e-mail and clicked Send. Callie watched in horror as the Message Sent notice popped up on the screen. Straightening, Lexi sighed.

Furious, Callie hit the Logout button and then stood, shoving the flash drive into her pocket. Pulling on her coat, she headed for the door.

"Have a wonderful trip home!" Lexi called at her retreating back. "Now that you're done you can finally relax over the—"

Callie slammed the door shut behind her, cutting Lexi's sentence short. Practically running, she stumbled down the stairs, finally giving free reign to the sobs she'd been restraining. She didn't dare let herself even glance across the street at Adams House when she burst outside—there was no telling when Clint would read the e-mail, but she would probably be on a plane to LAX before he even had a chance to open it. The flash drive was so lightweight she could barely feel it in her pocket bouncing against her thigh as she ran home to pack.

Her roommates were already gone when she arrived: Mimi had left the night before, Dana had departed earlier that morning, and Vanessa's LV luggage was no longer by the front door where Callie had spotted it a few hours ago. They hadn't even had a chance to speak since the ec exam, but in all honesty, Callie felt relieved to be alone. Right now she couldn't bear to face anyone.

Pulling her suitcase out of the closet, she began jamming her possessions inside. After a few minutes she pulled the tiny white flash drive from her pocket and stared at it. Now that she had it, what was stopping her from running over to Clint's and telling him not to open his e-mail? Perhaps because any explanation would involve telling him about the tape, which she couldn't imagine doing, having just been through hell to keep the contents a secret. But maybe it was the tiny voice in the back of her head reminding her that *all* of her problems that semester could be traced back to a boy. Make that *boys*, plural. She stuck the flash drive back in her pocket.

Yes, she had finally recovered the tape. But was it really worth the price?

Winter Break

THIRTEEN

"Congratulations, Callie!"

---

www.facebook.com/profile/calandrews

Clint Weber is now Single.

> 7 people like this.

Clint Weber, Anne Goldberg, and **Alexis Thorndike** were tagged in the album **Skiing in Vermont** by **Tyler Green**.

Gregory Bolton, Alexis Thorndike, Tyler Green, and **Vanessa Von Vorhees** attended the event **New Year's at the Ritz**.

Mimi Clement Je ne veux pas travailler, je ne veux pas déjeuner, je veux seulement oublier, et puis je fume. Also, Happy New Year!

Gregory Bolton is now friends with **Alessandra Constantine**.

Gregory Bolton, Alexis Thorndike, and **Vanessa Von Vorhees** were tagged in the album **It's a Ritzy Ritzy New Year's!**

> **Mimi Clément** commented:
>> Looks très fun! J'adore that dress, Vanessa.
>
> **OK Zeyna** commented:
>> Greg you look like a penguin.
>>
>> Also, who's the hottie?
>
> **Mimi Clément** commented:
>> Oi! Put a leash on it!

Alessandra Constantine added **Harvard University Class of 2013** to her schools.

Alessandra Constantine joined the **Harvard University network**.

Mimi Clément wrote on **OK Zeyna**'s Wall:

Bonjour, mon amour! Traveling in Switzerland.

Did you really have to sign us up for cooking class?

What were you thinking?!? Je te plaisante . . .

See you in a few days!

Gregory Bolton wrote on **Clint Weber**'s Wall:

Buddy! How's the break? Just saw the e-mail from Coach—

Better start practicing for the J-term scrimmage. Unless

you want to lose your spot to a freshman!

Dana Gray posted an album: **Habitat for Humanity: Collegiate Challenge**

Adam Nichols "likes" this.

Adam Nichols commented:

Such a great group! So sorry I missed the trip.

Glad you'll be back in time for HRC elections ☺

allie sat at the desk in her tiny bedroom in Wigglesworth and stared at her computer screen, absentmindedly clicking Refresh for what was probably the bajillionth time. Only this time, instead of the notice that "FAS Grades will be posted starting after noon on January 5th: please be patient and try refreshing the page if they do not immediately appear," the browser redirected. Her heart skipping, she keyed in her login information

Expository Writing 20:	B+
The Nineteenth-Century Novel:	A
Moral Reasoning—Justice:	A-
Economics 10:	B

She reread them twice just to be sure she wasn't missing anything. A sigh escaped her lips. Not bad! she thought, starting to smile. Well, sure, they *were* the lowest of her lifetime, but it's amazing how a small adjustment of standards—and thinking there's a good chance you'll fail everything—can help you see things in a different light.

Flipping open her cell, she dialed Matt's number. He picked up on the second ring. "Hey."

"Grades are up," she said. "Did you see?"

"Yep, I've been refreshing the page for the past twenty minutes and it finally worked."

"Ha. Great minds think alike."

"How'd you do?" he asked.

"Not too bad," she said. "Better than I expected."

"Me too," he said, yawning over the line. "B plus in Expos but—"

"That's what everyone gets in Expos," Callie finished for him.

"Mm-hmm," he said, yawning again.

Callie giggled. "What's with the yawning—were you up late last night or something?"

"Me? More like my roommate," he grumbled. "Slept on the couch again, but this one—this one was a loud one. Never saw her, but I heard her. Oh, I heard her. Man, I cannot *wait* to switch rooms this semester!"

Callie forced a laugh.

"Hey, how'd econ end up?" he asked suddenly.

"B. You?"

"A *minus*."

"I win."

"Speaking of econ," said Matt, "you did not have to get me a present for tutoring you!"

"It's not just for helping me; it's for Christmas, too. Does it fit?" She had bought him a royal blue sweatshirt from her favorite surf shop in Venice Beach and left the package outside his door late last night after she'd arrived from the airport.

"Yes. I'm wearing it now."

"Cool. What about Justice?" Callie asked.

Matt was silent.

"Matt? You still there?"

"Shit! Hang on."

"What?"

"Just got an e-mail from the *Crimson*."

Callie's blood ran cold. "What's it say?" she cried, tabbing over to her e-mail and clicking Refresh three times. No new messages appeared.

"Hang on . . ." he muttered, "I'm reading."

Callie's fingers tapped a tattoo on her desk, her foot bounced up and down, up and down, up and—

"It says they just posted the results in the offices for *Crimson* and *FM*."

"What?" cried Callie, leaping to her feet. "Now?" she added, flinging open her dresser drawer and pulling out the first pair of jeans she touched. Yanking them on, she hopped back over to her computer. "Ah, here it is," she said, clicking on an e-mail from "The Editors at *FM*" that had just arrived.

"So," said Matt, "meet me in the hall in two minutes?"

"Yes! Two minutes!" she cried. Dashing over to her closet, she started rifling through her clothes.

Matt chuckled across the line. "You nervous?" he asked.

"Nervous?" she echoed, only it came out sounding more like "Nerf-ush?" because she had pulled her sweatshirt on backward and the hood was now stuck over her head, her ear tilted to trap the phone against her shoulder. "Yes," she confirmed, twisting and hopping to straighten out the sweatshirt. "I mean, I did everything they asked, and—*gaaah*," she cried as her phone tumbled to the floor. She wrestled with the sweatshirt and, finally throwing it off, picked up her phone. "Sorry! Just—see you in the hall! In two minutes!"

Matt laughed again. "Okay, bye for now."

Thirty seconds later Callie was pacing the hallway, her hands jammed in her pockets to keep from knocking and yelling at Matt to hurry up already. In her rush she had barely stopped to greet Dana and Mimi and let them know where she was going. Dana had returned to campus, along with Adam, in time for the Harvard Republican Club board elections (Adam was running for vice president and Dana was managing his campaign—whatever *that* entailed), and OK had enrolled Mimi in a seminar called something like "Science of the Physical Universe 27: Science and Cooking, from Haute Cuisine to Soft Matter Science," which Callie was pretty sure was a cooking class. According to Mimi, Vanessa would be on vacation with her family for the next two weeks, which was probably—or so Callie assumed—why she hadn't returned any of Callie's calls over the break. Suddenly— *finally*—the door to C 23 popped open.

But it wasn't Matt who stepped outside.

Instead it was a girl: her long wavy hair, so dark brown it was almost black, swirled wildly down her shoulders, just below breasts so perky and perfect, it would be a crime if they were actually found in nature. She had full, heart-shaped lips, high cheekbones, and whether it was the low-cut sweater or the sultry pout Callie couldn't say, but everything about her radiated sensuality. She was by far the prettiest girl Callie had ever seen in these parts. Alarmingly pretty, in fact.

"Hi!" said the girl, smiling.

Callie nodded, embarrassed that she'd been so obviously staring. But then suddenly she grinned. Safe trip home to the state school from whence you came! she thought evilly, watching the girl disappear down the hall. And may you never return! Ha, no worries on that front. Those who came once never came back. This, it seemed, was the *only* matter in which Gregory was actually reliable.

"There you are!" Callie exclaimed when Matt finally walked into the hall. "Is that—is that gel in your hair?" she asked, peering at him.

"No!" Matt cried, his hands flying to his head.

She was somewhat curious to know why Matt had felt the urge to do his hair—not to mention lie about it—but she decided not to press the issue. "Let's go!"

They stepped outside, and the freezing air stung Callie's face, making her eyes water. The walk to the *Crimson* stretched out before her, feeling longer than usual, nearly endless. Her head felt oddly empty when they finally arrived in front of the old brick building.

Together they walked into the foyer stacked with newspapers and down the hallway that opened into the offices that had been the scene of many an all-nighter last semester. There, at the end of the corridor, a group of students was clustered around a spot on the wall. The lists were up; the results were in.

Two girls squealed, hugging each other and jumping up and

down while one boy high-fived another. A girl Callie recognized as a sophomore, however, bit her lip and then, shoulders slumped, ducked into the restroom down the hall.

Callie touched Matt's hand and then left him in front of the list of people who'd secured positions on the *Crimson*. The *FM* results were directly in front of her now. She could sense a dangerous feeling growing inside of her. It was hope.

Her eyes scanned the list once, then twice, and then a third time just to be sure.

Lisa Aberworth

Shaina Azarian

Jonathan Beale

Sarah Bretton

Ross Cademon

Dan Epstein . . .

Even though it was alphabetized and there was clearly no point to continuing, she read it a fourth time, all the way through. Then finally she tore her eyes away. No amount of rereading could add her name to the list.

Someone accidentally shoved her, and she let the inertia carry her sideways. She had failed. Not just at writing but at everything: grades, friendships, love life, proving that she could be excellent at something other than kicking a ball from one end of a field to another . . . All of the all-nighters, all of the rewrites, all of the time spent—no, time *wasted*—all of it was for nothing.

The walls of the *Crimson* suddenly seemed like the inside of a fun house: slanting down, sinister, waiting to crush her. Her chest felt tight; her breathing came in quick, haggard gasps. She had to get out.

Shoving her way through the crowd, she rushed down the hallway, oblivious to the pile of neatly stacked newspapers she sent flying.

Outside she gulped down icy air by the lungful. The sunlight hurt her eyes and she squinted, bending and placing her hands on her knees while she struggled to return her breathing to normal. In a minute she was on the move again. Matt would be out any moment to console her, but she knew that his kind words—or the look on his face as he tried to conceal his own excitement—would break her. And so, instead of heading home to Wigg, she made her way into the heart of Harvard Square.

She passed Grafton, Daedalus, Tommy's, and all the other restaurants and shops: the foreign landmarks of last semester now seemed strangely familiar. Slowing when she hit Mt. Auburn Street, she stared at the towering façades of Final Clubs: the huge mansions owned by the Fly, the Phoenix, and the Spee. This was Harvard: a massive ivy-encrusted enclosure that let only an elite set inside, populated by various brick buildings that were headquarters to clubs even more arbitrarily exclusive based on wealth, parentage, athletic prowess, race, or sex.

What . . . is the password . . . she imagined a disembodied voice might say if she were to knock on a door.

Whatever. Not like she'd be going out this semester. This semester would be about work, lying low, and staying out of trouble. Trouble: a word for which *boys* was a synonym—and antonym, as far as *staying out of it* was concerned. Boys/Trouble: that was Number One on the List of Things to Avoid This Semester. Number Two: Complications. Which meant no trying to reconcile with Clint— *even* though things were now definitively done with *FM* and that damaging file deleted forever so there was no real reason to stay away from him anymore. Right? Wrong! Wait—what?

She shook her head violently as she walked on. Boys were half the reason she had landed in this mess in the first place. It didn't matter how cute they looked in their cashmere scarves. Or the way they always held the door. Or picked the perfect movie for a cold winter night. Or taught you to build your very first snowman . . .

Oh, Clint.

She had spent a good deal of the break in bed absolutely aching for him but unsure what to do: call, don't call, explain everything, say her e-mail had been hacked or she'd had an aneurysm and suffered from momentary insanity. . . . He, on the other hand, had apparently read her e-mail, gone skiing, and then updated his Facebook status to "single" the next day.

Could she blame him for ignoring her completely over the break? She had been the one to type, *Please don't try to contact me.* She had also been the one to end everything through an e-mail, à la the world's greatest d-bag, i.e., her ex-boyfriend Evan Davies. It didn't matter that she had merely played puppet to Alexis's puppet master; *he* had no way of knowing that. Just like he had no way of knowing—because she hadn't told him—that she missed him.

And she did miss him. She missed the way his attention never truly left her, even when they were at opposite ends of the room.

She missed the way he made her feel like she wasn't a total outsider. She missed the little distractions and dates he had planned when she was completely swamped with COMP or final exams. She even missed all of the sneaking around that the last month had entailed: she missed the *ding* of her cell phone with a text asking when they could meet up, she missed the way he kissed her cheek when he thought no one was looking, and she missed the way his hair fell across his eyes when he leaned in . . .

When he leaned in over a steaming hot beverage toward the giggling girl sitting across the table from him, outside under the heat lamps at Finale—

Alexis MotherFreaking Thorndike.

Without thinking, Callie ducked behind the hedge lining the front walk of the Spee: for directly across the street, out in plain sight in the middle of the day, sat Clint, accompanied by the girl who had spent the entire previous semester making Callie's life a living hell.

MOTHERFREAKINGTHORNDIKE!

Callie peered over the top of the hedge. Alexis looked adorable in a thick, oversized white sweater with fluffy white earmuffs to match. How it was possible for someone to look so perfect no matter what a hundred percent of the time was still a mystery to Callie. She glanced down at her ripped jeans, dirty sweatshirt, held-together-by-duct-tape-Converses, and the hideous poufy green jacket that her dad had been so excited to find on sale right before winter break that she hadn't had the heart to tell him it made her look like a seven-year-old *and* a gigantic moldy marshmallow. But it was warm, so screw you, East Coast weather, and screw you, Lexi!

She watched Clint smile and take a sip of whatever was in Lexi's cup. *Don't touch that!* Callie wanted to scream.

Instead of inspiring her to run away—as it should, although there was the very minor stuck-in-a-bush issue—the sight of Lexi with Clint made her want him back that much more.

Was this a date? It couldn't be! Clint had made it very clear that things with Lexi were definitively over. But if that was the case, then *why* where they *sharing* drinks at Finale, which was famous for being one of Harvard Square's most romantic hot spots?

How very confusing. How very . . . clichéd. How very . . . *rage inspiring*.

Let's not forget the bigger problem here, she reminded herself. You are hiding in a bush.

The only way back to her dorm involved crossing the street. Even if she tried a roundabout way, she'd still have to stand up first, and there was a very real chance that Clint and Ms. Satanical Nightmare would see her.

What to do, what to do . . .

"Clint! Hey, CLINT!" a voice called from behind her.

Shit.

Turning, she spotted a boy emerging from the Spee, waving maniacally across the street.

Then it was all happening in slo-mo. First frame: Clint looks up from where his head was bent low over his friendly—romantic?— tête-à-tête with Lexi. Second frame: Clint, recognizing the shouter (aka Life Ruiner), smiles and waves as he starts to stand. Third frame: Clint, like a good Boy Scout, looks both ways before he crosses the street. Fourth frame: Clint cries, "Hey, Marcus, great to see you! When did you get back?"

" . . . my break was great, skiing in Vermont with some of the blockmates, you know, the usua— *Callie?*"

And . . . scene.

"Yes?" she replied, still crouched low, futilely imagining her ugly green coat had blended in with the hedge enough to conceal her through the duration of the exchange.

"What—what are you doing down there?" And then, perhaps worst of all, the corners of Clint's mouth twitched.

"I dropped . . ." *Double shit.* Her hands were completely empty. There was literally nothing she could have feasibly dropped. " . . . my shoe."

"Your shoe?" Now the twitch twitched again.

"Yeah, my shoe. It fell off. But I got it back now, see?" She pointed, wiggling her foot where the laces of her dirty old Converse were secured, as they had been ever since she'd put them on that morning. She straightened up.

Clint's smile faded when she met his eyes. But then, as he continued to look at her, his lips twitched again. "LaRhonda took first place in the competition, you know."

"She did?" Callie cried.

Marcus, who was tall, tan, and vaguely Hispanic looking, coughed pointedly.

"Uh, sorry, Marcus," said Clint, "this is Callie, my—ah—"

"Actually, sorry, but I've got to run," she said, turning to cross the street. Clint did not call after her. When she reached the other side, she resisted the urge to stop and fling the contents of Lexi's hot chocolate all over her snowy white sweater, barreling on toward the Yard instead. First her best friend, then her boyfriend, and now *FM*: Lexi had destroyed everything and taken no prisoners.

A plane whizzed by overhead, going west, and Callie wished she were on it.

She ducked through Dexter Gate, remembering how she had felt the first day she arrived. *Enter to grow in wisdom.* The words had seemed so full of promise: Welcome to Harvard: come in and we will nurse you to knowledge and greatness. Wrong, wrong, wrong. They were hollow now, these words: just words. Where was the class that told you how to fit in? Or the seminar on how not to mess up your life? Or the lecture on how to avoid falling for the boy across the hall who was so totally, utterly, and completely wrong for you . . .

Ha-ha, Universe, very funny: there, about fifty feet away on an ancient stone bench outside of Boylston with his back hunched over against the cold, was Gregory.

She hesitated, wondering how new, No-Complications Callie ought to handle any future interactions. Cool, No-Complications Callie might march right up to him and prove once and for all that she was totally and completely (and no, she does *not* protest too much) over him by saying a civil "hey" without dropping anything or fainting or peeing her pants. After all, even if he was still the same old Gregory, hadn't he also been unusually . . . *civil* as of late? She probably owed her B in economics more to him than to Matt. Were they . . . friends? Certainly not the kind who talked over break. Acquaintances, then? It had to be more than that when he clearly felt he had a right to comment on her love life during dinner. Ex-lovers? She pushed the thought out of her mind. One time does not a lover make. Also, the word *lover* was creepy. Ew.

She started walking toward him. *Hey, buddy*— No. *Yo, how was break? What's going on? Hi*— Well, she'd figure it out when she got there. She had closed half the distance when she stopped. He was on the phone. And, not only that, he was shouting.

She couldn't hear what he was saying, but the fact that she could hear him at all from this far away confirmed it: he was upset, angry even, which was phenomenal when his emotional range had hitherto seemed to vacillate between Totally Bored and Marginally Amused.

She stayed still for a minute, watching him, but then he stood and began to pace. Quickly she turned and headed toward C Entryway, wishing the snow wouldn't crunch quite so loudly under her feet. Any second now he might notice her and guess that she'd been staring. Hopefully he wouldn't think that she'd been trying to overhear his conversation, too.

She struggled to liberate her key card from the pocket of her jeans, finally biting the edge of her glove with her teeth and pulling her hand free.

She smelled the smoke before she heard his footsteps.

Flustered, she dropped the key card. Her fingers froze as she dug through the snow to retrieve it. Then, once she had found it, the damn thing was wet and it didn't seem to work. Scan, scan, scan: but no familiar click.

The smell of tobacco mingled with other familiar scents (pine needles, crisp winter wind, and that something extra indescribably intoxicating). The footsteps were drawing closer now.

"Dammit!" she cursed, scanning her card violently, repeatedly, faster and faster. Cool No-Complications Callie *should* be able to manage a stupid door—

"Need a hand with that?" Gregory asked. His tone hit the perfect middle point between Totally Bored and Marginally Amused that he seemed to reserve for moments when she seemed especially incompetent. Without waiting for a reply, he slid his own card from his wallet and scanned the lock. It clicked instantly. Pulling the door open, he stepped back, indicating that she should enter.

"Thank y—" she started, but swallowed the end of her sentence when he released an exaggerated, irritated-sounding sigh.

"So . . ." she ventured after a beat. "How was your break?"

"Fine," he grunted.

"Do anything fun?" she pressed as they mounted the stairs.

He sighed again. "Not particularly."

Why so grumpy? Was it that phone call or something more? "Rough night?" she asked when they reached the second-floor landing, hoping that teasing was permissible.

"What makes you say that?" he said sharply, turning to her.

Apparently not. "I don't know," she said, her eyes flitting across his face. "You look tired." In fact, he seemed exhausted. There were dark, purplish circles under his eyes, and a few days' worth of stubble lined his cheeks. She tried not to think about how, if anything, the beard only made him more handsome.

"I guess I was up late," he muttered, heading down the hall.

"So I hear," she murmured. They had reached the space between their separate suites. "So *everyone* heard, apparently," she added ruefully, facing the door to her room and digging into her pocket for the key.

"What I do with my time is none of your business."

Slowly she spun around. He was leaning against the frame of C 23, his arms folded across his chest. He had sounded serious, but there was a small smirk on his face: an accusation that she was obsessed with him, listening at his door and spying on his every movement. It was infuriating.

"I happen to think it *is* my business when the morning-after parade *tramp*les through *my* hall, not to mention Matt, who probably hasn't had a decent night's sleep all semester, not to mention . . ." She bit her lip. "I mean, do you ever stop to think about how *they* might feel when you just use them and toss them and never call them again? No! You don't."

"Right. Because I'm an asshole and a womanizing whore," he said, trying to deliver it like a joke—only the punch line fell flat.

"Couldn't have put it better myself!" she snapped.

He rolled his eyes. "Whatever. You were right the first time. Let's just try to stay away from each other."

"I believe that one was *your* genius idea," she retorted sarcastically, "but great. Whatever. Let's do it," she finished, jamming her key into the lock. Luckily the common room was dark because she didn't think she could handle dealing with anyone else right n—

"CONGRATULATIONS!" several voices cried in unison. Mimi flipped on the lights and yanked up the window shades to reveal Adam, Dana, and a disgruntled OK wearing party hats, standing in front of a huge banner that read CONGRATULATIONS, CALLIE! The room had been decorated with streamers, the coffee table was crowded with confetti and plastic flutes for champagne, and worst of all, someone had printed out a gigantic picture of her head and taped it to the wall.

"Félicitations!" screamed Mimi while Adam smiled and nodded. Only Dana seemed to notice that something was amiss, looking uncertainly from Callie to Gregory, who was still standing behind her.

"Can I take this off now?" OK asked Mimi, gesturing toward the lopsided party hat that was far too small for his head.

"You can all take them off—" Callie started.

"Ne sois pas stupide," Mimi said, seizing a bottle from the table. "We must celebrate *avec beaucoup de champagne!"* she cried, popping the cork and spraying fizz into a plastic flute.

Callie stared at her feet. Without lifting her eyes, she muttered: "I didn't make it."

"What?" Dana asked, yanking the glass out of Adam's hand that Mimi had just handed him and giving him a severe look. "What did you say?"

"I didn't—"

"Please!" OK shouted, trying to remove his hat, only to be intercepted by Mimi: "Let me take this"—Mimi held the hat down and looped the elastic back under his chin—"bloody thing *off*!"

"I said—"

"She didn't make it," a cold, high voice announced from behind her. Callie whirled around to find Vanessa, who, lugging her full set of Louis Vuitton luggage, pushed past Callie into the common room. Gregory was gone. Typical womanizing, a-hole behavior.

"She did not . . . *Quoi*?" Mimi gaped, her mouth hanging open.

Slowly Dana slipped her party hat off of her head. "Next time," she whispered. She took Callie's hand and squeezed it briefly.

"But . . . but you worked *tout le temps*!" Mimi cried. OK shook his head, trying to silence her.

Their pity, Callie decided, was definitely worse than not making the magazine. She wished that they would all stop looking at her like her dog had just died and let her be alone. At least Gregory wasn't there to laugh.

Vanessa, still standing near the door surrounded by her bags, was smiling. But it wasn't a I'm-so-happy-to-see-you smile, or a I've-been-waiting-to-thank-you-in-person-for-economics smile. More like a your-failure-is-pleasing-to-me grimace.

"Why is it you are returned so soon?" Mimi asked her. "You are supposed to be on family vacation, no?"

"Yeah, well, my parents got into some stupid fight—no big deal, it happens every other year—and we left," said Vanessa, hoisting two of her bags over her shoulders. "I didn't feel like sticking around to see them through another session of couples therapy so . . ." She shrugged. Then, pulling her luggage into her room, she slammed the door behind her.

"What the . . ." Callie muttered. It was almost like Vanessa was still mad. But she couldn't be—not after everything they'd been through—could she? Callie covered her eyes with her hands. Her head felt like it was about to split in two. It was too much: the magazine—Gregory—Clint—Vanessa—

She felt two arms wrapping around her and, opening her eyes, was surprised to find Mimi supporting her with ample strength, given that she was, in the words of certain jealous upperclassmen, "half the size of Kate Moss with twice the drug problem." Dana stood frozen in the corner looking awkward while Adam's eyes darted around the room, waiting to take his cue. Mimi led Callie to the couch.

"Bloody hell." OK sighed, reaching for the bottle of champagne, which was still fizzing over exuberantly, and taking a swig. "This is *so* depressing."

Mimi rounded on him, but before she could say anything, Callie started to laugh. It was the type of hysterical laughter that overtakes you at exactly the wrong time—the painful kind beyond your control. After all, what could be worse—no, what could be *funnier*—than a surprise party turned pity party in her honor?

"Did Matt . . . ?" Adam asked tentatively.

"Yeah," said Callie, finding that she didn't even have to force a smile. One sidelong glance at Matt's face before she had fled the building had confirmed it. "Yeah, he did—he really deserved it."

"*Les idiots.*" Mimi grunted, prying the bottle away from OK and pouring some champagne into a glass. "Well, Mama always had a saying back in France: 'Drink when you are happy and drink when you are sad as long as you do not drink in the bathtub while using an electronic device.'"

Callie took the flute from Mimi's outstretched hand. She hesitated only briefly—it was the middle of the day, but she wasn't in the bathtub, so . . . "To failure," she said. Adam tried to return the toast with a glass Mimi had set near him, but once again Dana swatted his hand away. Callie took a sip and grimaced. Not even the golden tide of sweet, fruity bubbles could wash the bitter taste away.

"So, OK, how'd calculus turn out?" Callie asked, wishing that Mimi hadn't deemed it necessary to print out that huge photo of her head.

"Grand," he said, smiling. "And I've got my fabulous tutor," he said, rising from the couch and making his way toward Dana, "to thank for it!" Dana's attempts at backing away were futile: he grabbed her as if she were a rag doll and lifted her in a giant bear hug.

"Put me down!" she cried, her eyes wide. "Adam?" she pleaded, turning to her protector, who, to his credit, seemed like he had put on a few pounds over winter break and now might even weigh more than Mimi. He looked on helplessly while OK danced Dana around the room. Suddenly the door to Vanessa's room opened.

"Hey," said Callie, hoping that Vanessa might be in a better mood now that her bags were put away.

Vanessa just frowned.

"So . . ." Callie tried again, "want some champagne? Help me drink away my woes?"

Vanessa looked at the bottle and then looked at Callie. OK, in an unusually perceptive moment, put Dana down. "Sure, I'll have some," Vanessa said slowly, staring at Callie. "To *celebrate*."

"Huh?" Mimi muttered.

"I'm *glad* you didn't make it," Vanessa continued, her voice rising steadily, "because if you had, then they would have published your pieces in the next issue—including the one you wrote about *me*."

Now it was Callie's turn to stare. "What are you talking about?"

"Really, I don't know why you bothered 'rescuing' me for the ec exam. I *thought* it was because I was wrong about you, but now I know that the only reason that you wanted to keep me from flunking out was so you could publicly humiliate me later!"

What? What kind of crazy pills was Vanessa taking? "I really don't know what she's talking about," Callie said to Dana and Mimi.

"'The Roommate from Hell has an inexplicably Dutch-sounding prefix to her name'?" Vanessa shrieked, her face turning red. "'The Roommate from Hell loses her diamonds as casually as you sometimes misplace your socks'!"

Callie's eyes went wide. "How did you . . . I mean, that was never supposed to . . ." She frowned. "What did you do, raid my room—again?"

"So you admit it!" Vanessa screamed, her eyes wide with triumph. "And you were going to try to have it published!"

"No, I was n—"

"Well, *thank god* you didn't make the magazine or *I* would have told the world everything there is to know about *you*!"

Callie cringed. "Vanessa," she said slowly. "Please, let me explain."

"No way," Vanessa said, violently shaking her head. "I'm done hearing what you have to say. From now on you stay away from me," she called over her shoulder. Turning at the last second, she cried, "The Roommate from Hell is LEAVING!"

The door slammed behind her with such force that the entire room shook.

Dana, Adam, and OK stared uncomfortably at their feet. "Party is over," Mimi murmured, tossing her plastic cup into the recycling.

"Yeah," Callie muttered. "It is." She hadn't realized she'd been holding her breath until it flowed out of her in a giant gust, like a balloon deflating. Suddenly she felt exhausted. The streamers fluttered gently in the air, mocking her. Setting her glass on the table, she stood. "Thanks for the . . . all this, you guys," she said. "I think I need to . . ." she gestured toward her room.

Fully clothed, she lay down on her bed and closed her eyes.

Some of the lessons she'd learned over the past semester had been committed only to short-term memory and were now—she was finding—proving difficult to consolidate. For example:

1. Gregory has no redeeming qualities, so stop talking to him, stop thinking about him, and stop Facebook-stalking him, because HE IS EVIL.
2. Never leave the house without a scarf and gloves; contrary to what you seem to believe, you *cannot* control the frigid Massachusetts weather by sheer force of will.
3. It would be unwise to un-break-up with Clint—*again* . . . or would it?
4. Pages 1–153, 174–359, and 426–803 of her economics textbook.

One lesson, however, had been branded into her brain: never, under any circumstances, should you leave your e-mail, documents, or even your laptop open in a place where somebody might find a file not meant for others' eyes, even if that place is your own bedroom, where you would *think*—stupidly, you would think—that you'd be guaranteed a little privacy.

When it comes to a college dorm room, nothing is private and nothing is safe.

FOURTEEN

Game, Set, Match

SCOPED!

All the latest GOSSIP on this year's Campus Characters,
brought to you by the one, the only:
Fifteen Minutes Magazine

New in Town: Which hotshot, self-proclaimed rock star of a visiting professor will be honoring us with his presence this semester? None other than the famous—or should we say, *infamous*—two-time winner of the Most Incomprehensible Academic Writing Award: the honorary professor J. M. F. C. Raja. And a very hearty thank you to Columbia University for sparing him this spring. No doubt he will enlighten us all on the topics of Post-war Fiction and Theory (Thursdays from 2–4), and Culturalism, a term he popularized in the late 1980s and now also a class (Tuesdays, 3–5).

Professor Raja is known for his distinguished British-Indian accent, tendency to bring wine to class in order to get his graduate students talking, and impeccable fashion sense, in addition to the major academic achievements with which he has graced the literati—at least those who can understand him.

List of publications include:
Where Is the Center?
The Center That Does Not Exist but for in Narrative
Relocating the Center
The Death of the Center
.*

*Yes, the title is just a period, like so: ".".

Harvard's Hottest Transfer: Which little stick of dynamite will be giving us all hot flashes this semester? Hint: her mother is a former Brazilian supermodel turned business tycoon's wife, which would make her father (for those of you who are on the slower side), a famous Captain of Industry.

Ding, ding, ding! Men, keep your pants on, and ladies, don't get your panties in a twist. We don't know how she did it (actually, we suspect construction of a new Constantine Center for the Arts to get underway immediately subsequent to her arrival), but sophomore Alessandra Constantine is transferring to Harvard effective for the spring semester from the University of Spoiled Children. Sorry, excuse us, but we meant to say the University of Stupid Chinese. (Sorry! But our Asian editors said that was okay? Don't sue us—you can't: it's anonymous!) Anyway, there is no doubt in this editor's mind that Alessandra stands to break a few hearts. Google-image that shit if you haven't already.

We hope that she can keep up, and for your sakes, ladies, we hope that *you* can hang on to your boyfriends.

We Can't Believe SHE Made Editor: Which dreaded feminazi has been elected managing editor of our beloved* "parent" organization, the *Harvard Crimson*? That's right: Grace Lee has finally done it, the first and only junior to hold the position since 1982. You may recognize her from any and all protests around campus; we here at *FM* know her fondly as the Woman Who Haunts Our Nightmares. This editor personally wonders how many she had to kill in order to secure the position. Heaven help us all. Amen.

---

*And by "beloved" we mean "incredibly oppressive and controlling." Unless you are reading this now, Crimachine, in which case by "incredibly oppressive and controlling" we of course mean "beloved." We swear.

Matt waved to Callie from the front of the classroom as she chose a seat in the back. She shook her head, wondering why on earth she had let him talk her into this. The wounds from her *FM* rejection were still fresh; she needed time to mourn and cycle through denial, anger, overeating too many vending machine cookies, depression, and kickboxing, or whatever the five stages of grief were and then heal. So throwing herself right into a *Crimson* COMP informational session—a form of "PTSD in vivo exposure therapy" (prescribed authoritatively by Matt after his single semester of psychology)—may have been a very poor idea indeed.

Nevertheless, here she was, pulling out a notebook and pen and watching Grace Lee take the podium. A panel of editors, writers, business staff, photographers, and graphic designers, some of whom were recently successful COMPers (including Matt) sat at a table behind Grace, ready to answer their questions.

"COMP doesn't officially start until next semester, so you can all stop looking so terrified," Grace Lee barked into the microphone. "The e-mail said 'informal,' people!"

General G. E. Lee, Callie scribbled in her notebook with a smile. Who was more frightening: Grace or Lexi? It was a toss-up. In the Fundamentally Evil category Lexi definitely had Grace beat, but it was just as easy, if not more so, to picture Grace making somebody cry.

"The *Harvard Crimson*, founded in 1873, is the oldest university newspaper in the country. We are also the only daily newspaper in the city of Cambridge, Massachusetts. As I'm sure most of you already know, many of our alumni have gone on to successful careers in journalism, including several Pulitzer Prize winners, and of course some of those who weren't as lucky had mildly successful careers as presidents of the United States."

Obligatory laugher ensued.

"Make no mistake," said Grace, silencing them, "we here at the *Crimson* take our newspaper very seriously. This isn't our Thursday pullout, *Fifteen Minutes* magazine," she continued, her gaze resting briefly on Callie. "And we're not here just to drink, pull pranks, and give fake awards to the Paris Hiltons of this world like the members of that semisecret Sorrento Square organization that used to publish a so-called humor magazine."

Ah. The *Crimson-Lampoon* rivalry was alive and kicking. Callie glanced at Matt. He winked at her.

"We deliver the news," Grace continued, "from on campus and beyond, and we do it every day in time for breakfast. It's a tremendous responsibility—"

"I'm so sorry I'm late," a low alto trilled suddenly from the doorway. Callie looked up. Even though she'd seen her only once before, there was no mistaking her: the dark-haired beauty from the hallway, who, Callie decided as the girl slipped off her coat to reveal another sweater of the extremely low-cut variety, would hitherto be known as Perky Boobs, Queen of the Amazon.

"It's fine; come in," Grace snapped in a tone that said, *lateness is the opposite of "fine" and I'd tell you so if you were important enough to be lectured by me directly.*

Perky Boobs smiled and slid into a chair at the front of the room, flipping her long hair back with both arms. Every set of male eyes in the room locked in on her—and some of the ladies' eyes did, too. Callie was certainly struggling not to stare. What the hell was this girl doing here? She didn't go to Harvard; she belonged at BU, or Tufts, or Boston Modeling Academy, or wherever it was she came from.

Before Callie knew what was happening, her hand had shot into the air.

"Question? Ah, yes, Ms. Andrews," said Grace, giving Callie a tiny smile.

Whoa. She remembered my name. Callie didn't know whether to feel flattered, or terrified, or both. Probably both. "Um," she said, "I'm sorry, but I was just wondering—you can't COMP the *Crimson* unless you go to this school, right?"

Everyone stared at her like she was a politically incorrect term for a mentally handicapped individual. Matt shook his head. "No," Grace answered slowly, "you cannot write for the school paper unless you are enrolled as a Harvard undergraduate and complete the series of requirements for the election process we call COMP."

Callie folded her arms and leaned back in her chair, staring at Perky Boobs's head. But Perky Boobs appeared to be staying put. Callie frowned.

"If there are no more questions," said Grace, "then I'll hand things over to our editors."

Callie doodled in her notebook as one of the editors began to talk about the business board. She knew she should probably take notes, but in truth she wasn't even sure if she wanted to be here. Did she really have the energy to survive another semester of COMP?

The business board editor finished speaking, and one of the writers took his place. She seemed happy and highly animated as she started discussing a series of articles she had written the previous semester on the asset allocation of the Harvard endowment. Callie sighed and wished she had COMPed the paper and not the magazine last semester. In fact, if she could do it all over again, there were a lot of things that she would have done differently.

Well, live and learn, she thought, flipping to a fresh page in her notebook. Surely part of being a freshman involved making one or two (okay, maybe three or four) epic mistakes. Weren't they the ones that made the best stories later?

Before she knew it, an hour had passed and the meeting was drawing to a close.

Matt ambled over, a goofy grin on his face. "So," he said, "what'd you think?"

"Sounds . . . like a lot of work," she said, standing and tucking her notebook under her arm. They started walking. "I'm not sure I'm ready to jump back in again . . ." Callie realized Matt's attention had gravitated elsewhere: specifically to the largest gravitational mass force in the room—in other words: Perky Boobs.

Not Matt, too! Suppressing a groan, Callie grabbed the edge of his sleeve and dragged him toward the door. They were almost there when Grace Lee intercepted them. "I hope you'll decide to COMP," she said, speaking to Callie. "You're a strong writer from what I saw in English class, and we could use a few more like you."

"Th-thanks!" Callie stammered.

Grace nodded curtly and walked away.

Matt gaped, speechless as they left the room. "I can't believe she just spoke to you," he finally whispered in a tone that bordered on reverential awe, like he was ready to tattoo *G. L.* on his bicep. "*And* she knows your name! She still calls me Robertson when she uses a name at all, but mostly it's just 'Hey, you!' or 'Where's my coffee?'"

Callie shrugged, trying to restrain her grin. She could already tell that Grace's compliments were probably rarer than diamonds and made you feel twice as sparkly. Maybe she *would* COMP the *Crimson*, she thought as their heels clicked down the hall.

"Excuse me," a sultry female voice called from behind them. They turned. Perky Boobs was hurrying to catch up.

"Yes?" Callie finally asked when it became apparent that Matt had momentarily lost his powers of speech.

"I recognize you," the girl said, her huge heart-shaped lips forming an enormous smile. "From the other day, in the hallway in uh . . . Waggensworth—"

"Wigglesworth," Callie corrected her. As you should know, she added silently, if you're going to pretend to go here.

"Right!" the girl said brightly. "I'm Alessandra," she added, extending her hand. Callie hesitated, but Matt, his eyes wide, reached for it. "I'm Matt Robertson—huh—Robinson," he said with a demented giggle. "It's Robinson," he repeated, placing a hand on Callie's shoulder, "I was just telling Callie here"—grudgingly Callie shook hands—"that Grace, who was my COMP director before she made managing editor, is always messing up my name."

Alessandra smiled at Matt like he was a perfectly normal, non-demented teenage boy. "That's a shame. If it were me, I would *definitely* remember your name!"

Great! So she's nice, too, Callie thought staring at her own feet. Not to mention a *huge* flirt!

"I just transferred here from USC," Alessandra explained, looking back over to Callie.

"Congratulations," said Callie. "Well, so nice to meet you," she added, starting to walk, "but we should really probably get go—"

"Do you need someone to show you around?" Matt volunteered at the same time.

"Actually," said Perky B—*Alessandra*, "I was wondering if you two could tell me where I might find the Harvard squash courts."

At the word *squash* Callie stopped walking. "Why do you ask?" she blurted.

"A friend of mine invited me to watch his scrimmage."

Callie stared at her, processing that tidbit and then biting back the urge to demand *which* friend. There's no way Gregory would invite a girl to watch him play. Maybe before he slept with her but certainly not after. Still, there was only one way to be completely sure. Plus, a certain teammate of his might be on the courts today, too.

"What a coincidence," said Callie, forcing her face into a smile. "Matt and I were on our way over there right now to watch the game!"

Matt, finally tearing his gaze away from Alessandra, looked at Callie. "We were . . . ?"

"We were!" she chirped, gripping his arm and squeezing.

"Ho-kay," Matt said with a shrug, apparently up for anything that involved spending more time with Alessandra.

Turning to her, Callie said sweetly, "Shall we?"

Fifteen minutes later, after crossing a bridge over the Charles River, they arrived at the Murr Center. Games were raging in all five spectator courts, and the bleachers opposite the glass back walls were surprisingly full.

Callie barely had time to register the shock of spotting Gregory, in one of the middle courts, playing a fierce match against none other than Clint, in light of the bigger surprise that awaited her: middle bleachers, far left, second row.

Alexis-MotherFreaking-Thorndike.

She wore an old maroon squash polo (CLASS OF 2012), faded from many washings, over her designer jeans, and even though it was the most dressed-down Callie had ever seen her, Lexi still managed to pull off the look impeccably. She held a Starbucks cup between both hands and was leaning forward, watching the game intently. She had yet to notice Callie, so there was still time to make a run for it—

"Aren't you going to sit?" Matt asked, patting the spot next to him on the bleachers.

"Uh . . ." Callie hesitated. Alessandra clapped her hands together as Gregory smashed the ball. Callie frowned and looked back over at Lexi: her eyes were glued on Clint, who was diving to return the shot. Maybe I really am stupid, she mused, watching Lexi watch Clint. It was Clint Lexi had wanted the entire time, not Gregory.

"Um . . . Actually, I think I might—"

Matt gave her a look that said, *Don't you dare*.

Lexi and Alessandra suddenly shrieked. Clint had just scored a point against Gregory, who had smacked into the back wall in his attempt to hit Clint's high lob into the far right corner. Turning, Clint saw Callie. His mouth fell open in surprise but twisted slowly into a smile. He gave her a little wave with his racket, and she found herself waving back, smiling as he adjusted the turquoise sweatband holding back his shaggy, light brown hair. Adorable.

"Scoot over!" Callie cried, sitting next to Matt. Folding her arms across her chest, she stared straight ahead. You don't own these bleachers, Lexi, and you don't own Clint! "Wahoo! Let's go Clint!" she cheered. Even though he probably couldn't hear her through the glass, her words were bound to encourage others . . . to feel extremely irritated.

"The other one's name is Clint?" Alessandra asked Callie, leaning over Matt.

"Mm-hmm." Callie nodded.

"Cute!" said Alessandra.

Callie's head jerked up, ready for a fight. But, seeing the goodwill in Alessandra's eyes, she said instead, "I know, right?"

Matt groaned.

"You're here to watch Gregory?" Callie asked, ignoring Matt.

"Yes," said Alessandra.

"Cool," Callie replied, surprised that she actually kind of meant it. Clint scored again and she clapped.

"I know him!" Matt offered excitedly. "He's my roommate!"

"Is he?" Alessandra asked. "You guys have a great room! Love the leather couches."

"You've been there?" Matt asked as if awestruck by the thought. But then: "You've been there," he repeated in an entirely different tone. "Oh."

Callie slid her arm around his waist and rested her head briefly on his shoulder. One day, she tried to tell him telepathically. One day the right girl for you will come.

"Excuse me," said Alessandra, speaking to a boy behind them. "Do you have any idea what the score is?"

"Seven to six. Weber's winning. Bolton was up, but it looks like he's lost his focus for some reason."

"And how many games in the set?" Matt asked, turning around.

"Best two out of three," the boy answered. "Bolton dominated in the first round, but Weber came back to win the second, slow and steady. That's why they call him the Tortoise."

"So whoever takes this game wins the match," Matt explained for Callie and Alessandra's benefit.

"Does it matter?" Callie asked. "I mean, isn't it only a scrimmage?"

"Yes, but they're competing for spots: number one and number two, I think. Greg said the team's leaving in a few days for the All

Ivy tournament at Brown, and if he wins this match against Clint, he'll be the first freshman to lead off in the tournament in . . . Well, I think, ever."

Alessandra was nodding. "He seemed nervous about it," she whispered. "He said he thinks his chances are slim."

"He said that to you?" Callie blinked. It was difficult to picture Gregory confiding in anyone, let alone a girl. Callie sighed. You do not care, she reminded herself. And stop reminding yourself!

"Oh!" Matt yelled. Gregory had slammed the ball low and fast along the far right-hand wall, and Clint, who had abandoned the T for the left side of court, hadn't made it in time.

"Seven all," the boy behind them cried. "Let's go, Bolton! Look sharp!" he hollered, clapping his hands three times.

Even Callie felt a slight thawing in her heart as she watched Gregory run his hands through his dark brown hair and wipe the sweat out of his eyes. She had never seen him look so intense about anything, or so exhausted. He arranged his feet, one inside the serving square and one out, and lifted his racket. The serve fell short.

Callie didn't need to be able to hear through the glass wall to know that the words he was shouting were curses. Dragging his hands across his forehead and over his eyes again, he bent to retrieve the ball and then, looking apologetic for the outburst, tossed it to Clint.

Clint nodded calmly. His serve soared high and perfect, bouncing off the back wall. Gregory barely returned it, hitting low and to the left.

"Isn't this exciting!" Alessandra exclaimed, gripping her cheeks with her hand. "Go—go—OH—*no!*" Gregory had dived and missed.

"Eight-seven," the boy behind them whispered.

"Game point," said Callie.

Clint served and Gregory hit it back with everything he had. Sprinting across the court, Clint sent the ball flying backward; it bounced off the glass wall and reached the front one just above the lower red line. Callie's fingernails dug into her jeans. Gregory scooped the ball up easily with his backhand, and it *zinged* down the far wall, moving deadly fast—only this time, Clint was ready for it.

All eyes in the bleachers darted back and forth, back and forth: Gregory, Clint, Gregory, Clint, Gregory, Clint, Gregory—

"WEBER WINS!" the boy behind them roared, leaping to his feet.

"*Eeee!*" Callie shrieked, standing and clapping wildly. Even Matt and Alessandra were on their feet shouting. Through the glass Callie saw Gregory drop—or was it throw? She couldn't tell—his racket on the ground. Callie's cheers caught in her throat. Gregory sank onto the floor after it, forehead in his hands. Clint stood still behind him, and then walked over and placed a hand on his shoulder. They stayed that way for almost a minute, until finally Gregory grabbed Clint's outstretched hand and let the older boy help him to his feet.

The glass door opened and snatches of conversation were suddenly audible: " . . . sorry, man . . ." Gregory was muttering, ". . . got a little intense there toward the end . . ."

"No worries, buddy," Clint said, slapping him on the back. They bent over their gym bags and grabbed water bottles. "You played a great game. Seriously. I'll be looking over my shoulder for the rest of the semester."

Gregory winced.

Callie and Matt hung back, but Alessandra approached the court. "Hey, you," she called, smiling at Gregory.

"You came," he observed, sounding less than thrilled. Probably because he'd just lost, Callie decided.

"It was a great game," Alessandra said, smiling at Clint. "Fantastic to watch," she added, leaning in toward Gregory.

Gregory just grunted and took a swig from his water bottle. Then he dumped the remaining contents on his head. As he shook out his hair, some of the droplets landed on Alessandra and she recoiled, but he either didn't notice or didn't care.

"So, what are you up to later?" Callie heard her ask.

"Gotta shower," Gregory muttered, zipping his racket into its case and throwing some extra squash balls into his bag. Looking up, he noticed Callie staring. Slowly a smirk spread across his face. "You wanna join me?" he asked loudly, throwing an arm around Alessandra's shoulders. She giggled and, looking embarrassed, pushed him playfully in the ribs. Horrified, Callie averted her eyes.

"Let me just say bye to Callie and Matt," said Alessandra, and before Callie knew it the other girl had returned.

"So nice to meet both of you," Alessandra said sweetly. "I'll see you again soon?"

"Nice to meet you too. . . ." Callie was transfixed by what was happening behind Gregory: Lexi had made her way over to Clint and was congratulating him on the match. If Callie strained, she could *just* hear them. . . .

"Yes, absolutely," Matt jumped in. "Great game, dude!" he called to Gregory.

"Thanks," said Gregory, ambling over to join the conversation. "Didn't go exactly the way I'd hoped . . ."

He kept talking, but Callie had stopped listening. Instead she had angled her left ear toward Lexi and Clint and was eavesdropping intently:

"You didn't have to come, you know," Clint said.

"I know," said Lexi, "but I wanted to surprise you!"

Callie missed the next part, biting her lip as Matt exclaimed loudly and reenacted one of Gregory's serves. Soon, however, she could hear again.

" . . . used to come to all of your games," Lexi finished.

Clint was silent for a moment. "There's a lot of stuff that we used to do when we were dating that *friends* don't do."

"Right," said Lexi shortly. "And I was just here to show a little *friendly* support."

"I appreciate that," said Clint. "I really do."

"Well, you can't win 'em all," Matt said with a shrug, and Callie snapped back into the conversation.

"No, you can't," said Gregory, his eyes resting briefly on Callie. "Let's go," he said to Alessandra. "See ya back at the room."

"See ya," Matt echoed. "Callie . . . Callie!"

"What!" she cried, furious. From the looks of it, Clint had just told Lexi he would be right back, but Callie hadn't heard so she couldn't be sure. Oh, wait—

"Hey," said Clint. "It's Matt, right?"

"Right," said Matt.

"Clint."

"Nice to meet you, man."

"You too," Clint said, looking at Callie. "So, what'd you think—of the game, I mean?"

Callie cocked an eyebrow. "Your nickname is the Tortoise?"

"Aw, dammit," said Clint, laughing. "Who told you? I'll have to have a word with him later."

Callie laughed. "Most nicknames usually have *some* justification."

"Freshman year I wasn't very good at sprints," Clint admitted.

"You seem okay now," Matt observed.

Lexi was still standing over by Clint's gym bag, watching Callie's every move. Eff it. "So . . . uh . . . do you want to get together later, maybe grab a cup of coffee?" Callie asked Clint. "I feel really bad about the way . . . um . . . yeah." Ugh. Callie waited, feeling about as uncomfortable as Matt looked right now. Possibly more.

Clint stared at her, saying nothing. No doubt he was mentally reviewing certain phrases from her e-mail that were completely at odds with her present behavior.

"There were reasons. . . ." Callie started. "I mean, factors . . . that made me act a certain way . . . only I—"

"Okay," Clint interrupted her. "I've got to hit the showers and take care of a few other things, but why don't you give me a call later and we'll figure something out?"

That . . . was not . . . a no! Callie felt so happy she could kiss him. Instead she nodded and said, "Yes, I'll call you later." Then, grabbing Matt's elbow, she turned her back on Lexi's seething glare.

On the walk home Callie felt a spring in her step. She wanted to lean over the side of Anderson Memorial Bridge as they crossed the Charles and scream *Freeeeeeeeeedom* at the top of her lungs. Lexi had nothing left to compel Callie to do her bidding. Now, instead of Callie's boss and blackmailer, Lexi was *Just another girl I know from the Pudding who used to have me occasionally run her errands. FRREEEEEEEEEEEEEEDOM!*

Clint had seemed confused, hurt, and even a little angry. But he had spoken to her and hadn't said no to coffee, and if she could see him, maybe she could figure out a way to explain what had happened. After all, there was nothing left to stop her from telling Clint whatever she wanted. From *doing* whatever she wanted. Maybe she could even describe how Lexi had orchestrated the breakup without revealing too many details. And then the breakup could turn into a make-up and then—

Callie's phone beeped in her pocket. They were just on the outskirts of Harvard Yard now, underneath the entrance to Dexter Gate. Callie grinned. Somehow she knew it would be Clint texting to say he couldn't wait to see her later. Still smiling, she flipped open her phone.

1 New Text Message
From Alexis Thorndike

267

THANK GOODNESS I ALWAYS SAVE
TWO COPIES OF EVERYTHING JUST
IN CASE ANYONE EVER NEEDS A
REMINDER TO BEHAVE. LEAVE WHAT
WE DISCUSSED ALONE AND I LEAVE
YOU ALONE. DISREGARD MY ADVICE
AND I GO PUBLIC. THIS IS MY FINAL
WARNING.
KISSES, LEX

"Callie, what's wrong?" asked Matt. "You look—"

"That FUCKING BITCH!" Callie exploded, hurling her phone into a snowbank. Spinning around and flailing wildly, she kicked the snow, blindly screaming a string of expletives.

Matt froze. Then he retrieved her cell phone and let her carry on for a while. Kicking the brick archway, she screamed, grabbing her foot and hopping around, wailing. Finally she grew quiet. Reaching out tentatively, Matt touched her shoulder.

"WHAT'RE YOU—" Wheeling around to face him, she stopped short. Then she burst into tears.

"Oh, Matt!" she sobbed, launching herself into his arms.

He wrapped them loosely around her, patting her head. "What is it?" he whispered into her hair. "What's wrong?"

She swallowed, taking several deep breaths. "Matt," she said eventually, speaking into his shoulder, "I need your help." Slowly she looked up. "But first there's something that I have to tell you."

social suicide

Transcript of Interview with C. Andrews

conducted by M. Robinson,

Reporting for the *Harvard Crimson*, 1/12/2011

"Testing . . . testing, one, two, three. Is this thing on?"

"There's a red light in the corner—does that mean anything?"

"Oh—yeah—On. Sorry. Never used one of these things before."

(Sound of female giggling.) "You look very professional, like a real journalist."

"Like Bob Woodward!"

"Uh . . . sure . . . or Bernstein."

"Nah. Bernie had the hair, but Bobby got all the ladies."

"Matt—you realize that you're recording all of this, right?"

"Right—sorry. Let's get going."

(A pause.) "Um . . . where should I start?"

"At the beginning. How did you meet your boyfriend— this Evan Davies character?"

"At soccer practice, my freshman year of high school.

The boys' practice was ending right as our team was starting. He screamed 'Girls can't play soccer!' as they were leaving the field." (A pause.) "I probably should have known right then."

"There was no way to know. Anyway—'girls can't play soccer'—then what did you do?"

"I kicked the ball across the field as hard as I possibly could. It hit him in the face." (Laughter.) "He had a black eye in all of his class portraits."

"Nice! Well done. Now." (Sound of a throat clearing.) "What was it about him that attracted you in the first place?"

"Is that—well—do you think that's really relevant?"

"Uh . . . probably not, actually. Er, sorry, moving on. So, when did the, uh, incident occur?"

"At the end of senior year."

"And what happened, exactly? You don't need to get into any specifics, just a general overview."

(A pause.)

"Maybe this was a bad idea. Callie? Callie, you know we don't have to do this."

"I know."

"There are other ways. We can figure this out."

(A pause. Sighing.) "No, this is the only way."

"Really, we can stop. I can turn this off right now—"

"No, I want to do it. I'm ready."

"You're sure?"

"Positive."

"All right. Whenever you're ready."

"Okay. So. It was my senior year of high school. We—

my boyfriend and I—had both just made captains of the varsity soccer teams, and we'd been entrusted with keys to the boys' and girls' locker rooms. Sometimes after practice when everyone had gone home we would sneak into the locker rooms and fool around. Toward the end of the year I guess Evan was bragging about it to some of the guys on the team, and they didn't believe him and so . . ." (A pause.) "And so they told him to prove it. Then, during our Senior Week, he did."

"By filming the two of you in the locker room without your knowledge or consent?"

"Yes. And it might have ended there if not for his fraternity initiation a few months later. They were having some kind of a sick scavenger hunt and 'turn in an X-rated video or photograph of you with a girl' was worth a lot of points . . ." (A pause.) "Well, I'm sure you can guess what comes next. . . . "

The day dawned dark, gray, and miserable. For the first time in weeks it was raining, not snowing, and the water poured down in torrents, mixing with the snow on the ground until it melted into wet, brown sludge and flooded the pathways that curved through Harvard Yard. No feet stayed dry; no good mood was safe.

Callie used to think that Harvard Yard was one of the most idyllic places in the world—now not so much. She was on her way back from the gym and soaked to the bone, ill prepared for the weather as usual in stretchy black pants and a hooded sweatshirt. Water splashed as she trudged through the puddles, hurrying home.

She was just passing the John Harvard statue when her cell phone started to ring.

"Crap," she muttered, pulling it out of her gym bag and watching it get wet instantaneously. It was Matt. "Hey, Matt, can I call you right ba—"

"Callie? Callie, we have a problem."

Callie stopped in her tracks. If there was a problem, she knew there was only one thing it could be about: the interview. Matt had assured her that, though it was "*technically* unauthorized" and that he wasn't "*technically* allowed to publish articles without following the 'proper protocol,'" he would somehow manage to get it into the paper.

"How soon could you get to the Greenhouse Café?" he continued, the edge in his voice becoming more and more pronounced.

"I'm only a second away right now, but I'm sweaty and soaking wet. Is there time for me to run home and—"

"No, no time. Get there as fast as you can. I'll be there in five, maybe ten. And, uh," he added, seeming to speak more to himself now than to Callie, "try not to panic."

Something was definitely very wrong. Callie tossed her phone into her bag and headed back toward the Science Center's Greenhouse Café. When she arrived, it was unusually empty— some students were still away on vacation, and everyone else was probably hiding inside their dorms. Callie ordered two hot chocolates through chattering teeth—one for her, one for Matt— and then chose a table in the corner.

She had been waiting for less than a minute when someone approached the table and cleared her throat imperiously.

Callie looked up, surprised to see Grace Lee staring down at her.

"You," she said. "Callie Andrews." It was less of a question, more of an accusation.

"Uh-huh?" said Callie as Grace sat without invitation. "We spoke after that review session for the Nineteenth-Century Novel and then again at the *Crimson* meeting—"

"Yes," said Grace, staring her down. "Apparently one meeting was all you felt the need to attend before attempting to hijack my page five. Of course, having never actually participated in any sort of *Crimson*-related activity, you had no way to know that I check my paper meticulously every night before it runs—*especially* on

Wednesdays, when our newest editors are responsible for doing the final read-through."

Callie swallowed. "I don't—I'm not really sure what you're—"

"Lee!" a voice, Matt's, called from across the café. He nearly tripped over himself in his haste to join the table. "Lee, listen to me—I'm so sorry—she didn't know—it was my screwup—"

"Robertson," she snapped, slamming a copy of the article he had written—the article about Callie—down on the table and jabbing a finger at the byline. "You are absolutely right: this is your screwup. In fact, I'd go so far as to call it a monumental fuck-up."

Matt gulped.

"I don't know what's gotten into this year's neophytes," she continued, shaking her head in disbelief. "You've been editors for five minutes and already you think you own the place. That you can just sneak your amateur excuse for a story into my paper without editing, or fact-checking, or any regard for the consequences."

Callie was finally starting to understand the difference between the way she feared Grace in the classroom—for her cold brilliance, unflinching analysis, and decimating counterarguments—and the way Grace was probably feared by her staff. It was wholly possible that Callie was about to witness a tiny Asian girl make a man twice her size start to weep.

"We have a reputation," Grace continued, after a beat. "A certain level of quality that we're expected to maintain. This isn't *Fifteen Minutes* magazine. This is the *Harvard Crimson*. There's a *reason* that new staff members aren't allowed to publish unsupervised.

But *you* think that you're above all that—don't you, Robertson?"

"Please," Callie cut in, "it wasn't him—it was my fault."

"Oh, excuse me. Are you on my editorial staff? Or are you the girl who came to one meeting and suddenly thinks she knows everything?"

Callie and Matt were both silent.

"I . . . I'll . . ." Matt whispered, looking close to tears. "Of course I accept full responsibility for violating protocol."

Callie's shoulders slumped. Matt had mentioned that it wasn't "technically" allowed to add last-minute, unapproved articles to the paper, but he had never said a thing about how he could get kicked off the *Crimson*. Hopefully Matt's "momumental fuck-up" wasn't something that you could be expelled over, or arrested, or executed, or— Calm down, she instructed herself. She was still soaking wet but too numb now to feel cold. Instead she felt defeated and trampled, like the leaves rotting outside in the gutter.

"You're damn right you will," Grace agreed. "The rules matter . . . even if this right here," she continued, holding up Matt's article, "is one of the most solid pieces of reporting I've seen from a freshman."

A pause.

"Wh—what?" Matt choked out when he could finally speak again.

"You," Grace Lee continued, pointing at Callie, "are very brave to tell your story in this paternalistic institution."

"I—uh—thanks," Callie stammered.

"And the writing," Grace added, turning to Matt, "isn't half bad either, though it could use some editing." She still wasn't smiling when she said, "It seems the main issue here is that we need to go bigger. I'm thinking front page, more direct quotes, references to last week's feature on privacy and technology, and maybe even an op-ed or two in section C."

Matt, who three seconds ago seemed scared to the point of peeing his pants, had started to nod enthusiastically.

"And, Robertson—if you think you're going to get away without showing the article to a copy-editor this time, you're dead wrong. In fact, forget the wrong—you're just dead."

"Of course," he agreed deferentially. "But does that mean that I'm allowed . . . well, that I'm still allowed to write it?"

Grace nodded. "I will oversee the article personally. And I want you to collaborate," she said, nodding at Callie. "Don't think for a minute that you'll be allowed to sidestep any aspects of the COMP process; this is strictly because I think it's crucial that we capture your voice and your perspective. We'll run the story sometime next week. Think you can handle that, Robertson?"

"Absolutely," he said, grabbing a pen and scribbling a note in the margin of the draft.

Callie hadn't really heard anything after "we need to go bigger." The front page? She'd been hoping to hide in the back of the paper behind the hopelessly under-trafficked sports section. Just a little article to out herself before Lexi had a chance. But a feature? Everyone in the school would read it. *Everyone.*

"I'm not . . ." she started, "I'm not sure this is the best—"

Grace Lee put on her most sympathetic grimace. "Look. I admire what you're doing. And I'm not going to lie: it will be tough, and there may be unfortunate consequences that you'll have to be prepared to deal with as best you can. But what you're trying to accomplish here—it's not something you can do halfway. It's up to you: all or nothing."

Callie closed her eyes and took a deep breath. All or nothing.

"Let's do this," she said. "No more secrets."

"You're making the right decision," Grace said, reaching out briefly to touch Callie's arm. Callie scrutinized her from across the table. Good decision, bad decision—great story, either way. But something told her to trust Grace, and when it came to Matt, she knew she was safe.

Abruptly Grace stood. "All right, then, you two. I expect the first draft to be on my desk by ten A.M. tomorrow. If you're late, you can both bid your spots on the *Crimson* good-bye."

"It's a date," Matt agreed. Then, realizing what he'd said, the color drained from his face. "I mean, uh—"

Grace cut him off with one shake of her head. She took a few steps away from the table, but then she turned back. "By the way, Andrews, just out of curiosity: would you mind telling me who it is that's threatening to expose you?"

Callie gave her a tight-lipped smile and shook her head.

Grace nodded. "Didn't think so," she mused. "No matter," she added in a low mutter. "I think I have an idea anyway. . . ."

After she had gone, Callie and Matt released a mutual sigh. Both of them had forgotten to breathe through most of the meeting.

"Whew! That was a close one." Matt whistled. Callie slid the now lukewarm hot chocolate toward him across the table.

"Tell me about it," Callie agreed. "I thought she was going to kick you off the paper."

"Hmm—oh—what? No, that's just how she talks. She likes me, I can tell."

Callie stared at him, one eyebrow raised.

"Didn't you hear? She thinks I'm a good writer! She said it was the most solid piece—"

"I heard."

Matt smiled. "Well, badass reporter genius skills or not, we should probably get started on this as soon as possible. Where should we work on it?"

"Why don't we get changed and head to Widener?" she suggested, deciding this was the safest—most secluded—option.

"Perfect." He smiled.

Callie tried to nod in all the right places while he chattered about their future at the *Crimson*—"how awesome was Grace" (apparently being verbally abused within an inch of your life and being referred to repeatedly by the wrong name was some kind of a turn on?)—and tried to reassure her that the article was certain to be a success.

But Callie was barely listening.

As Matt marched onward, out into the rain, out to greet his future at the *Crimson*, no doubt followed by *The New York Times*, two kids, a white picket fence, and a wife named Grace, Callie was marching somewhere, too: Certain Social Suicide.

Many hours later when the rain subsided and the sun had set, Callie and Matt were still burning the midnight oil in Widener Library. Back in Wigglesworth Vanessa had just poked her head inside of C 23.

"Yoo-hoo," she cried. "Anybody home?"

"Oi! Come in!" OK called from where he was sitting on the leather couch.

"Hey," she said, plopping next to him. "Do you mind if I put on *America's Next Top Model?*"

"Sounds interesting," he said, handing her the remote.

"Oh it is," she said. "Last week Gabriella pulled Furlawnda's weave at the photo shoot, and Anne Marie had like a total meltdown during the makeover because they cut off all her hair, and then Tyra was like '*Girl—*'"

Gregory emerged from his bedroom, or what was—from the looks of all the boxes and clothes lining the wall of the common room and the books and discarded papers on the coffee table and chairs—his *old* bedroom. Vanessa stopped talking.

"Hey, Vanessa," he said, carrying an armful of papers and notes and plunking them down on the coffee table. "These in your way?" he asked.

"No," she said, sitting up straighter. "You're fine."

"You like this shit?" Gregory asked, staring incredulously at OK.

"Uhhh!" Vanessa gasped. "*ANTM* is not shit! I did not hear you just say that," she cried, covering her ears.

OK examined the TV screen. "Fit girls?" he inquired rhetorically. "Brilliant television."

Gregory shrugged and returned to his room, emerging a moment later with his bedding.

"It is cool if I just dump this on the chair in your room and then you can toss it on your mattress whenever you're ready to move?" he asked OK.

"I'll never be ready to move," OK muttered.

Vanessa smirked. "You and Adam are switching into the double?"

"Please. Do not remind me," OK said, his eyes glued to the screen.

"You'd better be out of there by the time I get back from the All Ivy tournament," Gregory warned, "or you're going to be homeless and roomless."

"Vanessa: could you be so kind as to sock Gregory in the face? I'm busy watching *ANTM*."

"When's the All Ivy tournament?" Vanessa elected to ask instead.

"We're supposed to meet on Mass. Ave. in half an hour," said Gregory.

"Yikes."

"Yeah, I need to pack," he said, disappearing into his room.

"This is bloody brilliant," OK exclaimed, watching the models on the screen prance around in their underwear.

"*Told* you so," said Vanessa smugly, settling onto the couch.

For the next twenty minutes they watched uninterrupted while Gregory quietly moved the rest of his stuff into the common room, piled more loose papers on the coffee table, and put his gym and duffel bags by the front door.

During a commercial break Vanessa sat up and clicked Mute. Then she began rifling through the papers on the coffee table. "You're not saving your Justice notes?" she asked mostly to herself. "But I thought those were 'life lessons' that we ought to 'cherish forever'!"

Gregory came and stood behind her, leaning over the back of the couch to peer at the papers. "I probably will save those, actually," he said. "Haven't sorted out the trash from the treasured 'life lessons' yet, but there's no point to doing it until *somebody* cleans out his desk."

"All right, all right!" OK cried, swatting at Gregory's hands, which had landed vice-like on his shoulders. "Now buzz off, would you, it's back!" He seized the remote and restored the sound.

"You took calculus?" Vanessa called toward Gregory's room. "I thought you were supposed to be in, like, genius-level econ. . . ."

"Those are mine," said OK, glancing at the papers in her hands.

"Huh," she said, looking down. "'Notes on Triangles?' You have really girlie handwriting."

"That's Dana's," OK said with a wave, clearly irritated by the interruptions.

"What about this?" Vanessa asked, ignoring him. "*This* looks like girl's handwriting, too!"

OK turned up the volume and folded his arms. A few seconds later he stole a sidelong glance at Vanessa, presumably to see if she had gotten the memo.

Despite what one might infer about the private nature of the document that she held in her hands, Vanessa read it anyway. In fact, she read it three times, her facial expressions cycling through three stages of what appeared to be confusion, and then anger, and then finally amusement.

"I can't believe I never saw this!" she exclaimed, setting the note on her knee. "How on *earth* did it get over here?"

Gregory, who had just shut the door to his now almost completely empty room, paused on his way to grab his bags. Seeing the note, his eyes grew wide. Bending down, he snatched it away. "That was private," he said, his voice low and quiet.

"Obviously not," Vanessa countered, "seeing as everyone *except* me probably had a chance to read it."

"What the hell are you talking about?" said Gregory, stopping just as he was about to jam the note into his pocket.

"That note—*my* note—never reached me, so I'm assuming whichever one of you found it and stole it probably read it, too."

Gregory stared at her. "*Your* note? You mean *you* wrote this?"

"No," said Vanessa, turning around to face him. "Callie wrote it. That's her handwriting, right there," she said, pointing to the note in Gregory's hands. "And that's her signature. *Duh.* The part I can't figure out is how it ended up over here."

"She told OK to give it to me," Gregory said.

"Why would she tell OK to give my note to *you*?" Vanessa asked.

"*Uuuggh*," OK groaned, slapping his cheeks as the show's elimination process began. "Stop. Talking!"

"Why do you keep calling it *your* note," Gregory asked, "when Callie told OK to deliver it to me?"

"There is no way this note was meant for you," said Vanessa. "It's practically a point-by-point response to the note that *I* left taped to her window right after Thanksgiving break."

Gregory's brow furrowed. "The note that you left . . . ?" Then he shook his head. "I think you're confused," he said to Vanessa.

She shook her head right back at him. "I don't think so," she said, taking it from his hands. "Why would Callie bother telling *you* that she messed up our room dynamic? That's a direct response to *my* note where I accused her, I think word for word, of screwing up our room dynamic!"

"You go, Furlawnda!" OK cried as Tyra Banks handed the girl on-screen a photograph, indicating that she was still in the running.

"Or here: why would she say that she doesn't think there's any hope you can be friends?" Vanessa continued. "You guys were never friends to begin with!"

Gregory stood still. "I—"

"And *why* doesn't it say 'Dear Gregory' or anything like that at the beginning? I'll tell you why: because she was probably planning just to hand it to me or tape it to *my* bedroom window."

Slowly Gregory started shaking his head again. "No," he said. "Maybe *some* of this"—he pointed to the note—"fits in with that letter you say you wrote her first, but she actually handed this to OK and told him to give it to me."

Finally OK tore his eyes away from the screen. He took one look at the note in Vanessa's hands and shrugged. "I have never seen that before in my life."

"What?" said Gregory, his voice barely above a whisper.

"See?" Vanessa said triumphantly.

Gregory stared at the note and then at OK and then at Vanessa. "But then how . . ."

Suddenly Gregory jumped around the couch and kneeled in front of OK, grabbing his forearms and forcing him to look into his eyes. "You said that Callie had a message for me."

"Yeah, that she missed you and wanted to talk about Harvard-Yale or something, but *you* said she'd already told you herself," OK cried. "Now can you please move? It's down to the final two!"

Slowly Gregory stood. "I have to go," he whispered, starting for the door.

"Yes, you do," OK agreed, his eyes fixed on the screen. "You're already ten minutes late."

"Ten minutes—*fuck!*" cried Gregory, slapping his forehead. He stood in front of the door for a full thirty seconds, staring at it. Finally he shook his head and, muttering, slung his racket and gym and duffel bags over his shoulder. Hand on the doorknob he called, "Please tell Callie I'll be back in a week and that I need to talk to her. In person. Wait," he interrupted himself, surveying the backs of their heads. "Scratch that. Don't tell Callie anything. I'll tell her myself." The door slammed behind him.

"He has been so touchy lately," OK muttered as *America's Next Top Model* drew to a close.

"Tell me about it," Vanessa said with a snort, lifting the note. "'I may be a terrible person, but if I am, you are just as bad, if not worse'? Can you believe this crap? Who the hell does she think she is?"

OK shrugged. "What's really crap is that you two are still fighting. *Still.* I think you ought to just get over all of your girlie troubles by socking Callie in the face."

Vanessa giggled.

"Take the girls in this show, for example," said OK. "When they get mad, they fight, and pull each other's hair, and not only is it fantastic to watch, but everyone feels better afterward *and* everyone is a *model.* Well, only one girl can continue on in the hopes of becoming America's *next* top model, but I'd still bang most of them."

SIXTEEN

Extra, Extra,
Read All About It!

The Problem's Not the Man, It's the System

An anonymous op-ed in response to "Sex, Lies, and Videotape: The Story of an Initiation Gone Awry"

I take offense to the word *infringement* used in connection with *privacy* in the article published today on the front page of this paper. The *only* appropriate term that can be used in the case of Callie Andrews after the word *privacy* is *RAPE*. I cannot remember a time when I was more outraged by the actions of an individual: a male cretin mindlessly acting out a misogynistic dare from his peers with zero respect for the woman who deigned to call him her boyfriend.

But then I sat down and I thought to myself: is it really the man who is at fault here? Or rather, is it something greater: a larger problem that inflicts our society, rotting it from the very core?

The answer is yes. It's not the man. It's the System.

Readers: don't you dare think, not for one second, that what happened to Ms. Andrews is an isolated incident. Here at Harvard, do the Final Clubs and Social Clubs, sororities and even some of the extracurricular organizations not have initiations too?

How many X-rated videos or photographs have been made or taken without one party's knowledge or consent?

I'm guessing more than one.

How many individuals have been made to do something in order to fit in, against their better judgment, or worse, against their will?

I'm guessing hundreds.

It needs to end today. Stop obeying the criminally malevolent, if not simply criminal urgings of the fraternities and organizations that you answer to. Stop making information that should be private public. And stop having sex: stop having sex in high school, stop having sex in college, and continue to not have sex until you meet someone with whom you can be absolutely certain won't put a secret camera in the room.

Start thinking. This did not happen to Ms. Andrews because she was stupid; it happened because there is something wrong with society.

Whether that wrong gets righted is up to you. You can start here, today, on campus by boycotting the institutions that are, by extension, responsible. Or you can stick your fingers up your noses and wait until something like this happens to you. It's your choice.

(Please log in to leave a comment. If you wish to post anonymously, please allow up to 24 hours for your comment to be processed. Comments may be censored due to inappropriate content.)

Note: We have removed all postings purporting to link to the video. No such posting exists. We will continue to censor any requests regarding this subject matter. –Admin

Wow, not sure what I think about the "rape of privacy," but what that dude did was seriously uncool. You've got to love and respect your woman if you want to hang on to her. –Nicky C.

Callie Andrews, wherever you are: thank you. I went through something similar after a bad breakup when my ex was threatening to show naked photos of me to the entire school. It's nice to hear somebody stand up and speak out. Also, if readers can learn anything from me: do not send naked photos in e-mails or texts or anything, no matter how crazy "in love" you think you are. –Carrie P.

Personally I'm more "outraged" at the fact that a classmate would get a hold of the video and threaten to publish it for personal gain. Whoever he/she is, that is seriously *messed up. –John J.*

"Rick, I have to talk to you."

"Uh-huh. I saved my first drink to have with you. Here."

"No. No, Rick, not tonight."

"Especially, tonight."

"Please . . ."

"Why did you have to come to Casablanca? There are other places."

"I wouldn't have come if I'd known that you were here. Believe me, Rick, it's true I didn't know. . . ."

"It's funny about your voice, how it hasn't changed. I can still hear it. 'Richard, dear, I'll go with you anyplace. We'll get on a train together and never stop—'"

"Don't, Rick! I can understand how you feel."

"You understand how I feel. How long was it we had, honey?"

"I didn't count the days."

"Well, I did. Every one of 'em. Mostly I remember the last one. The wild finish. A guy standing on a station platform in the rain with a comical look on his face because his insides have been kicked out."

"Can I tell you a story, Rick?"

"Has it got a wild finish?"

"I don't know the finish yet."

"Well, go on. Tell it—maybe one will come to you as you go along."

Tears streamed down Callie's face at the familiar, yet never tiresome, images on the screen. She was watching *Casablanca* on her laptop, again, alone in her room, lying in bed, and it was not unusual for her to begin crying at Ingrid Bergman's "Play it, Sam" and continue weeping until long after "Louis, I think this is the beginning of a beautiful friendship," ended the film. At least, it wasn't unusual these days.

Today was day four of official "Hide in Your Room Week." Since second semester didn't even start until the end of the month, there was really no reason for her to do anything other than stay right here in bed. For food—though her appetite had all but disappeared—there was Dana, who seemed happy to drop off meals as long as she didn't have to stay and talk, which was fine, more than fine, by Callie.

Three things she avoided like the plague: answering her cell phone, checking her e-mail, and the online edition or any paper copies of the *Harvard Crimson*. (She was surprised that the HUPD had yet to burst into her room to verify that she was still alive, as her mom often threatened to call the police when Callie was unresponsive for over forty-eight hours.) After all, it was one thing to read the article but quite another to face the reaction. Or what she could only guess the reaction would be. The snatches she'd heard coming from the common room the day the feature ran had been bad enough. . . .

Mimi murmuring something about how it "explained a lot." Dana saying a prayer and then (and Callie was really starting to love her), banning the incident as a topic of conversation. She even added the ban to the official-looking document she had typed, printed, and taped to the wall above the couch to give them a fresh start for next semester: "Rules of the Common Room." Right underneath *All visitors of the male persuasion must vacate by 11 P.M.—preferably to their own homes, please; and Don't Ask, Don't Tell* (they were still debating exactly what she meant by that); she had written, *Please be Courteous and Respect the following Banned Conversational Topics when I am present: inappropriate behavior in the library, Paris Hilton, ~~Chelsea Clinton~~, The entire Clinton family, Anything X-rated including: tapes, files, photos, websites, or what Mimi did last night.*

And of course, there was Vanessa, who had remained oddly, uncharacteristically silent. Callie had listened particularly hard for her voice, but the anticipated commentary, like "can't believe she figured out another way to be the center of attention" or "at least now the whole school knows she's a slut," simply had not come. Perhaps, after a semester of ups and downs and in light of Callie's recent social kamikaze, they had finally reached a denouement. Or Vanessa was just busy or off with Tyler somewhere and still hated Callie's guts. Either/or, Callie had more important things to worry about.

In a lot of ways Callie felt relieved. She had been able to control the way the story came out, and she and Matt had phrased the article in a manner that would keep all but the most shameless people from seeking out the video. Even though Callie had stopped checking her e-mail, Facebook, Twitter, and voice mail—addictions that just a month ago she would have declared impossible to live without—she had a feeling that Lexi had been silenced. Yes, Lexi could still out the tape, but it would be at the risk of exposing herself as the "unnamed upperclassman who had secured a copy of the file and used it throughout the semester for coercive purposes" referenced in the article.

Callie imagined that she could probably watch *Casablanca* at least seven more times before she started getting bored. She turned up the volume, trying to drown out what sounded like OK and Mimi messing around in the common room. Laszlo's face filled the screen.

"I know a good deal more about you than you suspect. I know, for instance, that you're in love with a woman. It is perhaps a strange circumstance that we both should be in love with the same woman."

It sounded like Mimi and OK were arguing. Sighing, Callie reached for her headphones as Rick replied:

"You love her that much?"

"Apparently you think of me only as the leader of a cause. Well, I'm also a human being. Yes, I love her that much."

"BLITZKRIEG!" a male voice yelled, and Callie's bedroom door banged open against the wall. Two figures clad in black ski masks rushed inside.

Callie barely had time to flip her laptop shut before she heard

Mimi shrieking, "Red team, move! Now, go, do it now!" and Callie was lifted into the air.

OK slung Callie over his shoulder. "Red team to common room, we are a go, code red, code blue, blue forty-two now now NOW!" Mimi yelled as the three of them exploded into the common room.

"Put—me—DOWN!" Callie screamed, her arms and legs flailing ineffectually.

"Suit yourself," said OK, dropping her.

"OWW!" Callie yelled, hitting the floor with a thud.

"Whoopsie," Mimi muttered, removing her mask. The face underneath looked sheepish.

"What—the—hell," Callie asked, pushing herself to her feet, "is going on here?"

"Er . . ." said OK, glancing at Mimi for guidance. She nodded. "We came here to kidnap you—ow!"

Mimi, frowning and shaking her head, had just slapped him on the arm.

"Oh, right," he remembered. "What I meant to say is you *have been* kidnapped. And now you have to . . . uh . . ."

"Come with me if you want to live," Mimi finished in a surprisingly accurate imitation of California's former Governator.

Now that Callie had recovered from the shock of being "kidnapped" and held hostage in her own common room, she had a moment to take in her captors' outfits.

Mimi, who was always gorgeous no matter what—or how little—she was wearing, looked even more like a prostitute than she had the night she agreed to let Vanessa dress her for "National American Girl Slut Day" (Halloween). OK, on the other hand, in his baggy gold pantaloons (there was no other word for them) purple vest, which he wore without a shirt, and red do-rag looked like . . . Aladdin.

"What . . ." said Callie, starting to laugh. "Why are you guys dressed like that?"

"It is part of our so-called 'Pudding Initiation,'" Mimi explained. "Dress up. Go out. Experience humiliation. Etcetera, etcetera. We were assigned 'ho and pimps.'"

"Woman, I told you, I ain't no pimp—I'm a *rapper* pimp," OK said, making his best attempt at a "ghetto-fabulous" accent. It came out sounding slightly Australian.

Callie was now laughing so hard that she accidentally snorted. "You look"—she gasped, snorting again—"like Aladdin!"

"Who is this Aladdin?" Mimi asked, eyes wide with innocence. OK looked at Callie, looked down, then looked at Mimi and yelled, "MI-MI!"

"What?" she cried, unable to contain her laughter any longer.

"You told me you were going to make me a *rapper pimp!*" he cried, chasing her around the room.

"You think I know *ce que c'est?*" she shrieked, darting out of his grasp.

"*Arrête! Maintenant!*" Mimi gasped when he caught up to her. "We—are—supposed—to—be—on—une—MISSION!"

And it was then that Callie noticed the outfit on the armchair: a shiny minidress that her mother would describe as "cheap looking" regardless of what had probably been an exorbitant price tag.

"That," she said, pointing to the dress, "is not happening."

Mimi looked at OK. "OK?"

Nodding, he reached into the folds of his pantaloons and pulled out a small squirt gun. "Afraid you don't have a choice, love," he said, aiming it at Callie.

Callie laughed, holding up her hands. "Please don't shoot," she pleaded.

"Now, do as we say and put that on," he continued, gesturing toward the dress, "or I'm going to make it rain."

Callie laughed again.

"What?" he demanded, looking put out. "Rappers make it rain . . . right, Mimi?"

"*Oui,*" Mimi agreed. "But seriously, Callie darling, you must come with us to the Harvard pub."

"Harvard pub?" asked Callie. "I thought this was a Pudding thing."

"*Oui,* but the public venue is the key to the humiliation, you see?"

"Ah," said Callie. Public humiliation and initiation: two of my favorite things. "Sorry, but I'm going to have to pass."

"*Mais non,*" Mimi whined. "*Tu vas venir,* we have not been to an initiation event since Limericks, and this will be a perfect opportunity for you to . . . ah, how is it you say? 'Get back out here'?"

Callie considered but then shook her head.

OK looked at Mimi. "But last week Anne said that if she didn't come—"

Mimi gave him a look, and he stopped talking, but Callie got the message. "I don't care if they kick me out. I never cared much about the stupid club anyway." Since December 31 had long since passed and she had never paid her dues, and had been dutifully deleting every Pudding-related e-mail from her in-box without reading, her membership had probably already been deactivated and she simply had yet to receive the news.

"Listen," said Mimi, lowering her voice. "You have to face them sometime. You cannot stay in here forever watching old movies."

"Hells ya!" OK agreed, slipping back into rapper mode and flexing his muscles. "Old movies be trippin', yo."

Callie looked at Mimi and OK and realized just how much she missed them, and missed this. In fact, she missed *all* of her friends, even the one who presently counted herself an enemy.

How much longer could she stay in her room—really? It's not like she was going to drop out of school. Hadn't the point of coming out with her most intimate secret been about freedom anyway? So she could walk around without worrying about it all the time?

Mimi saw her advantage and pressed. "Matt will be there. . . ."

"Yeah, and Greg comes back toni—*ow!*" OK cried. Mimi had elbowed him in the ribs. "Woman be cramping ma *style*, know what I'm sayin'?" he asked Callie.

"I'm going to regret this later," Callie muttered, walking into the bathroom to fix her hair—if such a thing were even possible at this point. "And I'm still not wearing that!" she yelled back at Mimi, who had retrieved the mini-dress from the couch and was holding it up hopefully.

Mimi started grumbling something in French, but the sound of OK's whooping drowned out her words: he began dancing around the room, squirting his gun into the air and crying, "I'm makin' it raaaain! Yeah, baby, yeah!"

"*Dépêche-toi.* Hurry up!" Mimi cried. "We are already more than an hour late."

Half an hour later they were waiting in line at the Cambridge Queen's Head Pub: the bar that somebody at Harvard had the genius idea to build right underneath the freshman dining hall (but no underage drinking allowed!). Callie could see through the darkly tinted glass windows that it was very crowded inside. She wondered if everyone would be dressed like a pimp or a ho. If so, she was probably going to stand out like a sore thumb in her jeans and black tank top.

No matter, she decided. I'm used to it by now.

What she wasn't used to was not really caring. It felt nice.

The smile faded from her face when they reached the front of the line and she noticed that the girl at the door who was checking IDs had paused to stare blatantly.

"You're Callie Andrews?" she asked before Callie could even hand over her ID.

"What is it to you?" said Mimi, leaning in hostilely.

"Uh—nothing really, I just—I read the article and . . ."

"What about it?" asked Mimi, moving even closer.

"I—I thought it was really great. Inspiring. I'm in Theta, and for part of our initiation we had to flash a bunch of Owl guys. . . . I was so scared that I started crying—but in the end I did it anyway. I know it doesn't even begin to compare, but it was nice to hear someone else's story and get some perspective."

"Thanks," Callie whispered.

"Are we done here?" Mimi interrupted. "You going to let us in or no?" she asked, holding out her hands to get the Big, Black, Under-Twenty-one X.

"Oh," the girl said, clearly puzzled by Mimi's defensive attitude. Quickly she looked around before pressing three Over-Twenty-one bracelets into Callie's palm. "Find Marcus at the bar and tell him the first drink's on me. I'm Brady," she finished, grinning at Callie.

"Thanks!" said Callie, smiling back.

"Score!" said OK, sliding the bracelet onto his wrist.

"What's Theta?" Callie asked Mimi.

"Sorority," said Mimi, pushing through the swinging doors to the pub.

"We have sororities?" It was hard to believe that she'd been here for a semester already and there was still so much she didn't know.

The first thing Callie felt when they entered the pub—a large dimly lit space with dark mahogany-colored wood paneling and a huge circular bar in the middle like the hub of a wheel—was relief. It swept over her the moment she realized, glancing left to the room filled with couches and chairs arranged around low tables and then right at the booths over by the dartboards, foosball, and pool tables, that the majority of people present were dressed casually and were not members of the Hasty Pudding social club.

The second thing she felt was dread. The whole school wasn't here, but almost everyone she knew—and, as Vanessa might have said, everyone that *mattered*—was present. Clint: in the corner talking with some of his buddies from the Fly. Matt: on the other side of the bar yapping at Grace Lee's heels like an overgrown puppy. Vanessa: standing awfully close to Tyler, no doubt trying to mark her territory (or secure next semester's membership) by holding hands in public. Only Gregory was missing from the crowd. He was probably stuck in traffic on his way back from Brown or unpacking—or whatever.

And then, of course, last, least, and worst of all: Alexis Thorndike, over in a booth with Anne Goldberg, Ashleigh Templeton, and several other upperclassman girls.

Their heads were bent low, and Lexi, tossing her hair and laughing at something Anne had just said, either didn't notice or didn't care that Callie had arrived. Suddenly Lexi stood and, still without sparing Callie a glance, made her way over to the group where Clint was hanging out.

A reddish tinge that had little to do with the "mood lighting" colored Callie's vision.

"Drinks?" asked Mimi, steering Callie toward the enormous round bar.

"Drinks!" OK confirmed, snagging them three stools at the bar.

"Are you Marcus?" Callie asked the vaguely familiar student bartender who came rushing over.

"Depends who's asking," he said, eyeing OK's bizarre outfit with what seemed like appreciation rather than amusement.

"Uh, well, I'm Callie, and this is Mimi," Callie began.

"What's your name, sugar?" he asked, still staring at OK.

"Er, no. It's OK."

Marcus laughed. "Love the pants, by the way," he said, looking OK up and down.

OK brightened immediately. "See?" he asked, turning to Callie. "They *are* cool."

"So what'll it be, ladies?" Marcus asked, chuckling. "That's Mimi and Callie . . . Wait. Shut up. Stop!" he interrupted himself when his eyes finally settled on Callie. "Is this *the* famous Callie Andrews?"

"Um . . ." said Callie

"Yes!" Mimi nodded.

"Honey, you—are—*fabulous*! Saw the article. Read it. Loved it!"

"Thanks," said Callie

"But, honey, tell me," he continued, leaning in to take a closer look. "Why is it that when I'm seeing your face, I'm picturing a hedge behind it?"

"Uh . . . no idea?" said Callie, even though she knew exactly why, for she had just remembered this was the same Marcus who'd been coming out of the Spee when Clint had caught her spying on him from behind the shrubbery. That same Clint who was now staring at her from across the room, trying to make eye contact—

"What's a girl got to do to get a drink around here, anyway?" Callie asked, quickly averting her gaze.

"Nuh-uh, ladies, drinks are on me," Marcus said, throwing a dash of this and that into a cocktail shaker.

OK looked distressed that he had been included as one of the "ladies," but didn't seem to know quite what to do about it. "Allow me," he began, reaching for his wallet.

Marcus shook his head as he shook the shaker, swaying his hips. "*Your* money's no good here, *okay*?" he said, pouring the drinks. "That'll be zero dollars—unless you want to give me some sugar?" He pointed a finger to his cheek and winked.

"Can we get a little help over here?" a guy called irritably from down the bar.

"Uh-oh, duty calls!" cried Marcus. "Girl's gotta work for a living," he added, and then, with a snap of his fingers, he was gone.

"Well, he seemed nice," OK commented, reaching for his drink. "And did you hear him? He liked my pants!"

Callie and Mimi looked at each other and laughed.

"*I'll say* he did. . . ." Callie started.

"But he'd probably prefer," said Mimi, taking a sip of her drink, "to see you take them off—"

She stopped talking. Vanessa—apparently having detached herself from Tyler—sidled up to the bar.

"Hey, Meems; hi, OK—two rum and cokes please," she added to the bartender who'd approached to take her order. "Make one a diet."

Suddenly anxious, Callie took a huge sip of her drink and accidentally started to choke.

"Is something funny?" Vanessa asked, whipping around to face her.

"We will return . . . momentarily," Mimi said quickly, grabbing OK's hand and dragging him from the bar.

"Hey—Callie Andrews," said a girl from a group of three as she filled the newly vacant space to Callie's right. "Great article."

"You are just *so* brave," another girl added.

"I went over to my boyfriend's *immediately* after I read it to check for cameras," the third chimed in with a rueful laugh. "He's in the AD club, and you never know what they get up to: Sketch City!"

"Um, thanks," said Callie, acutely aware that Vanessa was listening to every word.

"Seriously," the first one said, starting to turn back to her friends, "you rock. Don't let anyone get you down."

Callie blushed. Then she stole a sidelong glance at Vanessa.

"What?" Vanessa said sharply.

"Nothing," said Callie, surprised that whatever nasty commentary she'd been bracing herself for still hadn't come.

Vanessa drummed her fingers on the bar while she waited for her drinks. Finally she murmured, "I can't believe you did it—coming out with everything that way, I mean."

Callie glanced at Vanessa, searching her face. She could discern no innuendo, criticism, or ridicule. Instead it seemed simply like a benign statement of fact. "I still can't believe it either," Callie said. "But I was out of options. Lexi . . ." she trailed off, watching Lexi, who was still talking to Clint, out of the corner of her eye.

"She's a heinous bitch," Vanessa jumped in. "The heinousest of the heinouses. If either of those are words."

Callie smiled. "By the way, I know you didn't tell her about the tape. Turns out I left my e-mail open in the *FM* offices. Like an idiot."

"Happens to the best of us," Vanessa said with a shrug.

The bartender plunked two rum and cokes on the counter. "That'll be twelve fifty," she told Vanessa.

Nodding, Vanessa pulled her Marc Jacobs wallet out of her purse. "Well . . . I guess I'm not gonna say I told you so."

Callie smiled ruefully. "You did tell me so, and I'm sorry that I didn't believe you when you said you didn't tell anyone about the tape. I'm also sorry . . ."

She watched Vanessa pull some bills out of her wallet and count them.

"I'm sorry for the things I wrote—in that other article," Callie said, trying again. "But you have to believe me when I say that it was *never* meant to be published. It wasn't even a real article draft—I just needed a way to vent after you trashed my bedroom, and so I wrote it all down. But nobody else ever saw it, and I swear nobody was ever meant to see it either."

Vanessa was staring down at the bar, making no move to take her drinks.

"I felt terrible when I reread it, and of course I deleted it immediately," Callie continued. She swallowed hard. "I know you can probably never forgive me. If not for this, then for everything, but I want you to know . . . that I'm sorry."

Slowly Vanessa nodded. "Deep down I think I knew that you were never going to publish it. And I'm sorry too, about what I did to your room. I don't know what I was thinking," she said. Callie leaned in, straining to hear her over the noisy group that had just sat down next to them at the bar. "Turns out the earrings were in my sock drawer the entire time. I was just so mad. . . . But then when you saved me with the ec exam, I thought . . ." She sighed, shaking her head. "You were right, though. I don't think I can forgive you. Maybe for the Gregory stuff, because it's obvious now that it was never me and always you, but that article—" She stopped, picking up her drinks. "It doesn't really matter what you were planning to do with it. The point is that you wrote those things in the first place. That you *believe* those things about me."

Callie was at a loss for words. Some of the things she had written were purely reactionary, but some of them did have a kernel of truth, even if they had been phrased in the meanest possible way. Callie bit her lower lip to keep it from trembling.

Drinks in hand, Vanessa turned to leave. She sounded sad, not angry, when she said, "I really am sorry it turned out this way . . . but I just don't think I can get past it."

Callie nodded even though Vanessa was gone and there was no one there to see. Blinking rapidly, she kept her eyes trained toward the bottom of her glass. She grabbed a cocktail napkin and a pen and tried to think of a three-digit number to factor into primes or whether she still had the Nash Equilibrium memorized. . . .

If she had looked up, she might have caught Clint staring at her, again, but her eyes stayed focused on her napkin.

"Andrews!" a voice barked from over Callie's shoulder. Grace

Lee slid onto a neighboring stool. Matt was hovering right behind her, golden retriever style. "What are you drinking?" she asked, summoning Marcus with a wave of her hand.

"Hey!" said Matt, his voice bordering on whiney. "How come you get to buy Callie a drink, but I can't buy one for you?"

"Because Andrews is neither my subordinate—yet—nor the current bane of my existence. Plus, I can't have you reporting me for sexual harassment."

Callie wondered if that joke-like-thing meant that Grace was in a good mood.

"Lee bebe!" Marcus cried, leaning over the bar to kiss her on both cheeks. To Callie's surprise, Grace submitted willingly. "Missed you at the meeting this week!" he added, pouting.

"I was getting my nails done," she said dryly. "And there's this paper I occasionally edit—you may have heard of it—"

"Yeah, yeah, yeah," he cut her off, pouring her a pint of very dark ale. By now Callie had guessed that they must be quite close: you had to be a very special friend of Grace's if you managed to interrupt her and live to tell the tale.

"Anyway, Andrews—to your success," Grace toasted her abruptly. "And yours, too, Robertson," she added before Matt could open his mouth. Then she drained her glass in one long gulp. "Fantastic responses all around," she said, slamming it on the counter. "Can't remember the last time a piece drew so many comments, and our circulation is through the roof. It's almost like the student body has finally figured out how to read."

Callie was all for literacy, but she couldn't help but wonder who specifically had read it. Had Clint while he was away at Brown? Or just a few hours ago after he'd returned?

Following Callie's gaze, Grace nodded toward Clint. Matt wandered away looking disappointed that Callie was hogging all of Grace's attention. "That's some friend you got over there," Grace said.

"He's not really my friend, exactly," said Callie, staring at her cup.

"No? It almost came to blows half an hour ago because of you."

"Really? Wait, *what*?"

"Some guys—or rather, chauvinist pigs—were over there earlier talking about you. Saying how they wouldn't mind getting their hands on a copy of that tape and some other things I won't repeat. That one stood up like he was ready to take on all three of them. He said something, and they all started apologizing like the little pansies that they are. Then he said something else, and they practically sprinted out of the bar." Grace chuckled.

Callie stared at Grace, looked at Clint, and then back at Grace.

" . . . good looking, too," Grace was continuing, "but not my type, if you know what I mean," she added. "Too bad he used to date The Devil Wears Prada. That's a deal breaker, if you ask me."

"Too bad he used to—what—date *who*?"

"Alexis Thorndike, of course—as in your former COMP director? Huge stick up her butt and a nasty habit of collecting other peoples' secrets?"

"Oh!" Callie cried. Grace had clearly guessed the identity of her blackmailer. "Great nickname," she said with a laugh.

Grace nodded. "You've got too much potential to waste on what is, between you and me, a sorry excuse for a magazine. And, if last week's article is any indication, you're going to be a great addition to our team."

Callie nodded absentmindedly, watching Clint throw back his head and laugh.

"Of course, you're going to have to work for it—harder than you worked for *FM*, but I'd say that you're up to the task, right, Andrews?"

"I—uh—what? You're saying I would be a good fit for the *Crimson*?" Callie asked.

"Yes, Andrews," Grace said, rolling her eyes. "Why don't you stop by my office next week after you've picked up your first COMP assignments and we can go over them together?"

"You would really do that? I mean, yes, of course, yes! That would be amazing!"Callie cried, temporarily forgetting everyone else in the room. "Thank you!"

"No guarantees, Andrews," Grace said gruffly. "Wouldn't offer if you didn't have potential . . . Anyway, got to get going now." She nodded, sliding off the stool. "Enjoy the party."

"Thanks," Callie repeated, but Grace was already gone.

Callie looked around the room. Mimi and OK were playing foosball, and Matt was sitting in a crowded booth with a bunch of the other *Crimson* editors. I need more friends, she thought, crumpling up her napkin and hopping off the bar stool. Back to the old alone-in-an-awkward-social-situation standby otherwise known as: bathroom time!

Callie picked her way through the plush couches and armchairs and rounded the corner to join the line. There were three girls ahead of her—and from the size of their purses and scope of their outfits, they all looked like they would take a very long time in the single-room stalls. Perfect. Callie leaned back against the wall and closed her eyes.

"Hi, Callie," said a cool voice on her right. "So nice to finally see you out again."

Aw, crap. "Hey, Anne," Callie said, turning. "How are you?"

"Good," said Anne, giving Callie a once-over with her ever-appraising eye. "No costume?"

"Nope."

Anne frowned. "Well, I guess all that matters is that you're actually here."

Callie nodded. Wait—what?

"Of course, participation in these events isn't *mandatory*," Anne continued, "but as secretary it is my job to ensure that everyone attends at least a few and makes an effort to bond with the other members."

Callie stared at her. Other members? As in . . . Am I still . . . ? "Um—about my dues—I know I'm super late—"

Anne silenced Callie with a wave of her hand. "You got them in eventually and that's what counts."

"I . . . I got them in eventually?" Callie repeated, dumbstruck.

"Yes," said Anne. "I received the envelope you left on my desk at the clubhouse, though next time you probably shouldn't leave so much cash lying around unattended."

"I . . ." Callie frowned. "But—"

"I think it's your turn," Anne interrupted brusquely as a door opened on their left.

Safe inside the bathroom, Callie stared at herself in the mirror. What—who—why—*who*—when . . . She splashed cool water on her face. Mimi, she decided, drying off her hands. It had to be Mimi. Opening the door and heading back toward the bar, she resolved to ask her right now—

"Callie."

Clint was there waiting for her.

"H-hi," she stammered, staring at the ground.

"Hey." He looked at her. "There's an empty couch in that alcove over there," he said, tilting his head toward it, "and it's pretty quiet, too. Sit with me for a minute?" he asked.

She nodded.

They sat, their knees angled toward each other but still a foot apart.

"Wow," he said finally, running a hand through his hair. "So that was the big secret, huh?"

She nodded.

"I thought . . . Wow," he said, shaking his head.

Say something else, Callie pleaded silently, praying that she wouldn't cry.

"Callie," he said, looking her in the eyes. "I am so . . . *incommunicably* sorry that this happened to you."

Not that! she thought, her chin starting to tremble.

"If I ever happen to see that guy . . ." He shook his head.

That's better. Thoughts of pounding Evan to a pulp always improved her mood. They were quiet for a moment, then Clint said, "And the upperclassman who had a copy . . . ?"

There was no need for him to say the name out loud. Callie nodded.

Clint exhaled. "Wish I could say I was surprised."

Callie suddenly found her voice. "That e-mail I sent you—I never wanted—I mean: *she* made me do it."

Clint looked thoughtful. "I'm going to be honest, I don't see how she could *make* you do anything. Yes," he continued, before Callie could protest, "she is capable of some pretty conniving behavior. But I think that ultimately the only real power she has over you is what you're willing to concede her."

Callie opened her mouth to object to his flippancy about all the things Lexi had made—yes, *made*—her do that semester. But when her eyes met his, the words got stuck. The more she thought about it as they sat there quietly on the couch, the more she wished that he had been around to voice this wisdom a lot earlier. But he had never had the opportunity, and that was also her fault.

As if echoing her thoughts, Clint said, "I just wish you would have told me from the beginning. I do understand why you didn't. But if you had . . ." He shrugged. "Maybe things would have turned out differently."

Now Callie wanted to cry again. "You mean . . . there's no hope that we . . . ?"

Clint looked at her and then cupped her chin in his hand. "I didn't say that."

"Well, then . . ." Her eyes were wide.

Clint dropped his hand. "First, I think there was one thing that you said that we need to address."

Callie cringed, not wanting to think about that horrible, horrible e-mail.

"Freshman year really isn't the best time for a relationship. Especially when you have so many other things that you want to do. I mean, you have your whole life to have boyfriends. But you get only four years of college."

Callie glanced around the room: the Cambridge Queen's Head Pub. She thought she had a pretty good idea of what constituted "college" by now—though there was still, no doubt, lots left to learn—and she knew that even in her plans for the *Crimson* and everything else she wanted to do, there was still room for Clint. After all, one of the things she had realized that semester was that happiness and sanity ought to occupy a high place on one's list of priorities.

"You're right," she said. "It *can* be tough to balance a relationship when you have all these other things you're not sure if you want to do instead." She paused. "But back then—before break—I was still trying to figure out what exactly it was that I wanted. Now I know, though," she said, looking at him and smiling in satisfaction with the full conviction she finally felt. "What I want is you."

He grinned. "Right back attcha, kiddo," he said, his laugh

lines crinkling. "You just gotta promise me one thing, though."

"Anything," she said, eager to hurry up and skip to the part where she leaped into his arms.

"From here on out, no more secrets."

She froze. This was it: should she tell him about what had happened with Gregory? Or should she leave the past in the past—as she was finally ready to do—and concentrate wholly on the future? Briefly she closed her eyes. He had said very specifically: "from here on out." She smiled. It was a promise she could make. "From here on out," she echoed. "No more secrets."

Leaning in, he kissed her. And for the first time, Callie kissed him back without worrying about who was watching.

A gust of wind whooshed through the pub as the double doors swept open, and a chill crept down Callie's back, despite the warmth of Clint's embrace. Snuggling even closer into his arms, she continued kissing him, angled away from the entrance and oblivious to the boy who, his hair rumpled and cheeks pink with cold, had just burst into the bar. Traffic, as she had rightly guessed, had kept him along with half of the squash team stuck on the road until less than ten minutes ago, when he'd texted OK and come running straight to the Queen's Head Pub.

His eyes darted around wildly, settling finally on the couple in the alcove on the left.

They were kissing.

He froze in his tracks. But after only a moment's hesitation, he was moving again. In another twenty seconds he was standing in front of the couch.

"Hey," said Clint, breaking away from Callie. Callie turned and, seeing Gregory, stared up at him in surprise. His blue eyes were, for once, devoid of irony, and radiating with the same intensity as when he had kissed her on the balcony in the rain. Another involuntary shiver shot down her spine.

Without bothering to return Clint's greeting, Gregory kneeled so they were at eye-level. "Callie," he said. "I have to talk to you."